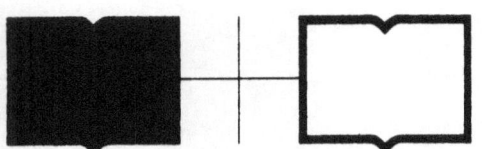

I0597119

Toronto Reprint Library of Canadian Prose and Poetry

Douglas Lochhead, General Editor

This series is intended to provide for
libraries a varied selection of titles of
Canadian prose and poetry which
have been long out-of-print. Each
work is a reprint of a reliable edition,
is in a contemporary library binding,
and is appropriate for public circulation. The Toronto Reprint Library
makes available lesser known works
of popular writers and, in some cases,
the only works of little known poets
and prose writers. All form part of
Canada's literary history; all help to
provide a better knowledge of our
cultural and social past.

The Toronto Reprint Library is pro-
duced in short-run editions made
possible by special techniques, some
of which have been developed for
the series by the University of Toronto
Press.

This series should not be confused
with Literature of Canada: Poetry
and Prose in Reprint, also under the
general editorship of Douglas Lochhead.

UNIVERSITY OF TORONTO PRESS

Toronto Reprint Library of Canadian Prose and Poetry
© University of Toronto Press 1973
Toronto and Buffalo
Printed in Canada
Reprinted in 2018
ISBN 0-8020-7527-4
ISBN 978-1-4875-8216-6 (paper)

No other edition located.

A ROMANCE OF TORONTO.

(FOUNDED ON FACT.)

A NOVEL.

BY

MRS. ANNIE G. SAVIGNY,

Author of "An Allegory on Gossip," "A Heart-Song of To-day," etc.

"I would like the Government to forbid the publication of all novels that did not end well."—DARWIN.

"What would the world do without story-books."—DICKENS.

TORONTO:

WILLIAM BRIGGS, 78 & 80 KING STREET EAST,

1888.

NOTE.

In the following pages are two plots, one of which was told me by an actor therein; the other I have myself watched from its first page to its last, being living facts in living lives of fair Toronto's children.

THE AUTHOR.

CONTENTS.

CONTENTS.

A ROMANCE OF TORONTO.

CHAPTER I.

TORONTO A FAIR MATRON.

WO gentlemen friends saunter arm in arm up and down the deck of the palace steamer *Chicora* as she enters our beautiful Lake Ontario from the picturesque Niagara River, on a perfect day in delightful September, when the blue canopy of the heavens seems so far away, one wonders that the mirrored surface of the lake can reflect its color.

"Do you know, Buckingham, you puzzle me; you were evidently happier in our little circle at the Hoffman House than in billiard, smoking, or reading-rooms, and just now in the saloon you seemed so content with Miss Crew, my wife and our boy, that I again wonder a man with these tastes, and who has made his little pile, does not marry," said Mr. Dale, in flute-like tones, distinctly English in accent. "I really think, my dear fellow, you would be happier in big New York city with some one in it to make a home for you."

"I am quite sure your words are kindly meant, Dale, but look at me," he says tranquilly, "I am not dwarfed by care, being six feet in my stockings, I have no worrying lines written on my forehead, and between you and I, I am fifty; to be sure I am bald and grey, but that is New York life, a bachelor life, then, has not served me ill; there is a woman at Toronto I should

like as my wife, but until I can give her the few
luxuries I now deem necessities, I shall remain as I
am."

"I regret your decision, Buckingham, it is a rock
many men split on, this waiting for wealth and miss-
ing wifely companionship."

"Perhaps you are right; but I should not care to
risk it," he says, calmly.

"And you a speculator!" his friend said, smiling. At
this they drifted into business and some joint invest-
ments in Canadian mineral locations, when Dale said:

"You must excuse me now, Buckingham, I promised
my wife to go and read her a letter descriptive of Toronto, as we, you know, have not been there."

"Who is the writer, if I may know?"

"Our mutual friend at Toronto, Mrs. Gower."

"Oh, I am with you then," he said, with unusual
eagerness, a fact noted by his friend.

Entering the saloon, Mrs. Dale, a pretty little woman,
fashionably dressed, with Irish blue eyes and raven
hair, said, lifting her head:

"Excuse my recumbent position, but I feel as if my
head wasn't level, if I try to sit up; ditto, Miss Crew."

"Where is Garfield, Ella?"

"Over there with those boys; now read away, hubby,
it will do my head good."

"Very well, let me see where the description com-
mences (the personal part I may pass). Here it is:

"Toronto is a fair matron with many children, whom
she has planted out on either side and north of her as
far as her great arms can stretch. She lies north and
south, while her lips speak loving words to her off-
spring, and to her spouse, the County of York; when
she rests she pillows her head on the pine-clad hills of
sweet Rosedale, while her feet lave at pleasure in the
blue waters of beautiful Lake Ontario.

"Her favorite children are Parkdale, Rosedale, and Scarboro'; Parkdale to her west, ambitious and clear-sighted, handsome and well-built, the sportive lake at his feet, in which his children revel at eve; her daughter, charming Rosedale, in society and quite the fashion even to the immense bouquet she carries at all seasons—now of autumn leaves, from the hand of Dame Nature; now of the floral beauties from her own gardens and conservatories, again, of beauteous ferns gathered in her own woods across her handsome bridges.

"Scarboro', fair Toronto's favorite son, of whom she is justly proud, is a handsome young warrior, fearless as his own heights, robust as his own trees, which seem as one gazes down his deep ravine, like so many giants marching upwards as though panting to reach the blue pavilioned heavens where they would fain rest their heads.

"From the time spring thaws the sceptre out of the frozen hand of winter, until again he is king, the breath of Scarboro' is redolent of the rose, honeysuckle and sweet-briar, with a rapid succession of the loveliest wild flowers in Canada beneath one's feet, a veritable carpet of sweet-scented blossoms has her son Scarboro'.

"Fair Toronto is also herself richly robed and jew-elled, her necklet being of picturesque villas, in Rose-dale and on Bloor Street; under her corsage, covered with beauteous blossoms from her Horticultural Gardens, her Normal School grounds, etc., her heart throbs with pride as she thinks of her gems, the spires from her one hundred and twenty churches glistening in heaven's sunbeams; of her magnificent University of Toronto, with its great Norman tower, which cost her nearly $500,000; her handsome Trinity College, in third period pointed English style; her Knox College, her hotels, her opera houses, her stately banks; with her diamonds, of which she is vastly proud, and which

2

are her great newspaper offices—the most valuable being those of first water, viz., her Church papers as finger-posts, with her *Sentinel* as guard; her independent, cultured *Mail;* her mighty clear-Grit *Globe;* her brilliant, knowing *Grip;* her often-quoted *World;* her racy town-cry *News;* her social *Saturday Night;* her *Life,* her *Week,* her *Truth,* with her *Evening Telegram,* the whole set being so valued by fair Toronto, that she would as soon be minus her daily bread as her newspapers.

"It would take too long to enumerate the many attractions fair Toronto offers—some of those within her walls having throats full of song, others in the 'Harmony Club,' others elocutionists, with orators and athletes; her Cyclorama of Sedan, her Zoo—to which only a trifle pays the piper—her interesting museums, her fine art galleries.

"And again, one word of her pet river, her picturesque Humber, where lovers meet, poets dream, and fairies dwell; yes, as Imrie says:

> "' Glide we up the Humber river,
> Where the rushes sigh and quiver,
> Plight our love to each forever,
> Love that will not die.'

"Such, dear Mr. and Mrs. Dale, is my lay of Toronto, which I hope you will like well enough to come and sojourn here awhile. You say, Mrs. Dale, that you have 'willed' to go to an hotel, if so, I shall say no more of my wish, for 'a woman's will dies hard on the field, or on the sward;' but when your will is carried out, should you sigh for home-life come to me—even then Holmnest will have open doors. You may be grave or gay, you may be *en déshabillé* in mind and robing, or you may have your war-paint on for the watchful eye of Grundy, be it as you will it, you are ever welcome, only tell dear Diogenes not to come

in his tub. I can give you both amusement enough in
many subjects or objects at which to level your glass,
for Toronto society is in many instances an amusing
spectacle, a droll conglomeration.

        "Yours as always,
              "ELAINE GOWER."

"Well, Buckingham, what think you of fair Toronto?"
asked Dale, as he finished reading.

"I think that, though unusual, a Fair Matron has
had ample justice from a fair woman."

"I want to-morrow and Mrs. Gower right now,"
said Mrs. Dale, "as Garfield says when he is promised
a treat."

"Toronto must be a fine city, and covering a large
area," said Miss Crew.

"Mrs. Gower has a taste for metaphor; I never heard
her in that style before, that is to any extent," said
Buckingham.

"I am intensely practical," said Dale; "but confess
Toronto described in metaphor sounds more musical,
at all events, than in plain brick and mortar style."

"Emerson says," said Buckingham, "men are ever
lapsing into a beggarly habit in which everything that
is not cyphering is hustled out of sight, and I think
he is right."

"We cannot help it, it is the tendency of the age;
but what have we here, Buckingham? What's the
excitement about?"

"Oh, we are only nearing Hanlon's Point; the ladies
had better come outside; every scene will be in gala
dress. Miss Crew, can I assist you?"

> "Where the blue hills of old Toronto shed
> Their evening shadows o'er Ontario's bed,"

said Dale, coming with the crowd to view the scene.

But since Moore so sang, the hills of the noble red

man have disappeared, save as a boundary to our fair
city ; the pale faces, in the interests of progress and
civilization, would have it so ; and Bloor Street, to the
north, is now reached by a gradual ascent of one
hundred and fifty feet above the lake level.   But
now the stately and comfortable palace steamer,
Chicora, with a goodly number of souls on board, is
rounding Hanlon's Point, and entering our beautiful
Bay, when the illumined city, with the Industrial
Exhibition of 1887 in full swing, burst upon the view.
The bands of music in and about the city, at the
Horticultural Gardens and on the fair grounds, with
the hum of many voices, fill the evening air with a
glad song of joy.

"What a sparkling scene," cried Mrs. Dale ; "see,
Garfield, my boy, all the boats lit from bow to stern."

"They look as pretty as you in your diamonds,
mamma."

"It is quite a pretty sight, and the city also," said
Miss Crew ; "I had no idea Canada could attempt
anything to equal this."

"So much for England's instructions of her 'young
ideas how to shoot,' as to her colonies, Miss Crew,"
said Dale ; "Come, confess that a few squaws, bearing
torches, with their lordly half smoking the calumet,
was the utmost you expected."

"Oh, Mr. Dale, please don't exaggerate our ignor-
ance in this respect ; I am not quite so bad as a lady
at home, who thought Toronto a chain of mountains,
and Ottawa an Indian chief."

"One of Fenimore Cooper's, I hope," laughed Buckingham, "who hunted buffalo on the boundless prairie,
instead of your lean gophers who hunt rusty bacon
from agents who, some say, use him to swindle the
public and line their own pockets.   But listen ; what a
medley of sounds."

"And lights," cried Mrs. Dale ; "it looks as if annexation was on, and they were firing up some of our gold dollars as sky rockets."

"It's pretty good for Canada, mamma," said Garfield, patronisingly.

"You say Toronto is quite a business centre, Buckingham?"

"Oh, yes; quite so; it makes one think of commercial union. Do you advocate it, Dale?"

"Well, as you know, Buckingham, I am not even yet sufficiently Americanised to look upon it from other than a British standpoint, and so do not advocate it, as it seems a slight to the Mother Country. What is your idea of advantages derived by Canada were it *a fait accompli?*"

"She would gain larger markets; her natural resources would be developed, especially her mineral, in which I am," he added, jokingly, "looking out for the interest of that most important number *one*, while also number two would benefit in home manufactures."

"You amuse me; I honestly believe number one is a universal lever; yet still in a way we are each patriotic; but, again, you must see that commercial union would be the forerunner of annexation."

"Yes, likely, though not for some time, but evolution will bring that about in a natural sort of way, as a final settlement of all vexed questions, whether," he addded laughingly, "of humanity or—fish."

"Oh, I don't know that, but you have the fish at all events and mean to keep them too; humanity may follow, but I should not like to see the colonies hoist another flag. But here we are at last, at the portals of the Queen City, and such a multitude of people makes one feel as if one might be crowded out," he said, uneasily, as the *Chicora* came in at Yonge Street wharf.

"Don't bother your head about your rooms, Dale, you secured them by telegram."

"I did, ten days ago, though."

"You never fear, they will be all right, the manager is a thorough business man," he said quietly, gathering up the belongings of the ladies.

"You are invaluable, Mr. Buckingham," said Mrs. Dale, "and are as gallant as if you had as many wives as Blue Beard."

"Rather a scaly compliment, Buckingham," laughed his friend.

"She means well, but the fish are not far off," he answered, picking up Garfield, and giving his arm to quiet Miss Crew.

CHAPTER II.

WHO IS WHO IN A MEDLEY.

"WHAT a moving sea of faces!" exclaimed Miss Crew.

"Yes, quite a few, and look as if they required laundrying—bodies, bones, and all."

"Here, Garfield, though you are 'very old' as you say, you had better take my hand," said Miss Crew, nervously, as Mr. Buckingham set him down on the wharf.

"Oh, no, he must go with his father," cried Mrs. Dale.

"Oh, I reckon a New York boy can elbow his way through that mean crowd." And darting through the mass of people, causing the collapse of not a few tournures, and with the aid of one of his mother's bonnet pins giving many a woman cause to scream as she unconsciously cleared his path by getting out of his way, he is on the outskirts of the crowd.

"Say, hackman, drive me off right smart to the Queen's!"

"Is it all square, young gent ?"

"Yes; dimes sure as Vanderbilt money."

"Oh, I mean you are but a kid to go it alone."

"Chestnuts!"

And taking another hack, "Pooh, Bah!" quieting his scruples by pocketing a double insult they are off.

"I feel sure Garfield is quite safe, Ella, and probably choosing a cab for us; here, take my arm dear, and don't be nervous, Buckingham is looking after Miss Crew."

But he is on ahead making inquiries.

"Yes, sir, the young gent is all right, if you take my hack we'll catch him, I lost him by being too careful like."

"Your boy is all right, Mrs. Dale, if you jump in quick we'll overtake him; allow me, Miss Crew."

"Thank heaven," said his mother fervently, "tell the man to go as quick as he can through this crowd; there he is, the young scamp, waving to us, there, on ahead, a pair of light greys."

"And here we are, and your boy of the period waiting to welcome us."

"Welcome to the Queen City," he said, pulling off his skull cap.

"You frightened your mother, my boy; see that you don't repeat this; remember she is nervous."

"Glad I ain't a woman, they are all nerves and bustles; here, give us a kiss, mamma, I only wanted to show you I aint a baby."

"There! there! that will do, my bonnet! my bangs! such a bustle as I've been in about you, I wish you were in long clothes."

"Then I'd have to wear a bustle too!"

"Ella you look tired, we had best let them show us our rooms at once; Buckingham, we shall have some dinner together, I hope."

"Yes, I shall meet you here, and go in with you."

"This is pleasant, rooms *en suite*, and you beside us, Miss Crew," said Mrs. Dale.

And now, while they refresh themselves by bath and toilette, a word of them : Mr. Dale, like his friend Buckingham, has reached fifty, is grey, also wearing short side whiskers and moustache. He is a man of sterling worth of character, honest as the day; a man whose word was never doubted, who, having seen much of life, was apt to be a trifle cynical; but withal, so generous that his criticisms on men and things are more on the surface than even he imagines. A good friend, a kind husband to the pretty, penniless girl, Ella Swift, whom he had married in New York eleven years ago, and though unlike in character, there is so much love between them that their wedded happiness flows on with never a rift in the rill; and though she does not look into life and its many vexed questions with his depth of thought, still, in other ways her brain is quite as active—a kindly, social astronomer, she loves to unravel mysteries in the lives about her, to set love affairs going to her liking, she not caring to soar above the drawing-room, leaving Wall Street, the Corn Exchange, and railway stocks to her astute husband, who has inherited English gold, to which he is adding or losing in speculations the American eagle. With some thought of changing their residence to fair Toronto, they had a year ago given up house, and have been residing at the Hoffman House, New York City; then engaging Miss Crew, as governess to their only child of nine years. Mr. Dale had been somewhat doubtful as to the advisability of giving the position to Miss Crew, who merely answering their advertisement in the New York *Herald*, stating nervously that she was without references, as the people she had been with had gone West; but she was a fair, delicate, lady-like, religious girl, interesting Mrs. Dale at once by her loneliness and reticence; above all, Garfield took to her, and she gained an influence for good over him at once; and by this time both Mr. and Mrs. Dale have come to consider her as one of themselves, though having decided to place their son at boarding-school until such time as they take up house.

Mr. Buckingham is, as we know, an eligible bachelor, fine-looking, tall, as we have heard, and a man of many dollars; a calmly quiet man (a trait from his German mother), who has lost two fortunes, but who will not play for high stakes again, as he does not care to begin over again at fifty, with nearly all he craves in his grasp; two women jilted him when fortune frowned, but taking it coolly, he merely told himself it was the dollar they had cared for, not he. Passionately fond of music, a skilled performer, the piano has been mistress and wife to him; if he marries he will be a good husband, but if he does not, he will be almost as happy in the best musical circle wherever his home may be.

Having dined, our friends gathered for a few moments' social chat before retiring, when Mrs. Dale said, "I expect, Mr. Buckingham, you feel as important as one of Barnum's show-men in your role, for you are aware you and Mrs. Gower must trot us round to see the lions."

"Any man, Mrs. Dale, would feel important as your cicerone, and in company with Mrs. Gower."

"How polite you are. Oh, Henry, I see by the *News*, "Fantasma" is on at the Grand Opera House; even if it is late, let us go."

"Nonsense, dear, we have seen it often enough."

"If you are tired, very well; but I wanted to make a spectacle of myself this time, and the ladies green with envy over my new heliotrope satin."

"Well, if that isn't self-abnegation," laughed Buckingham.

"Oh, you needn't sympathize, I only feel as the peacock when he spreads his tail."

"How many churches did Mrs. Gower say there are here?" asked Miss Crew.

"One hundred and twenty; so you will have a choice of roads heavenward, Miss Crew," answered Buckingham.

"Yes, there are a number of roads, and only one guide-book," she answered, thoughtfully.

"Mrs. Gower will put you on the right track," he said quietly.

Here Mr. Dale returned, saying in pleased tones, "Well, Ella, I have telephoned Mrs. Gower of our arrival, and she says she will call at 11 a.m., then do the Exhibition, where we are to remain until we see Pekin bombarded."

"That is in the evening, and the best part of it this perfect weather; may I come?" said Buckingham.

"Assuredly."

"Thanks, and au revoir."

"Good night."

CHAPTER III.

INSTANTANEOUS PHOTOGRAPHS.

"OTHING is more deeply punished than the neglect of the affinities by which alone society should be formed and the insane levity of choosing our associates by other's eyes," read a lady, musingly, as Emerson's essays fall from her knees to the soft carpet under her cushioned feet.

"Yes, nothing is more deeply punished," she half chanted in a musical voice, while a grave, troubled look came to the dark eyes, and a quiver of pain to the sensitive lips. "And well do you and I know it, Tyr, though you are only a dog," she continued, as she patted a brown retriever beside her. "Yes, you and I, Tyr, like only affinities; the others seem to us mongrels, and to us don't seem good. I wonder if they were so pronounced in the first week when the world was young; but fancy is travelling without reason; they were all thorough-breds in the good old days, and one does not read of anything like Emerson's words on affinities, or a case similar to my own; but I am half asleep, Tyr; watch by me, good old dog."

And leaning her head back against the soft green velvet cushioned back of the rattan chair, Somnus is not wooed in vain; indeed, one might imagine the god of slumber had wound a garland of poppies about her brow, so does she sleep as an infant.

As she rests, a word of her. A Canadian; a native of Toronto, with far-away English kin; above the medium height; dark, comely, and slightly embonpoint; a woman of thirty, but with that troubled look at present on her face looking older; generous, warm-hearted and conscientious; with more than the average force of character; too sensitive in days past; too impulsive, even yet, in this world of "they daily mistake my words." Even at thirty, she has had years of trouble; has been dragged in the dust under Fortune's wheel, that others might ride aloft at her expense; earning her "dinner of herbs" that "Pooh Bah" in the plural, may have the "stalled ox." But at last she rests, and summer friends would again know her, who fled at her first out-at-elbow gown; but experience is a good teacher, she will cherish only those who have cherished her in her dark days. Society also now desires her company in polite bids to its various webs, in shape of dinners and lunches, with its other numerous distractions, knowing she is in possession of a

rather pretentious little home, and is in a position to
repay; for society is a debit and credit system.

"Once a widow always a widow" was not the motto
of Mrs. Gower, and so she would have again wed,
again gone to God's altar; but the angel of death forbade, using his scythe almost as the words of the
church pronounced them man and wife, and the bridal
gown of the morning gave place ere the sun had set
to the black robes of a second widowhood.   Truly,
"Sorrow there seemeth more of thee then we can bear
and live;" yet still we live, was her cry.   The death
of her friend, just at the time manly counsel would
have saved her little fortune from vultures, habited as
Christian pew-holders! was very hard, not to speak
of that intense loneliness, the death of husband, wife,
or betrothed, brings into one's life; one is as though
struck mentally and physically blind, not knowing
where to turn or whose hand to take; for until such
relations are severed by death, one does not realize
how one has leaned on the one in the multitude.

"But," she would say, "one must harden oneself to
the inevitable, to Heaven's will, if one would keep
one's reason;" and in time the sudden death of the
man she had so passionately loved, was as some terrible
dream.   Not as she dreams away the moments now in
her pretty restful library, with its rattan furniture,
cushioned and trimmed in olive-green velvet; one side
a library of her pet authors, with Davenport near;
walls painted in alternate green and cream panels;
on the light ground are lilies from nature, gathered
from Ashbridge's Bay, and near the Island; nestling
in their bed of green leaves an English ivy trails
around the pretty Queen Anne mantel, with two tall
palms, which bring content to the canary as the perfume from the blossoms on the stand give pleasure to
the sleeping mistress of Holmnest.

Her own individuality is stamped upon its walls also,

for on each alternate dark green panel is some pretty
bits of painting, bric-a-brac, or motto ; one reads, "Let
ilka ane gang their ain gait," showing her dislike to
meddling in another's business ; another reads, "The
greatest of these is charity ;" and over a bust of
Shakspeare are his own words, "No profit goes where
is no pleasure taken; in brief, sir, study what you most
affect."

But she dreams, and what a troubled expression.
At this moment a coupé drives up a north-west avenue
of our city, stops at the gate of Holmnest, when a
gentleman, hurriedly springing out, saying, "come back
for me in about an hour-and-a-half, Somers," enters
the picturesque grounds, has reached the veranda
and hall door on south side of pretty Holmnest, rings,
when a boy, in neat blue suit, answers.

"Is Mrs. Gower at home, Thomas ?"

"Yes, sir ; in the library."

"Very well, you need not announce me, I know the
way ;" and hastening his steps he passes through a
square hall, done in the warm tints now in vogue, sunbeams coming softened through artistic panes of
stained glass, showing vases on brackets filled with
flowers, which would delight "Bel Thistlethwaite,"
with a few appropriate pictures, giving life to the
walls ; the door of the library is ajar ; he enters.

"Asleep !" he exclaims, softly ; "with Emerson's
thoughts for dreams and Tyr as watch ; but what a
troubled expression," he thinks, seating himself, evidently quite at home ; a man, too, one would like to be
at home with, if there be any truth in physiognomy, a
handsome man, five feet eleven in height, dark hair
and moustache, kindly blue eyes, amiability stamped
on his face ; a man who, had events shaped themselves
that way, would have made an heroic self-sacrificing
soldier of the Cross.

He is scarcely seated when the occupant awakes

with a start and a terrified exclamation of "Oh!" at
which the dog places his fore-paws on her knees, with
a whine of sympathy, as her friend, Mr. Cole, comes
forward with outstretched hand.

"When did you arrive; is it so late; you received
my message to dine with the Dales and Smyths with
me this evening? but I am half dreaming yet; of
course you did, for you answered 'Yes.' Getting
yourself in trim for leap-year, I suppose," she said,
smiling; " but how is it you are in your office coat? I
want you to look your very best, as you are to take in
a young lady, a Miss Crew, who comes with the Dales;
she is a super-excellent sort of girl."

"Has she money?" he says, laughingly.

"Oh, you need not pretend to be a fortune-hunter
to me; I know you too well for that; but remember,
I prophesy you will lose your heart to her. But, oh,
Charlie, I have had such a horrible dream," and she
presses one hand to her forehead, at which the lace
rufflings fall back from her sleeve, showing a very
good arm, her gown of ecru soft summer bunting, becoming her style, " that dream will haunt me unless
you let me tell it you, Charlie."

"Oh, that's the use you put me to, is it? all right,
fire away, I'll interpret; it was only a mistake the
baptizing me Charlie, when I have to play the part of
Joseph."

" Well, in the first part, oh Joseph, I had been reading this morning what held my mind as to the ascent
from Paris of the æronauts, Mallet and Jovis; their
courage, and Mother Shipton's prophecy impressed
me sufficiently as to dream, with the words of Emerson as to affinities also in my mind, that a party of
us—you, the Dales, Mrs. St. Clair, Miss Hall, Mr.
Buckingham, and myself, with a gentleman who was
masked—had been taking part in an entertainment in
the Pavilion, Horticultural Gardens, in aid of the Hos-

pital for sick children; we gave readings, vocal and
instrumental music, and laughed inwardly and glowed
outwardly, as we everyone, regardless of merit, received
repeated recalls, when afterwards the recalcitrant
balloon, which refused to inflate, when we gazed in
vain at the fair grounds, did ascend after our per-
formance, which fact emptied the Pavilion ere we had
concluded our last effort, everyone flying, as we do at
Toronto, as though there was a drop curtain with the
words in flaming colors, 'The de'il take the hind-
most;' the building was empty as our last supreme
effort frightened the few dead-heads who had slunk
in; we then laughingly made a rush to the balloon
ascension, and determined there and then to further
distinguish ourselves by becoming æronauts *pro tem.*
What made it ridiculously droll, Joseph, was the fact
that the men in charge chanted continuously Emerson's words that had impressed me ere I slept—
'Nothing is more deeply punished than the neglect
of the affinities.' I was nearest the basket, and wild
with reckless spirit. As I remember, myself stepped
in; the owners seemed at variance who was to pose
or rise," she said, smilingly, "as my affinity, that is of
yourself, Messrs. Dale, Buckingham, or the man with
the mask, when, finally, they signed to the latter to
enter; I was nothing loth, for his voice, a sweet tenor,
had charmed me; up we went, when to my horror
your *bete noir*, Mr. Cobbe, sprang from among the
branches of a tall tree into the basket.

"'Too much ballast,' he cried, throwing out all the
owners had provided us with; we ascended rapidly—
a feeling of faintness seizing me—up, up; I feel the
sensation now," she said with a tremor; "up, up, nearing the feathery clouds, looking like down from the
wings of angels. 'Too much ballast,' he again cried,
excitedly springing on the masked man, first tearing
off his mask, disclosing the essentially manly face of

a gentleman whom I frequently meet, but am not acquainted with, but in whom I take an interest, because of his tender care of a little lady I used to see with him ; Mr. Cobbe springing on him with the words, 'too much ballast ; down with affinities!' hurled the poor fellow to earth, at which I cried out as you heard ; his fall was a something too awfully real ; one's nerves for the time suffer as severely as though all was reality," she added in a pre-occupied tone, as though mind was burdened with latent thought.

"But 'all's well that ends well ;' Mr. Cobbe is in mid air, where I fervently hope he will remain."

"But you forget the poor man who was hurled to the earth ; I know his face so well."

"And I know yours, Mrs. Gower, and you are safe and so am I ; and as Joseph, I interpret that you are to give your charming self to an affinity, and don't fly too high."

"The first part of your speech is epicurean, in your second you play the mentor," she said, laughingly; "but in your face I see you have something to tell me ; go now to the telephone and tell them to send you your dress coat, for you have no time to go all the way to the Walker House and be back by seven."

"No use ; I cannot stay for dinner."

"Cannot stay ! Why ?"

"My father writes me he is going to sail for England at once, and wishes me to meet him at London."

"Well, you ought not to look so grave over such a meditated trip, Charlie, it will make a new man of you ; and instead of betaking yourself to the Preston baths, a sea voyage, I should say, will set you up, making you forget the word rheumatism better than any sulphur bath in all Canada."

"But," he said, in serio-comic tones, "what do you think of my being forced into annexation ?"

"Only that you use the word 'forced,' I should say I congratulate you."

"At the same time that you keep your own freedom, though," he said, despondently; seeing her look of gravity, he continued, touching her hand, "beg pardon, Elaine, I should not say that, knowing your past; but," he said brightly, "I should like to see you wed an affinity."

"I am afraid such pleasant fate is not for me," she said, gravely.

"Do you believe in predestination, Mrs. Gower?" he says, abruptly.

"What next! from annexation to dogma. Tell me all about yourself, and it is too lovely an Indian summer day to remain in the house, come to my favorite seat in the garden."

"Where I shall give you an instantaneous photograph, from my father's pen, of the girl I am predestined to change the name of."

"From your father's pen!"

CHAPTER IV.

THE FOOT-BALL OF CIRCUMSTANCE.

S they near a knoll under a clump of trees commanding a view of the road, a gentleman sauntering up the street gazes, as many do, at Holmnest with its pretty grounds.

"Look, quick, Charlie," said Mrs. Gower, in low and rapid tones, apparently intent on spreading a rug on the rustic bench, "there he is, I mean——"

"Well, I only see a very ordinary and thoroughly independent looking man, seeming as though he feared

3

nothing, not even you, and as if Toronto was built for him."

At this Mrs. Gower, laughing merrily, says, "And not for the Lieutenant-Governor, Mayor Howland, Archbishop Lynch, or the 'caller herrin'-man.'"

As the soft laughter fell on the air, the stranger looked towards them; and looked so intently, that involuntarily his hand is raised to his head and his hat lifted.

"You say you have not met him, Mrs. Gower; you are a very prudent woman, I must say, coming out here in your white gown, with ribbons the color of a peach, creating a sensation; you had better wed an affinity since you won't have me, and get a protector at once."

"That is the man I dreamed of whom the æronauts dubbed my affinity; it's too bad we are not acquainted, instead of only getting instantaneous photographs of each other."

"What a trial!" he said, ironically; "but still," he added, as with a sudden remembrance, "I have, strange to say, had occasion to say, hang the conventionalities, more than once, with reference to a fair-haired girl with blue eyes, that seem, when I think of her, to follow me; no later, too, than this morning at W. A. Murray's door, as you I have had only instantaneous photographs of her; once before at a window in New York city, also there in a suspension car; it is not that I have fallen in love with her—not by a long chalk, but she seems to have been in my life some time, that by a trick of memory I have lost; but I advise you, Mrs. Gower, not to allow that man to bow to you again."

"Oh, he only lifted his hat in apology; but I wish you were not going away, and that I could see this girl."

"I wish I hadn't to; but this is the way time flies

whenever I come to Holmnest; I am forgetting that I came to tell you I am just now the foot-ball of circumstance, which compels me to cross seas to have a halter put around my neck in wedding a girl whom I have never seen."

"Even if you have to, Charlie, you may love her at first sight, so don't take it to heart; if it is so that she is no affinity, you will suffer only as many others," she says gravely, "in having a taste of the tantalus punishment, in losing what we would fain grasp; but tell me all about it, as my dinner guests will be soon arriving, and I did so want you for—myself, as well as for Miss Crew."

"That's the first sympathetic word you have said, 'for yourself,'" he said, touching her hand, "but I am to be always for somebody else," he said, a little sadly; "but I see you think I am never going to begin, so here goes: My father, as you have heard me say, did not marry a second time, not that he did not again fall a victim to the tender passion, but that the mis-creator, circumstance, putting in an oar, sent him out of England, when his bride-elect that was to be, was coerced into marrying her guardian (one Edward Villiers, of Bayswater, London,) by his sister-in-law, a domestic tyrant, and his housekeeper; who, knowing to rid himself of her presence he would probably wed a woman of as strong a will as her own, when she, penniless, would be thrust out, told lies, not white ones, of my father, that he had married in Canada, intercepting his letters, and heaven knows what; at all events, Lucifer's agent triumphed, for on my father going across the water to claim her and scold her for her silence, he found her a wife with a baby girl, when, to reduce a three-volume story to a line, they, in despair, wept and raved, nearly heart broken, vowing that I and the little one should wed and inherit all the yellow sovereigns; and so, Elaine, it comes to pass in years of evolution this youngster has become of age, and I am presented with her as my bride. I have always known of this contract, but you know the kind of man I am, ever shoving the unpleasant into a corner; for the bare idea of marrying a woman for money has always been repugnant to me."

"I should say it has, for with you it has ever been 'more blessed to give than to receive.'"

"I don't know that, but to hasten, breathing time is at last not given me, I am summoned to England by those people and by my father's wish, who sends me a copy of the will of the late Mrs. Villiers, a clause of which I shall read to you; but what a bore I am to you."

"Nonsense; who have I poured my life puzzles into the ear of but your own kind self—turn about is fair play, and besides, yours is a sensational *life* story, and so more interesting than thoughts from the clever pens of Haggard or Mannville, Fenn, or our own Watson Griffin."

"Well, the will reads . . . . . 'on my dearly loved daughter, my little (Pearl) Margaret Villiers attaining her majority and becoming the wife of the aforesaid Charles Babbington-Cole, son of my loved friend Hugh Babbington-Cole, of Civil Service, Ottawa, Canada, my said daughter *shall enter into possession* of all my real and personal property, she to be sole executrix, and to inherit all, (with, I hope, the advice of Dr. Annesley, of London, and Hugh Babbington-Cole aforesaid,) and subject to the following bequests: To my step-daughter, Margaret Elizabeth Villiers, I leave my forgiveness for her unvarying unkindness to myself with my copy of the Christian Martyrs. To my dear friend, Sarah Kane, five hundred pounds sterling and my wearing apparel. To my husband's sister-in-law, Elizabeth Stone, I will and bequeath my piano and music for use in her mission work, with the hope that sweet notes of music will make her less acid to the children of God's poor to whom she brings the Gospel message of peace, etc., etc.' "

" So! your late mother-in-law made a point there, the self-righteous woman weighted religion then as now. I have always predicted, because of your open palm, that you would never be a rich man, Charlie; I little thought the precious metal with a wife would pour into your lap at the same time; if you only knew her and cared for her" she said, musingly, when, noting his troubled look, she said brightly, picking a beautifully tinted maple leaf from his shoulder, "See here, old man, take this crimson-hued leaf as a good omen, and we will read from it that your home-bound path, I mean back to Holmnest and Toronto, will be a path of crimson roses; and now tell me, does the girl write you, and is it in a stand and deliver manner? If so, I fear my verdict upon her will be lacking in charity."

" No, my pater has letters from her which he does not forward; but here is the last one from my father, in which he says: . . . 'I have received several letters from Broadlawns, Bayswater, England, and from Margaret also, in which they tell me time's up, your bride elect is of age, and naturally anxious to come into possession of her property. I need not go over the whole matter again with you, my boy, but I do most earnestly advise you to start at once, the daughter of my lost Margaret must be good and true, even though Villiers was her father; she should be pretty, also fair hair and sky-blue eyes (in woman's parlance). I saw her when her poor mother made her will in 1872. Pearl was then about five years old; she cannot fail to be attracted by yourself, if Dickson does not flatter you, and I don't think so; your good looks are honestly come by, so you needn't blush.

" 'And now to business; enclosed you will find a

cheque for five hundred dollars, for you are like me more than in appearance, you don't save. What an income you will have shortly, instead of bookkeeping on the paltry salary of $800 per annum, you and Mrs. Cole, ahem! will roll about King Street the envy of the town, with an income of £5,000 sterling per annum. While I shall have the pleasure of seeing some of your mechanical ideas patented, and their models in the buildings here, your nose and the grindstone will part company; how glad I am that you have not fallen in love and married; and now I ask you, believing it to be best, believing it to be for your happiness, to leave for the seaboard on receipt of this; my chief has given me a three weeks' leave, so shall run across, but to save time, as I have business at Quebec, shall sail from there; meet me at Morley's, London, Trafalgar Square. If my memory plays me no trick, I shall sail by the *Circassian*, Sept. 16th, you take the *City of Chicago*, one day later from New York.

"'And now, *pour le present*, farewell; you don't know how I have set my heart on this matter, if I were ill, the knowledge that the little daughter of my own love was your wife would cure me.

"'Social events are right down smart with us; in fact Ottawa is booming. Rumor says our next tid-bit will be an elopement in high life; even the soldiers can't keep the enemy from poaching; but we must be blind and deaf 'till Grundy says now.'

"'The American consul is a very knight of labor at present, minus their short hours, as quite a large number are leaving for, to them, the land of promise, the United States, whether they fly from the taxes or the cold; I have not interviewed them; by the way, you will be the better for a warm heart beating against your own this winter. And now one word of self, I shall be glad of the run across the water, for I feel any-

thing but smart. I wish we could have crossed to-
gether. Farewell, my boy, till we meet at Morley's.
"'Your affectionate father,
"'HUGH B. COLE.
"'C. B. COLE, ESQ.,
"'500 Wellington St. Toronto, Ont.'"

"How strange it all seems, Charlie," she said dreamily.
"I shall miss you so much, I do hope she is amiable
and lovable, you and she must come to me until you
get settled; poor fellow, you look stunned."

"I am paralyzed! it at last is so sudden, but why do
you smile?"

"At a remark you made at the Smyth's, or I rather
think it was when escorting me home, that 'you
deserved a good wife, for you had never sinned, never
told a lie.' So let us .hope in your case virtue will
have a reward."

"See! I must go, your guests are arriving; how I
wish you had no one this evening, and I might dine
with you alone."

"My wish too, on this your last visit, unfettered."

"That means you cannot bolster me up in this case,
as you have more than once heretofore; that I am in
for it," he says, looking at her sorrowfully.

"Yes, you are regularly hemmed in, and as I have
been before now, so are you at present the mere. foot-
ball of circumstances, but 'out of every evil comes some
good,' they say, and as your father says," she added
with forced gaiety, for she is sad at the thought of
snapping of old ties, "You will be the better of a
warm heart beside your own in our winter climate;
and above all, remember the good omen of this maple
leaf; here, take it with you," she says, pinning it to his
coat, the suspicion of a tear in her eyes.

"Good bye, Elaine, if it must be so; pray that I may
come out of it all right, for I feel horribly depressed;

and only you say I must go, would, I believe, show the
white feather; I wish I might kiss you good-bye;
there is that fellow, Cobbe, coming in, remember, that
'nothing is more deeply punished than the neglect of
the affinities.' God bless you; farewell."

And leaving by a side gate and entering a passing
hack, one of the kindest-hearted sons of fair Toronto
takes his first step to another land; easily led, yielding to a degree, he is now led by the wish of a dead
woman, by the iron will of a living one, his father
following their beckoning hand also.

CHAPTER V.

A BONA DEA.

N animated converse with her guests during the
half-hour ere dinner is announced, the mistress of Holmnest makes a picture one's eyes
dwell on—the folds of her soft summer gown
hang gracefully, while fitting her figure like the
glove of a Frenchwoman; fond of a new sensation—
as is the way of mortals—this of playing the hostess to
a few chosen friends in a home of her own once more,
is pleasurable excitement; there is a softness of expression, a tenderness in the dark eyes, engendered by
the fact of her sympathy having been acted upon by the
leave-taking, on such an errand too, of her friend Cole,
which lends to her an additional charm. The consciousness also that she is looking well, gives, as is natural
to most women, a pleasurable feeling in whatever is
on the *tapis*, with the knowledge also, that her little
dinner will be perfect, her guests harmonious—save
one.

"So you think Toronto is rather a fair matron after

all, Mrs. Dale, and that your New York robes blend harmoniously with the other effects at the Queens?"

"I reckon I do, Mrs. Gower; you did not say a word too much in her praise; I remember saying to Henry before we started, my last season's gowns would do."

"And you like Toronto also, Mr. Dale," continued his hostess.

"Yes, better than any other Canadian town I have visited; it is very simply laid out, one couldn't lose oneself if one tried."

"It is laid out like a what do you call it, like a chess-board," said Captain Tremaine, an Irishman.

"Yes, not unlike," continued Dale, "and as to quiet, one would think the curfew rang; I noticed it particularly coming from the Reform Club the other night."

"We all notice how quiet our streets are at night, and after your London and New York City, we must seem to you as if we had taken a sedative," said Mrs. Gower, taking his arm to the dining-room; "but where is Miss Crew, Mr. Dale?"

"She was too fatigued to come, she foolishly overtaxed her strength, taking my boy to the Industrial Home, at Mimico, I think she said."

"That's correct, it's a pet scheme of Mayor Howland's, and a worthy one too."

"Yes, so she said; they also visited your Normal School, and talked of the Cyclorama of Sedan."

"Indeed! they have overtaxed the brain and memory, I fear; what does Garfield say to it all?"

"Chatters like a magpie over the superior glories of New York, but is honestly pleased after all."

"I expect your little son is English only in name."

"Yes, and in his love for a good dinner," he said, laughingly.

"Well, from all we Canadians hear, there is every reason he should, an English dinner is enough 'to tempt even ghosts to pass the Styx for more substantial feasts,'" she said, gaily.

"Mrs. Gower is always up to the latest in remembering the tastes of her guests," said Mrs. Dale to her left-hand neighbor, Mr. Buckingham, as tiny crescents of melon preceded the soup.

"That she is," he said, complacently; "no man would sigh for his club dinner, did our hostess cater for him."

"Goodness knows what Henry would do if our bank stopped payment, or our Pittsburg foundries shut down; for I know no more about cooking than Jay Gould's baby," she said, discussing a plate of delicious oyster soup.

"He, I expect, makes himself heard on the feeding bottle," said lively Mrs. Smyth.

"But you are unusually candid as to your short-comings, Mrs. Dale," continued Buckingham, amusedly.

"Because I can afford to be; were I poor, I reckon I should pawn off my mamma's tea-cakes on my young man as my own, as men in love believe anything—they are as dull as Broadway without millinery."

"By the way, Mrs. Dale, talking of millinery, where are your bonnets going to, they are three stories and a mansard at present?"

"Oh, only a cupola, Mr. Buckingham, on which birds will perch."

"How so; I was under the impression the bird hunt is a thing of the past?"

"No, indeed! not while there are men in the field."

"How so; I do not follow you?"

"Stupid, you are born huntsmen, our bonnets are a perch for a decoy, and," she added, looking at him archly, "our faces are under them."

Here there was merry laughter from Mrs. Gower and Captain Tremaine, the former saying gaily,

"You would not accomplish it, the strength of will

of one of the party would keep the whole uppermost.
I appeal to Mr. Smyth."

"I am with you, Mrs. Gower; Tremaine must go
under, even though he is an Irishman."

"Irish questions always do get muddled, eh, Smyth?"
said Dale, jokingly, seeing that Smyth, intent on dinner,
had not heard the argument.

"That they do, Dale. Which is it, Mrs. Gower, the
Coercion Bill or Home Rule?"

"Neither," she said, laughingly, "we were on the
'Peace Party' (you remember the meeting at the
Gardens, on last Sunday); and I have been suggesting
that the Body Guard bury their pretty uniforms, and
Captain Tremaine raises the war-cry of, 'bury the
Peace Party, chairman and all, first.'"

"Oh, that's it! Tremaine knows the indomitable
will of one of them would cause more dust to be kicked
up than one sees on a March day on Yonge Street."

"Out-voted, Captain Tremaine, we weep 'salt tears'
over your becoming uniform; but seriously speaking,
though a High Court of Arbitration would be a grand
spectacle, it will be only after years of evolution, and
when, as Mr. Blake, the chairman said, 'the voice of
the private soldier, instead of the general officer, is
heard.'"

"If I should ever have the ill-fortune to be drafted,"
said Smyth, laughingly, "I should fight to the death
against my enrolment; an hospital nurse, like the
Quaker-love, would suit me better; such rations as a
man gets on the field."

"I know for a fact," said Dale; "that recruiting
during the present year in England, has been far below
the average of the last few years."

"Indeed! I was not aware," said Buckingham.

"By the way, Smyth," said Tremaine, "have you
seen, what do you call him, 'Henry Thompson,' in his
defence or answer to his critics?"

"I have, and he was able for them every time."

" Are you speaking of the journalist who went to jail in the interests of the *Globe* ? " asked Dale.

"Yes."

" His defence was capital, I thought," said Dale, " and I especially liked the way he stands up for his craft. 'There is no class of men,' he says bravely, 'in existence, animated by more humane motives than working newspaper men.'"

" I also read his reply with pleasure," said Mrs. Gower, "and reading it, thought what a clever and original fellow he must be."

"Talmage and Silcox have been lauding the power of the press to the skies," said Smyth; "they made me wish I surveyed the earth from an editor's chair, rather than from a tree I climbed to escape York mud."

" Have you heard how the Grand is going to cater to our dramatic taste this coming season, Mr. Buckingham ?" asked Mrs. Gower.

" Just a whisper, Mrs. Gower, as to Emma Juch, Langtry and Siddons."

"Yes; so far so good. Have you heard that the rail makes no special rates for travelling companies ? "

" I have; so you may expect that those who will pay the high toll, will be those of the highest standard."

" Then I suppose (though it seems selfish) we should be content with the rail rates as they are."

" You will enjoy the debates, Dale," said Smyth, "in the Local House during the session ; Meredith is just the man to lead our party."

" But I am not sure that it is our party, Smyth; I scarcely know how I should vote here; if Meredith is right, why doesn't he prove to Ontario that Mowat has held the reins too long ? "

"So he will before next election," replied Smyth, with a satisfied air.

" Don't be too sure, Mr. Smyth, eloquent though he

be," said his hostess; "while that clever Demosthenes of his party, Hon. C. F. Frazer, says him nay."

"Do you meditate a long stay, Buckingham, in this the white-washed city of the Dominion?" asked Tremaine.

"Yes, off and on all winter; you know I intend to purchase some of your mineral lands, since you allow them to lie undeveloped," he added, jestingly.

"You see, Capt. Tremaine," said Mrs. Gower, merrily, the American Eagle done in silver is not as yet plenty with us."

"Don't despair, Tremaine, Commercial Union is looming up," said Buckingham.

"Treason! treason!" laughed Tremaine, "for we know what it would father."

"Hear, hear," cried Smyth.

"Oh, I don't know," laughed Mrs. Gower, "they say it is the Main-e idea for settling; here's a pretty mess! here's a pretty mess—of fish!"

"We can wait," said Buckingham, quietly, "evolution will bring about the Maine idea, with you also."

"Did you say you are going to Maine, Mr. Buckingham, we cannot do without you now," said pretty Mrs. St. Clair, caressingly.

"Thank you, Mrs. St. Clair, I do not go; but even if so, you would, I fear, miss me less than your latest fad in the pet quadruped."

"How severe you are, Mr. Buckingham. Are all New York men so, Mrs. Dale?" She sighed, having a penchant for him.

"It's annexation, Mrs. St. Clair," said Mrs. Dale, mischievously.

"Annexation! is Mr. Buckingham going to be married?"

"I believe so." At this juncture Master Noah St. Clair, who had come instead of his father, was interested in other than his plate, while his mother said reproachfully :

"It *cannot* be true, Mr. Buckingham."

"Mrs. Dale is disposed to be facetious, Mrs. St. Clair; you must not swear by everything she says."

"That is an evasive answer, and I am dying to know; tell me, *dear* Mrs. Dale, what it means?"

"Which, annexation, or Mr. Buckingham?" said her tormentor.

"Oh, both, of course," she said, breathlessly.

"Both; well, when I come to take a good look at him, Mrs. St. Clair, he looks important rather than severe, his reason is, he believes, the best part of Canada pines for annexation; *comprenez vous?*"

"Oh, is that what you meant," she replied, with a relieved air, when, catching her son's eye, she said, with assumed carelessness, "I do miss my men friends so much when they marry."

"He is as cold as ice," whispered Mr. Cobbe, who, though a man of birth and breeding, prides himself upon being a flirt; "he is an icicle, I wonder you waste your warmth upon him."

"Nice man," she thought, "and only the second time I've met him; he must be in love with me, too, poor fellow," and, in an undertone, she says, "That's the way all you men speak of each other, but he is only so before people."

"You had better throw him over, an Irish heart is warmer than an American," he said, in his deep tones, into her ear.

"But the poor fellow would break his heart," she whispered, her cheeks flushing; he, equally vain, continued:

"Not he, a successful speculation would console him; and I—and I would console you."

"Are you always so susceptible?" she asked, turning her pretty enamelled face around to be admired.

"No, indeed; but a man doesn't meet as pretty a woman as you every day, as your mirror must tell you."

"How you gentlemen flatter," well aware that he is admiring her pretty hand and delicate wrist, as she holds aloft a bunch of transparent grapes.

"Not you," and for the moment he meant it; the particular she of the hour feasting on the nectar her soul loves, never dreaming that the next passable looking female in propinquity with him will be also steeped to the lips in the same food, "not you," he said, with a fond look.

"Thank you," she said, prettily, and with the faith of her early teens, "I must tell you a pretty compliment a gentleman paid me at the 'Kirmiss' last season, he said 'I was a madrigal in Dresden china.'"

"Too cold, too cold," he said, thickly, managing to press her fingers as they rose from the table, ere she laid her hand on the arm of Mr. Smyth, to whom she had been allotted, but who never spoiled his dinner by giving beauty her natural food.

"On Mr. Dale declining to linger, leading his hostess back to her pretty drawing-room, she said in his ear:

"You have dubbed me queen of Holmnest, therefore must obey when I bid you back to the dining-room for a smoke."

CHAPTER VI.

COFFEE AND CHIT-CHAT.

HAT a lovely little home you have, Mrs. Gower," said her friend, Mrs. Smyth, seating herself near her hostess, the pale blue plush of the padded chair contrasting well with her fair hair, pink cheeks and pretty grey eyes.

"That chair becomes you at all events, dear," said

her hostess, seeing that a maid deftly passed coffee bright as decanted wine, afterwards small bouquets of beautiful pansies and clematis among her guests, from huge glass and Japanese bowls.

"I could scarcely believe Will, when he wrote me of your good fortune, you know, the children and I were at Muskoka."

"Yes, I knew you would be glad. I bought this pretty little place the week you left, it seemed after years of waiting, my money (what is left of it) all came right in a day; you do not know how glad I am to at last see you in a home of my own—and in a chair pretty enough to become you, dear," she added more brightly.

"Oh, you always make the most of small kindnesses shown you, we were only too glad to have you."

"Be that as it may, I shall always remember the bright hours with yourselves in the dark days of my life," she said, warmly.

"When did you see Charlie?" asked Mrs. Smyth, in an undertone, for there are other ears.

"This afternoon."

"This afternoon!"

"Yes; and you will be surprised to learn he takes the rail for the sea-board to-night."

"To-night! Why, and whither, it must be a sudden move, for he was up for a smoke with Will the other night and said nothing of it; but," she added, laughingly, "he prefers a lady confidant when it's Mrs. Gower.

"Don't you think, Lilian, that the opposite sex is usually chosen to lend an ear?" she said, carelessly, to conceal a feeling of sadness at the out-going of her friend; for she is aware that the old friendly intercourse is broken, now that he has gone to his wedding.

"He has gone to be married; I suppose, he said something to us a long time ago about it, but he told it in a clouded kind of way; I wish he had confided in me, for Will would not care a fig, but every woman doesn't draw such a prize as I. Perhaps when you get number two he will not allow the opposite sex to confide; but talking of the green-eyed monster, reminds me of two scandals on our street." As she now raised her voice, the other ladies pricked up their ears. Mrs. Dale exclaiming:

"Scandals! sounds like Bertha Clay's novels. May poor Mrs. Tremaine and self come in. We have been on sermons, servants, and the latest infants; a scandal will be as refreshing as Mrs. Gower's coffee."

"I guarantee you an appreciative audience; Mrs. Smyth," laughed her hostess, "curtain rises over 'another mud-hole for us to play in.'"

"What a case you are, Mrs. Gower, but I must cut them short, for I would not for worlds Will and the other gentlemen come in while they are on."

"No fear of scandals in your home, Mrs. Smyth," said Mrs. Tremaine, "with Will always first."

"That's so; well, to begin, before I went to Muskoka, a lady and daughter came to reside near us. As they went to our church, Will said call; I did. Since my return, I heard from Mr. Cobbe," here turning suddenly to Mrs. St. Clair, to whom Mrs. Gower had overlooked introducing her, said: "I beg pardon, I should not name names." Continuing, "Mr. Cobbe told me the young lady had been married, and divorced. Some young fellow, in a good position down East, hearing she had some ready cash, wed and deserted her at close of honey-moon. Well, the other evening she was married again! at the house quite privately, and to whom do you think? to none other than, as the newspapers state, Norman Ferguson MacIntyre!"

"To Norman MacIntyre! oh, what a pity," cried Mrs. Tremaine, in dismay, "his mother and sisters are such pleasant people, and had very different hopes for him; it is simply dreadful."

"But he can throw her overboard, I am sure," cried Mrs. Dale. "If he only have his wits about him, the first marriage likely took place in Canada, the divorce across the line, don't you see; she is the precious prize of the gay deceiver, your friend is free."

"But, even if this be so, Mrs. Dale," said Mrs. Smyth, excitedly, "no girl will care to marry poor Norman afterwards."

"I am willing to stake our Pittsburg foundry on his chances," said Mrs. Dale, cooly.

"And I, Holmnest," echoed Mrs. Gower, "*poor* Norman has but to stand in the market-place."

"I think they have both lowered their social standing; don't you, Mrs. Tremaine?" said Mrs. Smyth.

"I do, indeed."

"It altogether depends upon their bank account," said their hostess, sententiously; and now for your next, for your mouth is still full of news, dear."

"Oh, yes; but my next is a *bona fide* married couple."

"But are they according to the Church Prayer Book?" said Mrs. Dale, with her innocent air.

"Oh, yes, certainly; and some say she is like a china doll, and the husband, a great big, ugly, black-looking tyrant; but the gentlemen are coming, and I must cut it short, and only say that a man handsome as Lucifer."

"Before the fall, I suppose," said her hostess.

"Yes, yes, you naughty woman. Well, they say this handsome fellow is there whenever the husband is out, and a pock-marked red-headed boy (some say their son) is there to watch the pretty wife, and their name is St. Clair." Sensation!

At this moment a pin is ran into the arm of the breathless narrator.

"Oh, mercy!" she cried, looking around discovering the boy Noah St. Clair, whom every one had forgot-

ten, seated on a footstool behind her, who said vengefully, indicating by a gesture Mrs. St. Clair and himself, "That's *our* name; it's *us.*"

"Gracious, Mrs. Gower, what have I done? Pardon
me, I was under the impression that this lady's name
was Cobbe. I don't know how I got things muddled;
I thought she was some relative of our Mr. Cobbe."

"Never mind, dear; I should have introduced you;
don't apologize; there are other St. Clairs in Toronto
than my friends."

"I don't mind it in the least," purred the pretty
doll; "some one is always talking about me. Women
are jealous of my complexion and all my admirers;
but I think my name is prettier than Cobbe."

"Yet 'tell my name again to me,' am always here
at beauty's call," said Mr. Cobbe, hearing his name on
entering with the other gentlemen.

"You, as a Bona Dea, have been our toast, Mrs.
Gower," said Buckingham, quietly, as he sank into a
chair near her own.

"And my inclinations, I hope," she said, laughingly,
"with no saving clause as to their being virtuous."

"I appeal to your memory of the 'Antiquary,' Mrs.
Gower; could any man living toast you as the Rev.
Mr. Battergowl did Miss Grisel Monkbarns?"

"I don't know; perhaps some would desire to make
a proviso."

"Then they would err; I should give a woman of
your stamp any length of line."

"Thank you; your confidence would not be mis-
placed, when in honor bound I have ever felt as though
I did not belong to myself."

"I should judge so; underlying your gaiety consci-
entiousness holds you to an extent few would dream
of; you have frequently sacrificed yourself to a mistaken sense of duty. Am I not right?"

"Yes; I have been a slave to what I used to think

the voice of conscience, but which I am now sure was
extreme sensitiveness, and a sort of moral cowardice;
but how strange you should read me so truly."

"Not at all, I am a phrenologist; if you will allow
me the very great privilege, I shall read your character
to you in some quiet hour."

"With very great pleasure. And now will you do
me another favor? Make my piano sing and speak
to us."

"Thank you; I should like to try your instrument.
It is from Mason & Risch, I see."

Having arranged a table at whist and euchre, Mrs.
Gower seated herself to enjoy the entrancing music,
while looking over some photographs to amuse the boy
Noah St. Clair, but it was not to be, for the voice of
Mr. Cobbe said in her ear:

"This won't do; you *must* come to the library with
me; I have not had a single word with you all evening, and am, as you are aware, an uninvited guest."

"Why invite you, Philip? Alas! there is invariably discord with your presence," she says sadly, in
the lowest of tones, moving away from the curious
gaze of the boy.

"Sit here, Elaine, if you positively refuse to leave
the room with me," he said excitedly, indicating a
tete-a-tete sofa not within ear-shot of her guests, managing to detain her until, the hours creeping on apace,
freighted with the music of soft laughter, and ravishing songs without words by the skilled performer, Mr.
Buckingham, when pretty Mrs. Dale's sweet voice is
heard, as she rises from the table, saying triumph-
antly:

"Win! of course we won. Why, Mr. Dale will tell
you, Mr. Smyth, that in our card circle at New York,
mine is dubbed 'the winning hand.'"

"Indeed! no wonder at our good fortune. Congratulate us, Mrs. Gower; we won three straight

games, all by reason of the admirable forethought of my partner," cried Smyth, exultantly.

"Forethought always comes in a head's length, Mr. Smyth. Now, if you could only gain a pocket edition of the winning hand, your surveys would yield you a gold mine," said his hostess, gaily.

"Instead of as now, a few promissory notes," laughed Smyth.

"The gentlemen have been envying you your monopoly of Mrs. Gower, Mr. Cobbe," said lively Mrs. Smyth, in an undertone; "she is an awful flirt, you had better take care of yourself," she added, mischievously.

"I mean to," he said savagely, and with latent meaning, adding, "she is as fickle as her clime; I hope," he said, endeavoring to control himself, "all you ladies are not so heartless."

"Oh, no; we are as constant as the sun, compared to her," she said, half jokingly.

"Would you be so to me," he said thickly, and coming near her.

"Go away, Mr. Cobbe; don't look at me like that, you awful man," she whispered, laughingly.

"When may I call, you are the right sort of woman," he continued, persistently.

"Will says so, any way," she said, archly.

"Say to-morrow," he persisted.

"Will!" she cried, mischievously, "Mr. Cobbe's compliments, and desires to know when he will find you in your sanctum, he wishes to smoke the pipe of peace with you."

"Hang it," thought Cobbe, "she has no ambition beyond Will; give me the Australian women after all."

"Almost any evening, Cobbe, I am always good for a smoke; but my wife says I'd better retrench, the house of Smyth is increasing so rapidly; good-night."

"May I see you home, Mrs. St. Clair?" asked Mr. Cobbe, fervidly.

"It would be too sweet—but oh!" and her arm above the elbow is rubbed, for the boy Noah has pinched her severely, saying,

"I'll tell papa."

At this juncture Thomas appeared, saying, a coupé had arrived for Mrs. St. Clair and Master Noah.

"I must see you to-morrow, Mrs. Gower, after office hours," said Cobbe, adding, on meeting the sharp eye of Mrs. Dale, "I have something very particular to tell you."

"Say the day after, Mr. Cobbe, please; I shall endeavor to restrain my curiosity so long, even though I am a woman."

"No, no, I must see you to-morrow at five p.m.," he said, impulsively.

"The yeas have it this time, Mr. Cobbe. Mrs. Gower belongs to us for to-morrow," said Mrs. Dale, drawing her wrap about her, over her cream-silk robe, slashed with blue velvet, and laced amid innumerable button-holes, her innocent look only apparent while, in reality, she is dissecting him, "our kind hostess does some of the lions with us to-morrow afternoon; the evening, she spends with us at the Queen's."

"Yes, we have no end of a bill for to-morrow," said Mr. Dale; "the Normal School, Mount Pleasant Cemetery, office of the *Mail*, and the University of Toronto."

At this there was a transformation scene, the face of Mr. Cobbe changing like a flash from inane sulkiness to jubilant triumph.

"To the University! then Mrs. Gower will tell you what a paradise we enjoyed, when I alone was her companion there," he said, with excitement; and having previously made his adieu, he departed, chuckling inwardly at his parting shot, and thinking for once she is nonplussed. "She is too high-spirited to sleep comfortably to-night, if so, she'll dream of me in spite of herself."

"What a funny man?" exclaimed Mrs. Dale, "reminds me of a Jack on wires. If I were in your place, Mrs. Gower, I'd hand him over to his mother to bring up over again; till to-morrow, farewell."

"*Au revoir,* dear."

"Good night, Mrs. Gower," said Buckingham, with a firm hand-clasp; "your evenings leave one nothing to wish for, save for their continuance."

"If your words have life, prove them by coming again; good night."

CHAPTER VII.

ACROSS THE SEA TO A WITCH'S CALDRON.

ROADLAWNS, on the outskirts of Bayswater, London, England, on the evening Charles Babbington-Cole, from Toronto, Canada, is expected, is all aglow with lights; its exterior a goodly spectacle with its many windows. A long, low, rambling house, the front relieved by cornice and architrave, and an immense portico from which white stone steps, wide and worn by many feet, lead to the lawns and gardens, which are gay with bright flowers, intersected with old-fashioned serpentine walks; one would call it not inaptly a garden of roses, such were their number, such their variety and beauty. Great masses of rhododendrons, with the fragrant honeysuckle, sweet-briar, and lauristina lent perfume to the air. Some fine oaks, with beach and graceful locusts, gave beauty to the lawns; stone stables, with farm and carriage houses at the back, with paved court-yard, and kitchen-garden luxuriant in growth, a very horn of plenty.

"A lovely spot, an ideal home," said numerous passers-by to and from the modern Babylon. Alas! that the interior should be a very *inferno*; in the library are assembled the family, for a family talk.

Miss Villiers, to whom did we not give precedence, would trample on some one to gain first place. Timothy Stone, her maternal uncle, and Elizabeth Stone, his sister and Aunt to Miss Villiers; the latter by sheer strength of will, since her babyhood, has ruled at Broadlawns, even though, owing to disastrous speculation, the whole family were penniless, save for the large fortune of her step-mother, Miss Villiers lived for, moved and had her being for kingdom. Intensely selfish, and totally devoid of feeling, an apt pupil of her aunt and uncle, she regards all sentiment, romance or disinterested acts of kindness as mawkish, unpractical foolishness.

A word of her looks. In height, five feet two, round shoulders slightly high, thin spare figure, a brunette in coloring; stony eyes of piercing blackness, always cold and searching as though planted closely in the forehead to read one through, as to whether any of her dark secrets have been discovered; a hook nose, thin, determined lips; hair black as the wing of a raven; the back of her head covered with short, snake-like curls, the front was drawn back in straight bands, thus giving prominence to features already too unclassically so.

As far as a man can be said to resemble a woman, so did, in looks and character, Timothy Stone his niece, save that his once coal-black hair is now white; his fishy eyes sunken, though keen as a razor; in height, five feet ten; of spare, alert figure, active as a prize racer, knowing as the jockey who rides him.

Elizabeth Stone is an older counter-part of her niece, save that she wears that fashionable mantle of to-day—the cloak of religion, in which, unlike her brother, she is so comfortable us never to allow it to fall from her angular shoulders.

The library, an old-fashioned, cold looking room, furnished in black oak, everything being in spotless order, from books biblical and secular, to Aunt Elizabeth's hands, folded just so on her stiff gown of black silk, as to cause one to long for *déshabillé* somewhere other than in the principles of those present.

"The only one whom we have to fear is Sarah Kane, and you, Margaret, *will* keep her about the place in spite of all I can say," said her uncle, in crabbed tones; "mark my words, you are housing a rod for your own back by your abominable self-will.

"I am no fool; did I dismiss her I should convert her into a deadly enemy at once; but, as I have before had occasion to remark, Uncle Timothy, that, thanks to your tuition and blood, I am quite able to take care of myself, and minus your interference."

"Don't squabble with her, Timothy, when the man Providence is sending her as a husband may be in our midst at any moment; as you heard at the hotel, he is now in the city."

"Oh bosh, Elizabeth, keep that tone under your church hymnal, as I do; between ourselves it is slightly out of place," and he smiled sarcastically.

"No, Timothy, in spite of the sinful example you set me, I shall keep my lamp trimmed and burning; providence is very good to us in laying low of fever, at Montreal, Hugh Babbington-Cole, thus giving him time to repent, as also preventing his presence at the wedding of Margaret."

"At which you have been making mountains of mole hills," said her brother, grimly. "Babbington-Cole could not possibly remember what Margaret and Pearl looked like in eighteen-seventy."

"Your memory is as usual convenient, Timothy, relentless time would have shown him the difference in years, of a girl just of age, and a woman of thirty-nine."

"Enough, Aunt Elizabeth," interrupted her niece, pale with rage, "I simply won't allow you to allude to the subject of ages; if I am to play the role of twenty-one, the sooner I get into the part the better for us all; we all serve our own ends in this game, self-interest is, and ever has been, our strongest motive. For myself, I hate Pearl Villiers as I hated my step-mother before her, and I shall not willingly leave Broadlawns merely because we have no income to keep it up, when, by personating my step-sister—fortunately of my own Christian, as well as surname, thanks to the British habit of perpetuating family names—I gain the where-withal to either remain in this peaceful English home," she said, ironically, "or roam across seas with the husband or crank I am about to wed—a crank! to re-volve the wheels of fortune, while I leave you both here like a pair of cooing doves. You, Aunt Elizabeth, gain your revenge on Mr. Babbington-Cole for his preference · for my step-mother to yourself; oh, you needn't wince, my ears have been put to their proper use. You, Uncle, were spurned by my angel step-mother, you, pining not for her, but her yellow sover-eigns, so . . . . "

"You are a witch, Margaret; how the d——l did you find it out?"

"Timothy, Timothy, be good enough not to swear in my presence."

"Oh, I have gleaned the truth in various devious paths from Sarah Kane in a weak mood, also letters, and I have not lost my sense of hearing; as you have told me since I could lisp that my wits are sharper than Rodgers' cutlery; yes, if Broadlawns went to its owner or the hammer, you joined the Salvation Army, and my step-sister dangled the purse, I feel it in my

bones that I could now rival my tutors in living by
my wits," she said, cruelly.

"You are not devoid of common sense, Margaret;
and as we may not have another opportunity before
your importunate suitor appears, I shall refresh your
memory by reading again a clause or two of your late
step-mother's will. . . . . 'to my husband, Henry
Villiers, I bequeath the life use of one thousand
pounds sterling per annum; at his death I will and
bequeath the whole of my real and personal property
to my only daughter (Pearl) Margaret Villiers. . . . .
on my little (Pearl) Margaret Villiers attaining her
majority, and becoming the wife of the aforesaid
Charles Babbington-Cole, son of my friend, Hugh
Babbington-Cole, of the Civil Service, Ottawa, Canada;
my said daughter shall enter into possession of all my
real and personal property, with the advice of Dr.
Annesley, of London, England, or Hugh Babbington-
Cole, Esquire, aforesaid, my said daughter to inherit
all, subject to the following gifts. To Sarah Kane,
five hundred pounds sterling and my wearing apparel;
my piano, harp and music, I will and bequeath to the
sister-in-law of my husband, Elizabeth Stone, for her
mission-work, with the hope that their sweet notes
will make her less acid to my poor little daughter, as
also to the daughters of the poor to whom she brings
the Gospel message of peace. To my step-daughter,
Margaret Villiers, I leave my forgiveness for her persistent and unvarying unkindness to myself, with my
copy of the Christian Martyrs.'"

"Fool!" muttered her step-daughter, vengefully.

"Poor, carnal creature, we are now ordained to be
almoners of the gold she would have spent sinfully on
her daughter; we are saving Pearl from the perils of
the rich, for easier is it for a camel to go through
the——"

"Enough of that cant, Aunt; please keep it bottled

up, it don't go down with us," interrupted her niece, hastily.

"The will is plain enough, considering that it was written by herself, and witnessed by Dr. Annesley, and that sneak, Silas Jones; how much the latter knows is hard to tell, I have pumped him indirectly without avail; Annesley, being a busy London physician, will not bother himself in the matter now that Villiers is dead; he has no more love for us than we for him; our card is to expedite your union with speed and privacy; you will most likely go to Canada, as I expect Charles (as we best accustom ourselves to call him) will prefer such arrangement; I shall pay you regularly——"

"Yes, you'd better not try any of your sharp tricks on me, Uncle; if the cheque is not forwarded to the day, Trenton and Barlow will interview you; my sword will also hang by a hair."

"How confoundedly smart we are," he answered, wrathfully.

"I have been brought up in a good school," she replied, sententiously.

"I am glad you are able to appreciate our many useful lessons to you," he said, sneeringly. "And now to business; three thousand pounds per annum will be a large income for Canada; especially, as knowing your generous nature, I feel sure it will be all spent on your own wants; had you not better leave us three thousand, and pinch yourself," he said, sarcastically, "on two thousand?"

"Not much! anything I don't spend on myself, as you observe, I shall invest in, I think, C. P. R. stock, or even Grand Trunk, as it is looking up, there being a rumor that next year it will form a connection by way of Duluth, with the Manitoba boundary rail, thus placing itself in competition with the C. P. R. You need not stare, I am making myself conversant with the state of the Canadian money market."

" How wise we are. I can tell you that only a fool would invest in such like, with that Red River Valley Railway bungle on. What I want to be made aware of is, have you determined on taking no less than three thousand per annum ? "

" I have positively so determined. I don't think I look like a fool."

" I do—in a pink muslin, with as much ribbon hanging over your bustle as would make a decent gown."

" You are neglecting your education, uncle, in your favorite game of gold grab. I'd advise you to go to the city and take a few lessons from the clerks at Swan & Edgar's; they will tell you that in society a bustle is a *tournure.* As for my dress, my role is twenty-one, and I must bear some resemblance to the sweet lines of the poet—of

> ' Standing with reluctant feet,
> Where the brook and river meet.' "

" Dear, dear, what frivolity, and the suburban train is due; we should unite in thanking Providence that this gold is in our hands; but previously, Margaret, you should stipulate in writing that your uncle may pay me the sum of one hundred pounds per annum for my good works. There is Meg Smith, actually pining for her drunken husband, who says he won't reform until he gets her again; but I have my foot down, and shall keep them apart even if we have to pay her board; there is no use in my telling them not to be ' unequally yoked with unbelievers,' and then give in. I could cite dozens."

" Pray do not. It's my belief all you women care for is power to rule ; the wretches would be far better without your government. Heaven preserve me from a woman with a mission," said her brother in disgusted tones. "As to my promising to pay you any stipulated sum, you will receive your allowance for wearing apparel, and anything you can crib out of the housekeeping you will (all women take to that card naturally); but remember, if I find myself on short rations there will be the devil to pay."

"One word more, as the speakers say," said Miss Villiers, "ere we dissolve this profitable (I use the word advisedly) meeting: what fable shall we concoct as to the whereabouts of my angelic step-sister?"

"What an unpleasant way you have of putting things Margaret," said her aunt.

"I prefer on occasion to call 'a spade a spade,' Aunt Elizabeth. Well, uncle, shall it be as to her self-reliant spirit, and that she (being a mistake which means anything) has fled to that broad and convenient field, the United States of America?"

"Yes, that will pass; but I scarcely think he will inquire, as he has never troubled himself about his betrothed or yourself until you hunted him up."

"At your instigation; so disinterested in you, never thinking of the feathers for your own nest."

"The suburban train is due!" exclaimed her aunt. "Do, Margaret, endeavor to act like a Christian."

"Never fear, Aunt Elizabeth; I shall act my part as well as you do, with self-interest as motive-power: our sex play without a prompter; and now to the drawing-room to awe the ignorant Colonial by our British gold and conventionalities."

CHAPTER VIII.

A TROUBLED SPIRIT.

ITH mingled feelings of disinclination and repulsion, also an undefined sense of dread and reluctance, poor C. Babbington-Cole left the *City of Chicago* and, again on *terra firma*, made his way up from the seaboard to London, where at Morley's Hotel he and his father had arranged to meet. "Hang it," he thought moodily, "I feel like an infernal frog out of Acheron, covered with the oóze and mud of melancholy. Jove, if I could only chance upon the Will Smyths or Mrs. Gower, what a tonic they would be; how they would enjoy this madding crowd with all the world abroad, with no blue blood in the beef they eat either, judging from red cheeks and stout ankles. What women! cotton batting would not be a safe investment here; I hope the governor is waiting for me at Morley's, but he must be, as he took the *Circassian* from Quebec on the 16th. I'll persuade him not to go out to Bayswater at all, but to abandon this debt of honor, as in his sensitive nature he dubs his promise to a dead woman, for I have no hankering after a martyr's crown. If I am coerced (for I am made of very limp stuff) into this union and she is not a girl I can care to spoon over, and must 'write me down as an ass' for selling my liberty to, then adieu to wedded bliss—I shall again content myself in a den by myself, and my craze for mechanism shall be my wife and my few real friends my mistress. Jove! though, I must strain my eyes and endeavor to see a glimmer of light in the black clouds; if she be a girl after my own heart she will sympathize after a more practical manner than did the 'twenty with Bunthorn,' in giving me the dollar to develop, and obtain a patent for one or other of my inventions. Yes, I'll be a soldier. I am nearing the battle-field; with the smell of powder in my nostrils, I will gain strength. Cabby is reining in his steed, so this, I suppose, is my hotel."

"Morley's, sir; and 'ere be a porter for your baggage, sir."

"All right," and springing from the four-wheeler he is interviewing the clerk.

"Has Mr. Babbington-Cole, from Ottawa, Canada, arrived?"

"No, sir ; are you Mr. C. Babbington-Cole ? "

"Yes."

"Then here is a cablegram for you, sir."

It was from his father, and ran thus:

　　　　　　" St. Lawrence Hall,
　　　　　　　　" Montreal, Sept. 20th.

" To C. Babbington-Cole, Esq.,
　　" Morley's Hotel, London, England.

"Your father has been very ill—typhoid fever; called me in ; is improving ; asks me to cablegram you to return by way of Montreal.　Longs to see you and your wife, which will be a panacea for him.

　　　　　　　　" John Peake, M.D."

"My father ill!　Oh that I could have foreseen all this," exclaimed Cole, flinging himself into a chair in the privacy of the bedroom assigned him.　"To have to face my fate alone," he thought, " and yet I have been aware for some time that this was hanging over me ; but the truth is, I thought the girl would never claim me, that they would arbitrate, divide, have a grab game among themselves, anything other than rope me in.　Had I been gifted with Scotch second-sight, or even caution, I should not be in this fix now; but I have been made of wax, and so absorbed in my loved inventions, filling in an emotional half hour with an occasional flirtation, with my nose to the grindstone the rest of my time, that this possible 'game of barter,' in which some one says 'the devil always has the best of it,' rarely occurred to me; but this will never do in action, only shall I now find repose.　I *must* go out to Bayswater, and I *must* wed this girl, unless Heaven works a miracle—no, unless I act the coward's part, cut and run, I am in for it.　If I could only moralize on the pantheon of ugly horrors half of our marriages are, and that one might imagine most of them were perpetrated in the dark, or on sight, as mine, then I might console myself by thinking that I have as good a chance of happiness as most. My brain is on fire; if I only had one friend in this vanity fair, wherein to me is no merriment, the babel of sounds seeming to me the guns of the enemy warning me to retreat; talk of *delirium tremens*, I have all the blue devils rolled in one; a stimulant is what I want, to be able to face the music."

And making his way to the bar, in a short time his spirits, with the aid of John Barleycorn, arise; though he knows in the reaction they will be below zero.

"And now for Bayswater and my skrinking young bride," he thought. "I declare," he said, half aloud, with a forced laugh, "I can sympathize, for the first time, with the fly who had a bid from the spider to walk into his parlor. Is there a roaring farce on anywhere?" he asked the bar-tender.

"Yes, sir; a reg'lar side-splitter at the Haymarket. You will 'ave time to take in the matinee and dinner at Broadlawns, Bayswater, too, sir."

"How the deuce did you know I was due there?"

"Mr. Stone and Miss Villiers have called three times to look you up, sir."

"Indeed!"

"Yes, sir; Mr. Stone, he came in, and Miss Villiers, she waited outside in the trap."

The mere mention of the people from Broadlawns having come to hunt him up, had such a depressing effect, that he abandoned all idea of distraction at the play.

"There is not a particle of use of my trying to sit through the farce with this thumping headache; have a hansom here for me in a couple of hours, to convey me to Broadlawns; I shall walk out and get a glimpse of the city."

5

"All right, thank you, sir."

"Some one hath it," he thought, entering Trafalgar Square, "that the grand panacea, the matchless sanative which is an infallible cure for the blues, is exercise, exercise, *exercise!* so now for a trial; here goes for five miles an hour."

"On, and ever onwards, with, and yet apart from, the stream of busy life, alone and lonely amidst the throng, not once staying his steps; winging his flight in the vain effort to flee from self, drifting on the waves of unrest, they engulfing him, his face white and worn as a ghost, his blue eyes weary and with a hunted look, a neuralgic headache driving him to the brink of madness; the panorama of wonderful sights on which, under other circumstances, he would have feasted his eyes. Peers of the realm, having gained notoriety in one way or another, passed unnoticed, with lovely women, from professional beauties reclining in their own carriages, whose toys were men's hearts, with the world as a stage, to the avowed actress, whose bright eyes looked from a hired equipage, who played for men's gold on the stage of the theatre; far-famed Regent Street was traversed with less interest than he would have accorded to Lombard Street, Toronto; for man loves freedom as a bird—there he was free, now he feels his fetters.

"Take care, sir," said a policeman, kindly.

"Blockhead! it would serve him right to come to his senses under the feet of my horse," said the only occupant of a low carriage, in the voice of a shrew, as she drove on.

At this juncture Cole shook himself to rights, as it were.

"She was ugly enough to give a fellow a scare, after our pretty Canadian women," he said to the policeman.

"Oh, she isn't no type of what we can show you, sir; she's but small, but enough o' her sort, say I."

"Ditto ; and now be good enough to hail a cab for me."

" Yes, sir; here you are, and thank you, sir."

" To Morley's hotel."

" All right, sir."

On reaching his destination he learned that Mr. Stone had driven in to ascertain whether he had arrived, when, on hearing that he had, but was out, had waited ; when a lady, calling for him, had gone, leaving a note for him, which on opening read thus :

" DEAR BABBINGTON-COLE,—Am very pleased to hear of your safe arrival ; have important business, so cannot wait ; in fact arrangements for the immediate marriage of my niece to yourself ; kindly come out at once, on your return.

" Yours sincerely,
" TIMOTHY STONE."

" The net is well laid," thought poor Cole ; " they are bound to rope me in ; how strange it all seems ; even my name sounds unfamiliar, having at home, in dear old Toronto, dropped the Babbington ; but I must adorn myself for the altar." And once more he seeks retirement in his own chamber. " Hang that evolution of a woman's corsets and curling tongs, viz., the modern dude ! such a choking and tightening a fellow's throat and legs undergo ; I wonder if my shrinking bride will expect me to kneel to her. Ah ! there goes for a rip ; under the knee, though, as luck would have it ; not being quite educated up to a chamois pad and face powder, my modest Pearl will have to be satisfied with candle and throat moulds. I wonder if she will compliment me on my handsome black moustache, as my women friends at home do ; and now to fortify myself with dinner, or at least oysters and a glass of stout. Hang it, how faint and dizzy I feel."

CHAPTER IX.

VULTURES HABITED AS CHRISTIAN PEW-HOLDERS.

N due time his hansom enters the gates of Broadlawns; at the door he is met by Mr. Stone.
   "Welcome to England and Broadlawns," said
the spider to the fly, his ferret-like eyes scan-
ning his victim eagerly, as if to read whether
he would give him trouble. "We have been expecting
you for twenty-four hours; the ladies have been most
anxious. Simon, bring this gentleman's baggage upstairs, to the east room; and put in an appearance soon,
Babbington-Cole, or the ladies will think you a myth."

"Thank you; as I dressed at Morley's, I shall be
with you in a few moments," responded Cole, in sub-
dued accents, feeling that struggles would be now of
no avail, that he was well in their net; but the
house itself would have depressed him under any circumstances. It was solid, massive, thick-set gloom;
happiness and mirth were far away; the cold, chill
atmosphere of distrust, dislike, deceit and hypocrisy
dwelt in its dark corridors and gloomy apartments.
The last gleam of "Home, sweet home," had fled with
the spirit of the second wife of its late master; she,
poor thing, was wont to say, "Broadlawns is like a
lovely, smiling face, with a black, lying heart; its exterior is bright with Nature's beauteous flowers, its
interior a very Hades."

Miss Villiers and Miss Stone rose to greet Mr. Cole
on his entering the gloomy, but handsomely furnished
oak drawing-room; his first glance at the former
served to show him that the lady who had wished he
might come to his senses under the feet of her horse
and Miss Villiers were one and the same."

"Jove! that vixen," he thought; "but, thank Heaven,

there are two daughters; the other is my one, for my father says she is the prettiest girl in all England, and this one, ugh, she makes one's flesh creep."

"My conscience, 'tis that dolt," thought his bride-elect, giving her hand with her false smile. "We expected you to dinner, but cook has my orders to get you up something, so come with me to the dining-room," she added, insinuatingly.

"Don't trouble about me, Miss Villiers, I beg; I had a bit of dinner at Morley's."

"Muff," thought Miss Villiers, spitefully, "not to have taken his chance to become acquainted."

"Margaret is, as you are aware, Mr. Babbington-Cole, the Christian name of my niece (and a beautiful name it is); she will be better pleased if you drop all formality, and call her so, eh, Margaret."

"Yes, under the circumstances," she answered, with a meaning glance.

"Thank you; I have not seen your sister yet; is she quite well?" he asked, timidly; for, with a forboding of evil, he unconsciously looked to the sister as an escape.

"Margaret's fascinations fall flat," thought her uncle, with a malicious chuckle.

"I don't take; he wants a milk and water miss, but no you don't, young man; you are *my tool*," thought his bride-elect, setting her teeth.

"My poor step-sister is well—I hope, but we never name her; she is a—a mistake; however, *she* is not your one."

"But is she not here?" said Cole, nervously, now really frightened, "does she not reside with you? My poor father said—" here he utterly broke down. Accustomed ever to lean on some one, of a clinging, trusting nature, with a strong spice of feminine gentleness, which caused him to turn to some woman friend for advice or moral support, so that here, in the hour of his greatest need, he feels doubly alone, as he gazes

around at the three hard, cruel faces, each with a set
purpose and false smile perceptibly engraven, he is in
despair.   Miss Villiers especially; will he ever cease
to be haunted by her as she sits in a high Elizabethan
chair, an ebony easel exactly on a line with her face,
and partly behind her, on which is a frightful head of
Medusa, the reptiles for hair looking to him, in his
highly nervous state, like the tight, crisp curls and
braids covering the head of his bride-elect, and the
lines from Pitt's " Virgil" recurred to his memory :

> "Such fiends to scourge mankind, so fierce, so fell,
> Heaven never summoned from the depths of hell."

Mr. Stone broke the momentary silence by saying, in
matter-of-fact tones :

" It is natural, I suppose, to a man of your seemingly
nervous temperament, to be a little upset at not
meeting your father ; but, in my opinion, life is too
short for sentiment, especially when wasted as in this
case, for your father, according to cablegram sent us,
is improving, and is, I dare swear, kicking his heels
about St. Lawrence Hall, Montreal, waiting impatiently
for your return."

" Yes, Uncle Timothy, yours is the practical view of
it ; sentiment is, or should be, a monopoly of the poets;
self-interest, with pounds, shillings and pence, are good
enough for us."

" Margaret means to convey, Mr. Charles, that you
should be thankful to Providence that you have been
spared to come to us ; to a land, also, flowing with
milk and honey, ready to your hand and purse," said
her aunt, sanctimoniously adding, " How is religious
life in Toronto ? "

" Religious life ? " he said, half dazed, wholly absorbed in the thought that he was to be held in bond-
age by that stony-eyed woman with snake-like hair—
his Medusa.

"Alas, I fear you are dead in sin, Mr. Charles. You do not even know the meaning of my words. I have heard that New York is the most wicked city in America, and you, I fear, frequently go there to participate in the pleasures of sin. I dread to allow my niece to go out, even as your wife ; it was only the other day I read, copied from one of your newspapers, that at Tahlequah, which I suppose is near you, that a Chickasaw Indian was arrested by a deputy United States marshal with three assistants; the company camped on the prairie, with the exception of the marshal, who, riding on, reached his goal; waited there until weary, he rode back, and what did he find ? The entire posse with heads cut off, and the Indian fled. America must be a very Sodom and Gomorrah. But I see you are not listening to me, Mr. Charles. We have a saintly young man here, the Rev. Claude Parks, whom I must ask to influence you to a better frame of mind, with an intense gratitude to Providence for the favors about to be showered upon you."

Thus did Miss Stone give vent to her feelings to unlistening ears. Fond of hearing her own voice, it mattered little to her that she received no replies but to be told impatiently that "he was ill," and to be compelled to waste the eloquence she seduced herself into believing she possessed, upon a man with now his hands pressed upon his feverish brow, now his eyes fixed on vacancy, now upon the entrance as though he would fain flee, incensed her almost to rage; during the absence of Mr. Stone and his niece she had determined to improve the occasion, and so read him no end of lectures. The two absent ones, after a few minutes' whispered conversation in the library, had crossed the lawn to a neat cottage where the clergyman in charge of the Bayswater Mission existed on one hundred and fifty pounds per annum. As they stepped through the flower beds, which the moon rising in unclouded splendor lit with her soft white light, Miss Villiers in cold, hard tones, said :

"Yes, you are right ; he showed his hand, and of how much he loved me at first sight, as he asked in that scared way for my sweet sister, but bah! such maudlin folly in our wasting our precious moments over *his* feelings in the matter ; they are of no more consequence than are the blades of grass we crush beneath our feet in reaching our goal ; let him laugh who wins, even though the goal be reached by a foul."

"Yes, the sooner we hold the lines the better ; he has not spirit enough to be a runaway horse."

"Let him but try, there is the curb bit and halter."

"Oh, you need not tell me, Margaret, that you will have him well in hand. Yes, and before that paradise of fools, the honeymoon, is over," laughed her uncle sardonically.

"Yes, the grey mare will be the best horse this time ; but what a blessing his father is laid low ; it would have been all up, when he saw how cut up our precious Charles is. I did hope, had they come over together, they might have been shrewd as their Yankee neighbors, and gone in with us. Now, if his father should die, we have nothing to fear ; if he lives, we must exercise our wits, that is all.' And, now, as to your little fiction as to the telegram summoning you away at daybreak, where will you stay ?"

"Oh, anywhere, in some quiet cheap boarding-house in East End, London ; perhaps Tom Lang's."

"I suppose it's soft of me, uncle ; but I may not have a quiet word with you again. You must mind, I mean what I say. You must pay aunt one hundred pounds per annum for her own requirements and beloved mission work, though what she gives would not buy salt to their porridge, unless to that of her pet parson himself."

"When you know this, Margaret, why make such

an ass of yourself as to give it her; for, in my opinion, she is hoarding."

"It is in the blood; but you are a monopolist," she said sententiously as, merely tapping on the door of the cottage, they entered *sans ceremonie*, meeting the Rev. Claude Parks in the hall, who, shaking hands with both, said: "I had some calls this evening, but expecting you in, postponed them. At what hour to-morrow am I to tie the knot?" he asked smilingly.

"Never put off till to-morrow what can be done to-day, Mr. Parks; you may take that for your text next Sunday," said Miss Villiers decidedly.

"Nothing like it, Parks," said her uncle in oily tones, rubbing his hands.

"I shall give you another," said the curate rejoicing in his coming fee. "'If, when done, 'twere well, 'twere well 'twere done quickly.' Do you desire me to return with you?"

"Yes," said Miss Villiers, "and at once, if we are to act on our joint quotations, for it is only two hours until midnight; come, get your robes of office, and let us be off."

Thus it was that the ways and means did duty, the curate standing much in awe of Miss Villiers, as well as of Miss Stone; some saying the latter was his curate, others facetiously protesting that he was hers. And so she considered him not as the ambassador of Christ, but as a paid servant of her own, for so does too often the Anglican Church pay its clergy only sufficient for a dinner of herbs; knowing that man, be he priest or sinner, being a dining animal, has, at a weak moment, a craving for the "stalled ox," and if his appetite be too strong for him, sells himself, like Esau, for a "mess of pottage."

But now to return to Miss Villiers and her uncle, with the Rev. Claude Parks, as they make their entrée to Broadlawns and its oak drawing-rooms.

CHAPTER X.

A LUCIFER MATCH.

"EV. MR. PARKS, Mr. Babbington-Cole, of whom you have heard us speak, from Canada," said Miss Villiers; and Bengough's modern curate of the conventional type flashed across the memory of poor Cole. He was a meek young man, though a true Christian, who spoke in a monotone, his hair parted, to a hair, in line with the bridge of his nose, and wearing his hands meekly folded.

After their going round and round the barometer, English and Canadian, Miss Stone said, primly:

"It matters little whether the poor carnal bodies suffer from the cold. I fear, out there, souls are cold unto death, starving for spiritual life and heat. I have been telling Mr. Babbington-Cole, and I feel sure you will coincide with me, Mr. Parks, that with so many infidels and wild Indians in his land, they should have their lamps trimmed and burning."

"You are always orthodox, Miss Stone," chanted Mr. Parks, meekly. "You look ill, Mr. Babbington Cole; was the sea too much for you?"

"Yes, and now my head is in a whirl. I feel as if I am in for brain fever. Would to God I had remained in Canada," he answered feverishly.

"Tut, tut; a night's rest will set you up," said Stone hastily. "You Canadians are pale in any case, looking as though you feed on gruel."

"Cablegram, sir," said Simon, tapping at the door.

"It's for you, Babbington Cole," said Stone, handing it.

"From my father's medical man," said Cole nervously, as, on reading it, he returned it to the envelope, and was about pocketing it, when Miss Villiers said, putting out her hand:

"I presume we may see it."

Cole, though with visible reluctance, handed it to her, when she read as follows:

"ST. LAWRENCE HALL,
"MONTREAL, 25th Sept.

"To C. BABBINGTON-COLE, ESQ.

"Typhoid fever left; but taken cold, sore throat; looking most anxiously for the return of yourself and Mrs. Cole. *Pray don't delay.*

"JOHN PEAKE, M.D."

"Too bad, too bad; but you may yet find your father quite well," said Stone, with assumed feeling.

"'In the midst of life we are in death,'" said Miss Stone. "I trust your father has not been a careless liver, Mr. Charles; as a young man, I remember he was much given to the things of the world.

"My father is no smooth-tongued hypocrite, but has a truer sense of religion than many representative men and women in our church of to-day," said Cole, warmly; while thinking, but for his mistaken sense of honor, I would not now be in this abominable fix.

"You will, I am sure, be anxious to return at once, Mr. Babbington-Cole," said Mr. Parks, in measured tones. "And as the first step towards it, as it grows late, if you will arrange yourselves, I will proceed at once with the service."

"To-night!" exclaimed the victim.

"I think it best, Babbington-Cole," said Stone, firmly, "for you are not the only one who has received a telegraphic message this evening; mine summons me away at daybreak for the Isle of Wight, on urgent business; and as you have crossed the pond to marry my niece, what do you gain by postponement?"

"By delay," said Miss Villiers, fixing her stony eyes on him, as she motioned him to stand beside her, "by delay we may miss seeing your father alive."

"True," said Cole, "and I must find him alive to explain all this," he added, with feverish haste. And while the service was said in monotone by the clergyman, so intent was he in performing hidden rites of vengeance upon his bride for the pantheon of hideous idols she was making him walk through life in, that he was deaf to the words:

"Wilt thou take this woman to be thy wedded wife?"

And the first caress he received from his bride was a pinch, sharp and telling; he said, excitedly:

"Take it all for granted, Mr. Parks, I am really too ill to take part."

At the words, "I pronounce that they be man and wife together," etc., muffled footsteps and the noise of panting breath is distinctly heard, and a pale woman, who had evidently come from a distance, with flying feet entered; the clergyman only seeing her, the others having their backs to the entrance; but she nears, staying her feet to listen as she hears the words which add another couple to the long line of loveless unions, her hurried breathing falls on the ears of those present. All turn round. Miss Villiers eyes her menacingly, while Miss Stone and her brother simultaneously point to the door, as she interrupting Mr. Parks' congratulations, says in heart-rending tones of despair:

"Yes, I will go, for I am too late, too late, alas! for my poor young mistress and my oath to protect her." And she vanished noiselessly.

The fetters securely fastened, Mrs. Babbington-Cole said, wrathfully:

"A lunatic asylum is the only fit home for Sarah Kane." Turning to her new-made husband, she says explanatorily, "an old servant, and a crank. Uncle

Timothy, you had better see her caged up somewhere, or pay her off, and dismiss her."

"Yes, I must; we can't have a madwoman going about like this."

"Alas! how ungrateful of Sarah," sighed Miss Stone. "I fear the seed we have sown fell on stony ground, Mr. Parks."

"I fear so, indeed," echoed Mr. Parks, as he departed, his heart gladdened on thinking of the good British gold in his pocket; and from Mr. Stone, mean though he was, it was worth paying a sovereign to become the possessor of a yearly income of two thousand pounds. The poor bridegroom thought not of the parson's fee, which, had he wedded a woman of his own choice, he would have paid with an overflowing heart, he, poor fellow, being as generous as morning sunbeams on a beauteous June day.

The ceremony over! the fraud consummated! the bird snared! the man fettered! all joy in living, all hope in his heart crushed by a woman. Cole since hearing the solemn words of the agitated woman, felt as he threw himself into a chair, burying his head in his hands, as he leaned forward elbows on knees, as though did some one put a knife to his heart he would be grateful; he felt feverish and his brain throbbed as it had never throbbed before. Starting to his feet, he said brokenly, "It is now my turn to dictate; you will excuse me, I *must* have time to think, *and in solitude;* I go to my own apartment."

"You had better have some supper with us first to celebrate the event," said his bride, jocosely, for she feels triumphant.

"No, I thank you, food would choke me, and I am in no mood for revelry."

"You had better, Babbington-Cole," said Stone (who never offered a meal that he had to pay for), "you had better; an empty stomach is a cold bed-fellow."

But he was gone. Six ears sharp as needles listened to the sound of his retreating footfalls, slow and heavy, in ascending the stairs; they heard him go in and lock his door.

"A loving bridegroom," said Stone, malevolently. "You have evidently made an impression, Margaret."

"As you did on my sainted step-mother, when she spurned your offer beneath her feet, history repeats itself, most affectionate of uncles."

"'The tongue is a fire, a world of iniquity,'" said Miss Stone, reprovingly; "let us show a Christian spirit, and prove we are thankful everything is settled; we have worked hard for it, and have a right to partake of the feast prepared for the wedding party."

"Had you not better call your recalcitrant spouse, Margaret," said her uncle, as they repaired to the dining-room and seated themselves; "perhaps you do not know that the way to a man's heart is through his stomach."

"No, I shall not disturb his peaceful slumbers; by leaving him to himself he will the sooner come to his milk. For a beggarly eight hundred-dollar clerk— Colonial at that—he does not show gratitude as he should for a three thousand pound per annum wife."

"I agree with you, Margaret, but I doubt not you will bring him to a more Christian frame of mind," said Miss Stone, dwelling on each mouthful of veal-and-ham pie with the relish of an epicure.

"Alone once more, thank God!" said Cole to himself in despairing tones, throwing himself on to a sofa of stiff, cold horse-hair; "and now to collect my unwelcome thoughts," he sighed wearily, now walking restlessly to and fro, now flinging himself down, lying perfectly still.

Some one says that "locality is like a dyer's vat." This room assigned to Cole would in itself have lent a gloomy, funereal aspect to one's tone of mind, from the

cumbrous bedstead of dark mahogany to the darkest
of hangings and carpet, every article as cold and
polished as the black hair-cloth furniture. No pretty
feminine knick-knacks, no bright pictures, nothing to
relieve the eye.

"Alone," he groaned, "yes, but for how long? She
will. I expect, think she has the right to come here;
had she forced her hateful presence upon me to-night
I feel that reason would have fled. What could my
father have been about to sell me like this? But
there has been some devil's work. He has been
deceived, and I have been completely hemmed in by
the moves of the miscreator circumstance, the cablegram of his physician to them and to myself to-
night. She a modern Medusa, to be a panacea for him
or any one! Poor father, how you have been duped.
That they are all playing some devil's game is clear
even to my throbbing brain, no wonder that ever since
I set foot on England's shore I have had a terrible pre-
sentiment of evil hanging over me, and now the very
worst has come to pass: they have roped me in. I
have given her, that awful woman, my name! God
save me from madness! Hist! what sound was that?
They come! and yet the hideous midnight revelry is
still on below; but they come, a tap! Jove's thunder-
bolt, or Vulcan's hammer would be of no avail. I
shall feign sleep."

CHAPTER XI.

THEIR "RANK IS BUT THE GUINEA'S STAMP."

" ND what does our Diogenes find to say?" said Mrs. Gower, gaily, as on the night of the 9th November she gathered a few friends to supper, after an evening at the Grand Opera House. "Come, Mr. Dale, like a good man, confess that Mrs. Langtry is worth letting your tub go to staves for."

"Well, on the whole, yes. I think she has improved."

"Improved! but I suppose one must be content with even such admission from you."

"But, my dear lady, when a man has seen the best that London, Paris, and New York can put on their theatre boards, what you in Canada offer is merely *pour passez le temp.*"

"Yes, I suppose one grows to feel like that; but I am glad I have yet a few sights to see, if, by seeing everything, one loses one's zest for anything."

"But you surely do not admire her choice of plays?"

"No; but I do really deem her a born actress, as clever as she is charming."

"One could easily see, Mrs. Gower, that you got the worth of your ticket in emotional feeling," said Mr. Smyth, laughingly, "for you visibly trembled when 'ex-Captain Fortinbras' made his triumphant *exposé.*"

"Malevolent wretch! a thrill of horror did run through me, as well as of pity for his unfortunate victim."

"My feelings are not so easily acted upon," said Mrs. Dale. "I was very coolly watching to see if she could disentangle herself from the villain's clutches, and her arms from her odious lace sleeves."

"The latter absorbed me," said lively Mrs. Smyth; "if I had such arms I should never cover them, not even in mid-winter; you ought to pay more for your ticket than we do, Elaine, you get more—more feelings —than we do."

"Yes, I must trouble you for some more oysters, Mr. Dale; 'nerve tissue is expensive,'" she laughingly answered.

"Her gowns, her robings, were in perfect taste," said Buckingham.

"Yes, Oscar Wilde would have breathed a sigh of satisfaction," said Mrs Gower.

"Speaking of our color-blending pet," said Mrs. Dale, "he wishes his baby was a girl; he says girls drape so much better."

"Just fancy a thing like that living in our stirring times, and calling itself a man," said Dale, contemptuously; "picture him beside the two liberated Chicago Anarchists."

"Poor fellow! he would feel badly had the Communists the control of his wardrobe," said Mrs. Gower.

"His would be a capital garb for a surveyor," said Mrs. Smyth; "I wish Will would adopt it."

"Then would surveyors be on the increase when his measure would be taken," laughed Mrs. Gower.

"Lilian has vivid recollections of my last homecoming, when I was a mass of sticky York mud to my knees," said Smyth.

"I remember, Dale, you were disgusted at the Emma-Juch concert by reason of large hats and small chatter," said Buckingham. "What did you think of the manner of the audience to-night?"

"I think that, on the whole, when one considers the antecedents of the moneyed people of Toronto, that they behaved themselves better, showed more consideration for the feelings of others, in fact, ignored their fine feathers—remembering that they were not

6

the only occupants of the theatre—better than at any other gathering of ' beauty and fashion ' (in newspaper parlance), that I have made one at."

" Yes; so I thought," said Buckingham ; " and at the theatre, one escapes the worrying nuisance of recalls, as felt at Toronto." .

" I wish some star in the concert world would have the courage to insert after her name, no encore," said Mrs. Gower, " for though we do recall, it is astonishing how *ennuyeux* the best numbers are in repetition."

" Will did an awfully daring thing at the Carreno-Juch concert," said Mrs Smyth, eagerly ; " we had seats immediately behind the Cawsons ; and you know, Elaine, what a rude, boisterous——"

" My dear," said her friend, in mock reproof ; " they are in society ! have, of course, the dollar, and, perforce, are fashionable ! what in poor people we should designate as rude and underbred, we must call' in the Cawson's, and that ilk, ' quite the thing, you know.;' but proceed, *ma chère.*"

" Well, Will fidgetted, and they chattered across each other in audible remarks, on acquaintances in the audience, on a luncheon they were to give, as to the war-paint of a lady friend who had been presented to Queen Victoria, when I, the meanest of her subjects (I use the words figuratively, as Burdette says), pitied royalty ;' but the climax was reached when in Raff's ' Ever of Thee,' a particular favorite of Will's, the ' unruly member ' was heard with renewed vigor, when this husband of mine rose in his might, and to his feet, saying audibly, ' Come, let us try if the low price seats hold better-bred people.'"

" Bravo! bravo!" cried Buckingham.

" Very well put," said Dale ; " short a time as I have been in Toronto, I have observed that for culture and refinement one must look to the people who live on modest incomes, or salaries ; middle class is a phrase I find no use for. In this country there are the 'vulgar rich,' whose 'rank is but the guinea's stamp,' and well-bred poor; there are impoverished gentry, with an innate refinement showing in their too often struggling descendants; there are the moneyed people, lacking what filthy lucre cannot buy, namely, good breeding, and who never weary in parading their jewels, furniture and fine clothes."

"Very true," said Mrs. Gower; "I have frequently thought at some of our large social gatherings, that it is a pity one's blood cannot be analyzed instead of one's gown."

"What a resurrection there would be," said Buckingham; "not a few would long to pocket their own heads."

"A sympathetic artiste must feel any want of oneness in her audience," said Mrs. Dale; "I should throw my roll of music at them and retire."

"At which, dear, they would only give their unwearied cry of 'encore,'" said her hostess; "it is very evident we are all at one in a very decided distaste for mongrels; but, Mr. Buckingham, during your run on the Kingston and Pembroke rail you missed hearing the Rev. Jackson Wray."

"Yes; did he please you?"

"Extremely; both in his sermonizing and in his lecture on George Whitefield; he is eloquent, and his imagery and figurative language charmed me."

"Indeed; in that case I regret to have missed him. Did you hear him, Dale?"

"Yes, and though I regret the not being at one with Mrs. Gower in all things," he said, smilingly, "must say he pleased me not."

"Pleased you not!" echoed his hostess; then I abandon you to your tub; the scholarly, the literary world, would be a desert did your sweeping criticisms prevail."

"But how so, Dale? one would almost make sure of finding in him a rather superior excellence, knowing that he holds a pulpit in such a city as your London."

"Granted, Buckingham; but not only at London, but over the whole Christianized world, mistakes are to be found in the pulpit."

"Oh, no, Dale, I cannot go with you; 'tis in the pew that mi-takes exist."

"I go with you there, Buckingham," he replied, wilfully misunderstanding him; "the pew system is selling out the Gospel by the square foot," at which his friend laughed.

"Mr. Dale," asked Mrs. Gower, "do you never allow the critic within you to go to sleep, allow your really generous nature full play, and give yourself up to enjoyment?"

"I do; for instance, now, here is a real enjoyment; but, pray, do not dub me a critic."

"I fear I must in some of your moods; but see, the mere word, or the silvery chimes of midnight, are lending wings to your wife, and Mrs. Smyth: they are deserting us. Are you examining the heavens, dear?" she says, following Mrs. Dale to a window.

"Look quick, Mrs. Gower, he won't see you if you peer through the slats; and how awful! in among the bushes, out in that torrent of rain, there is a——"

"Don't alarm Mrs. Gower," said Buckingham, quietly, who had neared them unnoticed; "if there is anyone loitering about, let me open the shutters and window, and step out."

"Good night, Mrs. Gower," called Smyth, from the hall; "our carriage stops the way, and if I don't make a move, Lil never will," he says, meeting her.

"Mr. Dale is too fascinating," laughed his wife. "Good night, Elaine; Will thinks he hears baby crying, or he would not stir."

"Nice little baby, don't get in a fury 'cause mamma's gone to a play at the theatre," sang Smyth, jokingly.

" Did you *really* see anyone, Mrs. Dale ? " had asked Buckingham, in a grave whisper.

" I really did; the—but hush, she returns."

" You look pale, Mrs. Gower," he said, kindly, " put me up anywhere to mount guard over you for to-night."

" Oh, no, I thank you, not for worlds," she said, nervously; but recovering herself, added, " you know I have Thomas, and Mrs. Dale may only have seen a shadow, like a cloud which will pass."

" Clouds sometimes precede a storm."

" But not always," she says, with a sudden resolve, " for if Mrs. Dale will stay with me all night, she will be its silver lining."

" Indeed, I shall with pleasure," she said, eagerly, adding, in mock condescension, "Good night, Mr. Dale."

" What do you mean, Ella; our cab is here ? "

" I am going to stay with Mrs. Gower, Henry, so good night, dear; an extra blanket and night-cap must be my substitute," she said, as he kissed her good night.

" Good night, Mr. Dale; you are keeping up your character for generosity," said Mrs. Gower.

" Come along, Dale," said Buckingham, glad of the arrangement; " I shall be with you as far as the Rossin House."

Oh, Henry," called his wife, as he was entering the cab, "don't forget the schools are on for to-morrow; Mrs. Gower says to come up at one, to luncheon; don't forget Garfield and Miss Crew; and tell Miss Crew to send me first thing, by electric despatch, 82 Yonge Street, my plum walking dress, and bonnet to match, and——"

" No more, dear, please; you should have given it to me in manuscript form, I fear I shall not remember it."

" Poor Capt. Cuttle, when found make a note on,"

said Mrs. Gower, jokingly, but rather nervously, peering out, in and among the dark bushes.

"I'll coach him," laughed Buckingham.

"Etc., etc., etc.," called out Mrs. Dale, as the hack rolls away.

As the friends turn from the door, Mrs. Gower herself seeing to the fastenings and putting the chain on, Thomas said:

"Beg pardon, ma'am, but can you step this way, please?"

"But, Thomas," she said, trying in vain to battle with her fate.

"Yes ma'm, I know it's a shame to be a pestering of you at this hour, but it's——"

"Very well, Thomas, I shall attend to it; excuse me, dear Mrs. Dale, for a few moments, and then we must really go to bed."

"That's all right; I know what the calls upon a housekeeper are."

"Quick as a flash, on the exit of her hostess, the portière hangings are drawn, the gas at one end turned out, the window flown to.

"Yes, my lady crouches there still, and—yes, that is he on the kitchen steps; the light from the window points you out to me, my dear cupid—done up by a west-end tailor; the door opens, which shows me my kind hostess; and now for the woman—for ferret out this mystery I shall—for in some way, unknown to me, this gentleman and follower are worrying the life out of my friend."

With a waterproof on, noiselessly she opens the window and shutters; a step and the veranda is reached; with beckoning hand she endeavors to attract the attention of the woman, but without success, as she is wholly absorbed in watching the door by which the man entered. Afraid of attracting attention by calling out, she twists a couple of buttons off her waterproof, throwing them on to the gravel walk; her object is gained and defeated simultaneously, for the woman, taking fright, makes for the gate, at which Tyr, who had made his exit on the man making his *entreè*, swift as a deer, ran barking after her; but she is safe outside the gate, at which Mrs. Dale quiets Tyr, who has come up to her, rubbing his cold nose to her still colder hands. And now to make another attempt. In a few moments the gate is reached ; yes, the woman is standing under the the shade of a tree on the boulevard, the lamplight falling full upon Mrs. Dale.

"Down, Tyr, be quiet; down, I say. Come here, young woman ; don't fear, I only wish to speak to you."

"I won't go there ; let me alone, for I warn you, I am a desperate woman," she growled, in threatening tones, Tyr making a dash to be at her.

"Come here, Tyr, it's all right. But what is your trouble ? If you will only trust me, I feel sure I can help you," she says, breathlessly, for she does not wish her friend to miss her.

" *You help me !* go away with your smooth serpent tongue; away to that other hussy, in her silks and jewels, robbing an honest woman of her——"

But her sentence was never finished, for the man is coming; and quick as a deer she is out of sight.

Mrs. Dale is quietly seated by the cheerful grate, apparently absorbed in "Cleveland's winning card," as given in *Judge*, when her hostess returns, looking sad and troubled.

" I don't know how it is I feel so nervous to-night, dear," she said, seeing to the window fastenings; I am so glad you are with me, but you will find me very doleful."

" Not a bit of it, Mrs. Gower; I am no relation to an acquaintance of mine, who is not content unless one is making a buffoon of oneself for her especial delectation."

"I fear she would cut my acquaintance in my present mood. I am going to ask you a favor, dear; it is to call me Elaine; I shall feel less alone in this big world, and can talk to you more freely, hearing my Christian name. I dare say it is a childish fancy for a woman of my age, but——"

"But me—no buts. Elaine, we are true friends, and you have some secret trouble which I ought to share, else, what use is my friendship to you; you will tell it me, dear?" and the pretty Irish eyes look up into the dark ones bending over her with a questioning look.

"Tell me first, dear, did you recognize anyone in the garden to-night?"

"I did, Elaine."

At this, covering her face with her coldly nervous hands, she said, brokenly:

"God help me, I am driven by the winds, and tossed; I must sleep on it to-night, and if I feel strong enough, tell you all to-morrow."

"That's right, and to insure your being brave enough, you must take the best tonic, sleep; so let us mount," she said affectionately, rising and taking her friend's arm.

"Very well, dear; and the dropping rain shall be my lullaby in wooing the god of slumber."

CHAPTER XII.

ON THE RACK.

T was no heated fancy of a half-delirious brain of our poor friend, Cole, that he had heard a tap on the gloomy door of the east chamber, at Broadlawns, on the night he was snared by the huntress; held by the fetters of a loveless union with Margaret Villiers; but he paid no heed to the stealthy tap, repeated whenever the revelry below was loudest; but as silent as the grave, he almost holds his breath as he watches the door, a look of agony in his tired eyes, which throb as does his head in neuralgic torture; but now, his strange midnight visitor, as if driven to desperation by his silence, says through the keyhole:

"For heaven's sake, let me in !"

But no response; he will trust no one under the roof of this hateful place, to which he has been trapped, in which he has lost his freedom, in which the terrible conviction has seized him that he is going to be laid low by the fell hand of sickness. What is that ? Yes, he sees a slip of paper passed under the door; his midnight visitor is evidently bent on obtaining an interview; pale as a ghost, and trembling in every limb, he creeps noiselessly to the door, picks up the paper, and reads the following words:

"I am the woman who came in *too late* to stop your marriage; *your own friends*, who are far away, would tell you to see me. For God's sake, let me do what I can for you, even *now*."

But for her wording, as to his "friends far away," he would have paid no heed; he remembers now, in a dazed sort of way, amidst the medley he has been in ever since his arrival, that there was some woman who appeared, was maligned, and vanished, all in a few seconds. Yes, if he could only feel sure the oak door only separated him from one not in league with his enemies, as he now feels them to be, the lock would be immediately turned ; but, should it be a fraud whereby to obtain admittance for the terrible woman he has wedded, and whom he loathes and fears at the same time ; and so, with his cold, nervous hand upon the lock, he hesitates, when she again appeals a last time through the keyhole.

"I must go, and leave you to your misery, if you will not open the door; they are preparing to come up stairs."

At this, the dread of loneliness, the craving for sympathy, with the sinking feeling of sickness coming over
him, the natural instinct of self-preservation impelling
him to risk something in endeavoring to secure one
friend to be about him if he cannot shake off this
feeling of intense lassitude, low spirits, head and brain
on fire, and throbbing as with ten thousand pulses,
cause him with a sudden fear lest she should go, to
turn the key, when noiselessly, a pale woman with an
intensely sad expression in her whole countenance,
and prematurely grey, enters.

"Poor fellow! and a kindly, handsome face, too;
what a sacrifice! God knows how willingly I would
have saved you; but their moves were hidden from
me." she said piteously, in a low whisper, gazing into
his face tearfully, while taking his hands in her own.

In the reaction he flung her off, saying, brokenly,

"Why were you not in time? What trust have you
broken so, blighting my very existence? Out upon
you, woman, you may go and leave me to despair."

"No, no, I must stay; I *will* stay; you are ill, but
will be more calm; though with *her!* God help you,
you will never find peace, never be at rest."

And throwing her apron over her face, she, too, sank
on to the sofa where he was; but he is, after a few
moments, quiet again, and drawing the covering from
her face, which she has used as if to shut out the view
where all, all is misery to the last degree, she turns to
look at him; both hands white, cold and trembling,
cover his face, through his fingers drop scalding tears,
silent tears of woe.

"Do not give way so, sir. Poor fellow, you are indeed to be pitied, away from your home, away from
your own land. They sent me off to London on mes-
sages—to get me out of the way—for some things for
Miss Villiers, as then was."

"Don't remind me. God help me. Swear, woman,

swear !" he said excitedly, "to stay by me to get me well; quick, for my inner consciousness tells me I shall be, nay am, ill; elucidate this mystery, is it money they want, how can I escape? swear, swear to stay by me in this place, smelling of brimstone. Swear!" he continued, forgetting time and place, as he raised his voice, only remembering his wretchedness.

"For heaven's sake try to calm yourself; they have heard you, they come; not a sound; they will turn me out, and you will have only them. I conjure you, curb yourself; not a sound." And taking both his hands to her knee, with motherly tenderness, seeks by gently stroking or holding them in hers to soothe him to even momentary calm.

"I say, Cole, are you sleeping?" said the voice of Stone, turning the handle. "You should have been down with us; we have been feeding like fighting cocks."

"I am sure I heard him talking," said Margaret. "Mean fellow he is; feigning sleep."

"Good night, Cole, or rather, morning; pleasant dreams," said Stone, malevolently.

"Look, uncle, at aunt rolling into her bed-chamber; veal pie and stout will be her nightmare. Good night, spouse," she said, through the key-hole.

At this, Sarah Kane had great difficulty in quieting him. "I kiss my hand to you"—for she is hilarious; a glass of beer, a change of name, three thousand per annum secured, have been a powerful stimulant.

"It's my belief he heard every word we said, but wouldn't give in," said her uncle, as they went along the hall.

"Of course, he did, the mean pup; but never fear, I'll make him knuckle under."

"That you will," he said, chuckling.

When all is again quiet at Broadlawns, Charlie Cole and Sarah Kane again breathe more freely.

"Tell now, *now*," he says feverishly, "how I am to get away from here and without, remember, that woman? You will have to stay by me, for I am too ill, God help me, to act alone"

"First, you must undress and get into bed; my, but you are weak!"

"I am; please take this key and unlock my trunk; I am not equal to any exertion."

"Were you ill crossing the ocean, sir?"

"I was, but nothing like this; the medical attendant on board said I must have some mental worry which preyed even then upon my bodily health."

"Your name, Charles Cole, how well I remember it," she said, reading it on his linen. "My poor dead mistress and friend trusted me—God help me if I have seemed unfaithful to my trust. Perhaps I should have found out and followed my young mistress, but Silas and I thought I had best watch her interests here. God pity me," she said tearfully, falling upon her knees. "Good Lord, watch over her, lead my steps to her, for I have failed in preventing their black deeds here; so I shall go to America to try and find you, poor, dear, wronged Miss Pearl."

Here Cole, with a groan of weakness and dizziness, falls half undressed upon the bed, at which Sarah Kane flies to him, takes off his boots, assisting him to get under the clothes.

"Poor, poor feet, like ice," she says pityingly; "I must do something for him. Heaven help him among such a horde of cruel hearts; I must at any risk go down and get a foot warmer. Poor fellow, so gentle and amiable-like, he deserved a better fate, and should have a physician at once; but the mind, the poor sick mind, as well as body, how will that be calmed? There, there, don't mind anything; try to sleep. I am going down stairs to get a foot-warmer for you."

"No, no," he said nervously, "you must not leave me."

" I have listened in the hall, and they are all snoring, sleeping heavily after the late supper. I must, indeed, sir, see to the warming of your feet ; it will only take me five minutes ; please consent, for your own sake."

" Well. go ; and I will lock the door after you, lest the wretches come in ;" and attempting to sit up he feels too weak, falling backwards with a heavy sigh.

Sarah Kane, now really alarmed, slips off her shoes, silently unfastens the door, making a speedy exit ; passing the doors of the sleepers without detection, not so though on entering the servants' wing—the cook and man-servant seeming both restless, she hesitates, then on with flying feet accomplishes her object, bringing also mustard ; up again this time, not risking the back stairs and the servants, the front stairs, which, being thickly padded, cover her footfalls.

Back again, she finds him staring fixedly at the door in terror, lest any but herself should appear. She now applies the foot-warmer, also putting mustard plasters to the nape of the neck and pit of the stomach.

" You look tired," he said languidly, " but I cannot say go and rest, I am not brave enough."

" I am accustomed to do without sleep. I nurse many sick. Since my poor mistress died, and they sent sweet Miss Pearl out to the States, I have no regular duties here, but thought it wise, as they did not bid me go, to stay on and watch them. They often quarrel over my being here, Mr. Stone wanting to drive me out, Miss—I mean—but no, never mind— there, there," stroking his hands, " the aunt and niece thinking, and true, that I know too much. It's a fact, sir, but I have not known how to check them for all. God help me, but when I see you well and away from this home of the Pharisee—this place with a heart of stone and a tongue of oil, or evil, as it suits—I must see what is best, even so late."

And so the poor, half-distracted thing talked on and

on, often in a disconnected sort of way, but her tones were soothing."

"Go on," he said, opening his eyes; "what trust have you broken," he repeated, "bringing me to this?" Here he grew excited, but, evidently too weak to talk, said languidly, putting her hand to his brow:

"Feel that, their work," he said feverishly, "and in part yours, as you have not exposed them; why have you not?"

"What would the world heed had I, *in their employ*, lifted up my voice against them? they are all Phari-sees, all strict church-goers, and would turn the wrath against myself, for I do not make loud prayers, their hypocrisy driving me to my closet, instead of to the be-seen-of-men sort of religion; no, no one would have believed me, though I think now of one who would, and he is Dr. Annesley, of the city. I have erred in judgment, but never thought they would marry you to Miss Villiers; nay, look at it calmly, if you can, sir, and get well sooner. My father was an attorney, but rogues fleeced him, and I was penniless; my late mistress took me here, and I was her friend and con-fidant, for they were cruel to her and her child. Silas Jones and I knew of Miss Pearl and yourself, and Silas said——"

CHAPTER XIII.

LUCIFER'S VOTARIES RAMPANT.

"YES, Silas Jones shall hear of how we found his precious Sarah Kane alone in a man's bed-room," sneered the coldly cruel voice of Mrs. Cole, entering, and not making a seduc-tive picture in bright green dressing gown, with large purple flowers, her hooked nose as red as her high cheek bones, her awful eyes fixed, staring and stony, her uncle and aunt following.

"Oh dear, oh dear! Heaven help us! I forgot to lock the door when I brought the poor fellow the foot-warmer," thought Sarah Kane, distractedly.

"I thought I heard a jabbering going on before you called me, Margaret," said her uncle, savagely.

"How dare you bring disrepute on a virtuous home by coming to a man's bed-room at night, and alone, Sarah Kane?" asked Miss Stone, quivering with rage at being disturbed after her late supper.

"Sarah Kane, go and pack up, and see that you develop no light-finger tricks; you leave Broadlawns at daybreak," hissed Margaret, between her teeth.

"Please let me stay, ma'am, until Mr. Cole recovers; indeed, indeed he is very, very ill."

"That is *my* affair—go!" and she points to the now open door.

"She has been kind to me, she must stay; I am too ill for her to leave me; if she goes she must take me," said Cole, sitting upright, his pulse rapidly rising.

"We don't harbor women of her stamp," said Margaret, beside herself with rage at her having gained the ear of Cole; she would willingly have torn her limb from limb.

"Get out of here, and at *once*, Sarah Kane, unless you would have me use violence," said Stone, savagely; for from the words of Cole he sees she has made a favorable impression.

"I implore you not to go and leave me here," said the sick man, excitedly; "my brain is on fire. I am weak and ill; oh! by everything you hold sacred, stay by me and nurse me; if not, I go too, if I have to crawl to the door;" and he attempted to rise.

"This is nonsense, Cole; she must go; I have wanted to turn her adrift before this. We shall procure you a medical attendant at once; though, I think, did you take a berth in a steamer immediately for America. it would be best, and set you up all right, especially with Margaret as nurse. Sarah Kane, what are you waiting for ? "

"For the impetus of someone's foot, I presume," sneered Margaret.

Sarah Kane, with a pitiful look at Cole, her lip quivering and whole frame trembling, prepared to leave the room, saying, as she smoothed his pillows :

"Try and keep calm, sir, you will get well all the quicker, and I shall go and tell Silas Jones, and see if he can help you."

At a sign from Margaret, her uncle followed her from the room, when she said, hurriedly :

"I am going t give the wretch permission to remain until morning, to prevent an interview with Silas Jones ; after breakfast, you say you will drive her in to Mrs. Mansfield's. We have never let her know she wants her. but now she will be capital bait; Sarah Kane will bite, and so be hooked, when you can lodge her for safe keeping at Tom Lang's, who, if needs be, may give her the luxury of a straight-jacket."

"I feel inclined to say No, and kick her out at once; otherwise, yours is a good plan."

"It is the only gag to fit the case ; but out of that room *she shall go.* She may go and pack up. I'll show them who is mistress."

"Yes, do ; besotted fool, that Cole is, to have turned us against him. You don't think that viper will go to Silas Jones at daybreak, do you ?"

"No ; his shop won't be open until seven. By that time cook can have an early breakfast for you, and you will then at once drive off to London, and if Silas Jones comes prowling around here after her, leave him to me, that's all," she said, cruelly, returning to the sick room.

"Go to your room at once, Sarah Kane, pack up

your things, and be ready to leave this house at seven sharp; go," she said, stamping her foot. Don't pollute us by your presence any longer."

"I pray of you to let me stay and nurse him; I will do just what you wish, spare you from fatigue, be no trouble, only let me stay," she cried, imploringly.

Margaret turned her stony gaze upon her. "Put her out, Uncle Timothy, or I shall."

"Get out, woman," he said, taking her by the shoulder, Miss Stone shoving her, and saying:

"Be thankful, hussy, you are getting off so well."

"At your peril send her forth; it will be the worse for you all when I recover, if you do," said Cole, with the utmost excitement.

"Keep cool, Cole; you don't know what a viper we have harbored. I am only going to take her to a Mrs. Mansfield's, and, if she can speak so much truth, she will tell you she is a friend of hers," said Stone, vengefully.

"You are heaping coals of fire on the viper's head by taking her there, Timothy," said Miss Stone, wonderingly.

"Is this person a friend of yours, Sarah?" asked Cole, forlornly pressing both hands to his throbbing temples. "How cruel they are to send you from me. Do you know of a good physician, Sarah?"

"Oh, yes, sir; Dr. Annesley, of London; he——"

"Hold your prate, Sarah Kane, and mind your own business," cried Margaret, trembling with rage. "Get out of here," and with a smart push she is outside and the key turned.

For a few moments Sarah Kane stood irresolute, when the clock struck three.

"Yes, that will be best," she thought, "but I have no time to lose," and, quickly flying to her own apartment, she hurriedly picks up, but not the handsome wardrobe willed her by her late mistress, of which she

7

knows not, but simply her own modest apparel; this
she places in two trunks, weeping silently the while
for the evil come upon the poor sick man in yonder
east chamber, for her own forced desertion of him into
the cruel hands of the inmates at Broadlawns. for her
own undefined plans to find her young mistress, and
endeavor to reinstate her in the fortune willed her,
which she is in doubt now that the law will give her, as
she has not married Charles B. Cole. She weeps on, as
she thinks of the fearful fraud that has been committed;
for here is Mr. Cole married! actually married to Miss
Villiers, in Sarah Kane's estimation, the most wicked
woman that lives, when he had been the intended husband of her sweet, gentle Miss Pearl.

"Woe, woe, that I did not go to Dr. Annesley, and
tell him of the prolonged absence of Miss Pearl, instead of watching here, or to a lawyer; but I dreaded
their fees, as they have paid me no salary for five
years. nor can I claim it, as they told me if I staid I
should get nothing. I have erred in judgment. God
help me and that poor sick man. Yes, I must slip away
and tell Silas. It is fortunate Mary is with him still, or
they (if by some mischance they miss me) might again
make occasion to malign me as to going to see a man;
how easily those smooth-tongued hypocrites can take
away one's character, and they doing the real harm all
the while. My grey ulster and hat will not be too heavy;
it is quite a cool morning, and being up all night, and
supperless to bed, makes me feel chilly. How surprised Silas and his sister will be. I know he will
want me to marry him at once, but I feel too old and
grey; but, as he says, so I have told him for years; and
he has waited and waited until the clouds at Broadlawns would lighten, and now they are blacker than
ever. Kind Silas, good and true Silas, what will you
say to this terrible marriage of poor Mr. Cole to awful
Miss Villiers?"

And now her expeditious fingers having set her house in order, her grey hair rolled back from her brow, her small, regular features, sensitive mouth, and good blue eyes looking wan and anxious, locking her door, she slips down the back stairs, and out into the chill dulness of an October morning. In fifteen minutes she knocks at the house of Silas Jones, the front room of which he calls his shop, selling in a quiet way stationery and current literature. The city clocks are ringing the last quarter before four, and Mary is the first to hear the unusual sound on the knocker at that early hour. Waiting to hear it repeated, she lifts the window, when, at Sarah Kane's voice calling Silas, they both hasten down to open the door.

"Dear me, Sarah; what's up?" said Mary, kissing her. "What a scare you gave me!"

"You have been up all night, Sarah," said Silas Jones, reproachfully, leading her in, as he again locked the door. " However, as this is the earliest kiss I have ever had, I shall not scold you too much; but whom have you been looking nearer your own grave for this time, Sarah? You have been nursing again, I suppose, and are returning to Broadlawns?"

"How you chatter, Silas, dear; Sarah can't get in a word edgeways," said Mary, kindly, but curiously.

"I was only giving our Sarah time to catch her breath, she has been running and is cold," he said, rubbing her hands. " Make her a hot drink over the spirit-lamp, Mary, please."

"The very thing, Silas, dear; what a good man you will make our Sarah; here, drink this, Sarah, and promise to marry Silas this day week (my wedding-day too, Sarah), for indeed, you want someone to make you stay in your bed o' nights."

"Yes, Sarah, dear, Mary is right; for it's my belief the wretches at Broadlawns wish to see you in your grave, seeing as you know too much."

"Oh, Silas, that young man, Mr. Cole, came; and they have married him to Miss Villiers, instead of our sweet Miss Pearl," blurted out Sarah, in trembling tones.

"You don't say, Sarah; what a fearful piece of wickedness," cried Mary, with distended eyes.

"I am not surprised at any villainy on their part," said Silas, with knitted brows. "Let me see, the will reads, on Miss Pearl coming of age and marrying young Mr. Cole, she inherits all (so Dr. Annesley told me, and, by the way, he sent me word he wants to see me); well they have got rid, the de'il knows how, of Miss Pearl, and this ugly vixen marries the man to inherit; bad business, their having similar Christian names; so it's from there you come, and not from sick nursing ? Tell us all, dear."

"Well, Silas, that's just what I ran here for, for they've as good as turned me out, at least, I am to go at daybreak, and——"

"Did they dare to turn you out. you a lady born, though their drudge—faithful in nursing, faithful in your housekeeping. Shielding them, when you could have put the blood-hounds of the law on their track, hoping things would right themselves in this very marriage; but to Miss Pearl—turn you out, after wasting your youth and mine in a martyr's life, to see that right was eventually done to the innocent daughter of your dead friend, growing literally grey in this self-imposed duty, while we both lived lonely lives apart, when they should be in a felon's dock for breach of trust; never mind, it is my turn now, they shall be exposed, and compelled to disgorge; Miss Pearl must be found, Mrs. Mansfield may know something."

"Mrs. Mansfield, yes, Silas, that is were Mr. Stone is going to drive me at seven sharp this a.m., and, oh dear, it is near six; I must hasten back. else they may make me black in Bayswater, for they have called me a hussy to-night, Silas, because I went to poor Mr.

Cole's bedroom, who is very ill, and he was sorry when
they turned me out, Silas, for he knows he has fallen
into their net, and he is ill in mind and body; God
help him. He is kindly and handsome, is yielding and
pliable, and so an easy prey; he was to have met his
father, he tells me. Ah, he would have saved him, but
he is ill, he learned on his arrival, and away off across
the sea at Montreal; but I had to come and tell you,
Silas, for I missed you last evening, when they sent me
to the city, so I should be out of the way, and alas! I
came back too late to save him," she said, tearfully.

"Don't go near them again, Sarah," said Mary,
sympathetically.

"Yes, Sarah, that's it; stay with us, and we will pet
and nurse you, and you will be my wife."

"No dears, I could not remain inactive so near poor
Mr. Cole; he hates them as his enemies, it is best for
me to go to Mrs. Mansfield, I shall be near Dr. Annesley, and must see what can be done; you will come
and see me at Mrs. Mansfield's, so good-bye, now, dears."

"I shall come to the city to-morrow, Sarah, so look
out for me, dear," he said, buttoning her ulster.

"You shouldn't be parting us at all, Sarah," said
Mary, tearfully.

"But only for a few days, Mary."

"You must marry me this day week, Sarah, dear,
for somehow I feel as if evil will come to you parted
from me; promise, it will bridge the time," he said,
following her out into the grey morning light.

"I promise." And there and then, in the dim gaze
of the earliest bees in life's hive, she is pressed to his
loyal heart.

CHAPTER XIV.

FENCING OFF CONFIDENCE.

HE knowledge that, with the morning, her friend would look for a confidence as regarded the intrusion by a man into the grounds of Holmnest on the evening previous, unless, indeed, by fencing she could ward off such confidence, caused Mrs. Gower to pass an almost sleepless night; and so, with the natural desire to put off the evil day, she arose later than usual, lingering over bath and toilette. But now in warm morning robe of a pretty, red woollen material, with ecru lace rufflings, she is worth a second look; though her thoughts are sad, for under the dark hair on her brow, her eyes wear a wistful expression, and on her sensitive lips is almost a quiver of pain, as she stands at her window, looking mechanically on the familiar scene.

"He always looks up," she thought, as a gentleman passed, and must now either reside in the neighborhood, or take it in in his morning outing. How a lonely woman notices any seeming interest taken in herself. I have not seen much of him since poor Charlie Cole went away, and strange; but I miss his face if I don't see him for some days. I remember telling Charlie of a dream I had of this very man, and his *bete noir*, Philip Cobbe. That reminds me again of my promised confidence to Mrs. Dale, it was weak in me to make any such promise—I, who have never had a confidant, even when a girl. I have met some who would have been staunch and true enough, I feel sure, but I never thought heart secrets were altogether one's own; and as to this chatter over men's kind or loving attentions to one, is just about the meanest thing a woman or girl can be guilty of. It is

sufficient to deter men from being commonly civil.
I have known women prate and boast by name of
those who have paid them the highest compliment a
man can, that is of asking them to be their wife; yes, I
positively shrink from meeting my kind, little friend,
Ella Dale, she has a positive craving for knowledge,"
she thought, with a half smile; " and had she been Eve
she would have cut short the eloquence of the serpent's
tongue, and have succumbed, merely out of curiosity.
And yet she is a dear little woman, craving to be
'trusted all, or not at all,' and meaning good to me;
and perhaps I should be less lonely did I empty my
griefs into the lap of another's mind; but again, in con-
fiding in a married woman one confides in her husband
also. It is natural, but, at the same time, not altogether pleasant; but at that peremptory ring I must
give up dreaming here, or my 'Madonna of the Tubs'
will be giving me notice."

"Good morning, dear. Pardon my not having
been down to welcome you," she said, warmly, finding
her friend and the morning papers ensconced in a
rocker by the grate, Tyr stretched on the rug.

" I have just come down, Elaine, and have had my
mirrored reflection as company, and don't I look comi-
cal, encased in this dressing gown you lent me? Won't
I have to eat a substantial breakfast to fill it out?"

"All right, dear, if my seraph of the frying pan
condescended to fill my orders, we have bloaters on
the menu."

"I am ready for them, Elaine, and feel bloated
already," she said, as they seated themselves at table.

"I wonder what kind of a day we shall have for
your review of the city schools? Old Sol does not
seem to have made up his mind whether to laugh or
weep," said Mrs. Gower, as she touched the bell to
remove the fruit.

" I hope he will be good enough to weep over some

other city, for I am sure Henry will not bring my
waterproof."

"But Miss Crew will, she seems so really thoughtful. What do you intend doing with her when you
place Garfield at school?"

"That's just what I am in a quandary about. I like
her, for she puzzles me."

"What a droll little creature you are, Ella; you have
a perfect craze for working out problems, even to a
woman," she said, laughingly."

"Now you musn't think, Elaine, that my interest
in you has the remotest connection with the mystery
at Holmnest," she said, opening her blue eyes in apparent innocence, but in reality her words being a
reminder to her hostess.

"The mystery at Holmnest? What a tragic sound
you give it, it makes one's flesh creep, but I have not
forgotten how large-hearted you are, dear, when you
do not forget, 'Share ye one another's burdens.' "

"Yes, you must tell me all, Elaine, and I feel sure
that with, or without the advice of Henry, your trouble
will either vanish or lighten by your sharing it with
me."

"Yes, perhaps so," she said gravely; "but we must
not spoil our breakfast, and the play of knife and
fork. My little tragedy must be the afterpiece this
time."

"As you will, Elaine, but don't bear it too long alone.
Tragedy is heavy. How cozy and home-like break-
fasting with you is after hotel life."

"I am glad you think so, Ella."

"Your dark leather chairs and handsome sideboard
look well against the brown paper on the walls, and
oh, you won't mind telling me who hung your drapings,
portière hangings, and all that, they are in such good
taste."

"Murray did them for me; it was a case of two

heads being better than one, where I was at fault he set me right."

" Your home is small, but all so home-like, except for one great want, a man to hang his hat up in the hall as your husband, and a child to call you mother."

" Quite a tempting picture, Ella," she answered, a little sadly, " but *'l' homme proposé Dieu dispose.*"

" Take the man, when he proposes, Elaine; I cannot bear to see you alone."

" That is my advice to my friends also, Ella; but, speaking of living alone, will you and Miss Crew come to me when you place Garfield at school, and during the absence of Mr. Dale north-east with Mr. Buckingham; say you will, it won't be for long."

" It's the thing above all others that will please me, Elaine. Excuse my Irish blood, but I must give vent to my feelings by giving you a hug," she said, merrily, as they rose from table.

" Angels and ministers of grace defend us, Elaine, here's a lady visitor; and now that her umbrella is down, I see Mrs. Smyth. But, fond as I am of her, I wish her back to her home, for I wanted the morning alone with you."

" You are both looking charming, it's a pity I am not a gentleman caller, but what lazy people you are," said lively Mrs. Smyth.

" Now that I have emerged from the under side of Fortune's wheel, I do believe I am growing epicurean," said Mrs. Gower, gaily.

" Don't I look too sweet for anything, Mrs. Smyth?" said Mrs. Dale, promenading up and down the room; " haven't I grown stout?"

" But you are all uneven," laughed Mrs. Smyth.

" Now, that is cruel, Mrs. Smith; 'tis ' love's labor lost,' after having utilized all the mats, towels and pillow-shams in my bed-room as stuffing, to be simply told I am uneven."

"Stuffing never goes down with me, Mrs. Dale," laughed Mrs. Smyth.

"It's a good thing for us you are not a man," said Mrs. Dale, demurely.

"Women all angles would cry ' hear, hear!'" laughed Mrs. Gower.

"But you don't ask me what brought me in this morning."

"No, I am too glad to have you; but is it a call of a mouth full of news?"

"Yes, which I shall stuff you with 'as pigeons do their young.'"

"Me, too!" piped Mrs. Dale.

"Mr. King is in town, Mrs. Gower; there, I thought I should electrify you, but you don't seem to care."

"I do, for we shall now have news of the Coles."

"And is that all you will welcome him all the way from Ottawa for?"

"That is all, Lilian; these little flirtations, *pour passez le temp*, soon burn themselves out."

"What a funny woman you are, Elaine; sometimes I can't make you out at all."

"Don't try to, dear, when I puzzle you; life is too short for problem-solving, though our little friend here doesn't think so. But did Mr. King name the Coles?"

"He did."

"Thank you, Thomas," said Mrs. Gower, receiving her letters, which had been put in the letter-box by the letter-carrier.

"One moment, you will excuse me, dears, while I run my letters over." One marked "Immediate," she read to herself as follows:

"THE QUEEN'S, Wed. Eve., Nov. 9th.

"MY DEAR MRS. GOWER,—It is with extreme pleasure I again find myself in the same city with yourself, and am anticipating with intense eagerness an

interview. I go west to-morrow p.m., so shall go up
to Holmnest in the morning.

"As ever, yours devotedly,

"CYRIL KING.

" MRS. GOWER,

"Holmnest, West Toronto."

"Oh, dear! oh, dear! he may be here any moment,
and I am in a quandary as to what I shall do with
him. This little settling up of one's *affaires de cœur*
is distasteful, but I have not been a bit to blame here,"
she thought, quietly tearing up the note, and making
a holocaust of it.

"Oh, I can assure you, Mrs. Dale, she had scarcely
any waist covering at all," said Mrs. Smyth, in disgust,
"she looked simply dreadful."

"Who is the woman this time, dear?" asked Mrs.
Gower, amusedly, as she fastened some camellias to her
gown; "what fair one are you throwing mud at now,
Lilian?"

"Oh, that Mrs. St. Clair. Miss Hall walked down
with me as far as College Street this morning, and she
says, or rather mouthed, for she is too full of affecta-
tion to speak plain, but managed to convey that Mrs.
St. Clair's dress began too late during the Langtry
season. Her dress was *couleur de rose* (what there
was of it), no sleeves, well there was an invisible band,
Miss Hall said (I wondered at her, the way she talked,
as she is so thick there). Now, what do you think of
Mrs. St. Clair, Elaine?"

"I think that she would be the cynosure of all eyes
—men's, for she is very fair to look upon."

"But, Elaine, she is enamelled! Miss Hall's description reminded me of how an American paper describes
such—as if they in their opera boxes sat in a bath
tub."

" Oh, that's hard, said Mrs. Dale; " who was she with, and was the boy Noah ready with his pinchers?"

" No, it was that horrid boy's night off, I suppose, for his father was on duty; the little wretch nearly gave me cancer; the two Wilber girls and our Mr. Buckingham were the party; oh, Elaine, it's most absurd, but Mr. Buckingham is the 'foreign count' gossip said Mr. St. Clair is jealous of."

" I am not surprised; all Grundy's scandal brews are a froth of lies, Lilian."

" But it *is* true that Mrs. St. Clair flirts and enamels."

" If so, she is very pretty, and has a husband with an eagle eye—and," she added gaily, " a son with claws that even you speak feelingly of."

" Well, good-bye, it is getting near our dinner hour, I must off; and, as I live, here is the King from Ottawa ; you are here opportunely to play gooseberry, Mrs. Dale; oh, I must tell you, you know, how quiet Mrs. Tremaine is. Well, she went back in the dark last Sunday evening for her dolman, it was so cold, but when she hung it over the front of the pew it proved to be the Captain's trousers ! "

" How do you do, dear Mrs. Gower ? " he said with *empressement,* his strikingly handsome face aglow with pleasure.

" ' Mrs. Dale, my friend, Mr. King,' from the tower-crowned city, dear."

" And you come to a spire-crowned one, at which, Mr. King, don't become unduly elevated."

" I am in the heights," he said, with a swift glance at Mrs. Gower.

" Then beware of the attraction of gravitation," laughed his hostess, thinking, " I shall have to do a little fencing, I can see by his face."

" Excuse me, Elaine, I see my family are arriving."

" Quite a cavalcade, Mr. King," she said, gaily.

"And mercy me, that young monkey is on horseback, while the driver is giving his attention to bell ringing; I must fly. May I bring them upstairs, Elaine?"

"Certainly, dear; and as your colony will want you all to themselves, send Miss Crew to the drawing-room; she will be happy with the piano."

"How handsome he is; I wonder if he thought me uneven," mused Mrs. Dale, as she left the library.

"Thank heaven, they are all despatched," he said, fervently, leaning over the back of her chair; "look around at me, dear, and tell me I am welcome."

"You are;" and turning her face, her cheek was brushed by his whiskers; "but I am going to be very proper, and tell you to take that very comfortable chair, at the other side of the room."

"Why, what have I done; don't send me away, when my heart is bursting to take you in my arms."

"With your temperament, how full, metaphorically speaking, your arms must be."

"No, no; you only, with your warm eyes and handsome mouth."

"Come, come; no more of this, Mr. King."

"Since when have you dropped Cyril; I cannot bear my surname from your lips."

"'Tis safer so; and you *know* I have tried to act up to this, since knowing you have a wife."

"Yes, yes, you have; but you magnetized me from the first, and had it not been for that meddling fellow, Dubois, telling you, I believe, dearest, you would have learned to love me, wholly, and alone."

"Thank heaven he did tell me, and in time."

"I think there has been every excuse for me, dearest; you are aware of the circumstances of my marriage; then, after fifteen years of *such* wedded bliss, I find you, my heart's mate. I often think how tame life is before the meeting with the one that is to fill one's being with rapturous content; well, if they come to one while one has one's freedom, if not, what miserable loneliness; what an array of jealous fears. Do not turn me out of some corner in your heart, Elaine," he pleaded, "just because the Church and the law come between us; it is no fault of mine that I have met you too late to offer you my name; therefore, pity my misfortune, be kind to me; give me a corner in your affections; you will, won't you, darling," he pleaded, earnestly, his winsome voice coming on the air like sweet notes of song to the accompaniment of 'Il Trovatore,' exquisitely rendered, by Miss Crew, across the hall.

"You must never again talk to me in this strain, Cyril," she says, putting her feelings aside, for she pities him intensely; "it is harmful for both of us; be a man, be brave. I, too, have trials; help me to bear them by seeing you at the post of duty; let us forget that we have hearts; let us harden ourselves by looking at life teeming with ill everywhere.

Let us, from this moment, begin over again, and talk as though the room was full of a gaping crowd; let us talk of anything but ourselves. Of Chamberlain and the fisheries; of who will run for mayor; of how that hot pickle, the French cabinet, will be formed; of whether Bishop Cleary wishes he had been tongue-tied before his imagination went without bit or curb on our girls; *anything* but *ourselves*, Cyril, for pity sake."

"No, it will not do, dear; we can never be as common acquaintances, though you charm me in any mood."

"Very well; if that be so, you must go. Those songs, without words, by Miss Crew, with the scent of flowers, have been enough to intoxicate one; but you *know* that since the knowledge came to me of your having a wife, that I have told you, repeatedly, our acquaintance must end unless you always remember, in our intercourse, the fact of your being bound to another. If you care to meet Mr. and Mrs. Dale, and a young lady friend, stay to luncheon, if you will not more than look at me as a friend—for I will be that."

"I cannot face strangers now, and shall go, but shall write you from the west; and pray let me have a line in answer, saying you will see me on my return?" he said, beseechingly, his handsome face clouded.

"I see I must tell you something I had not intended," she said, nervously, "they are coming downstairs to luncheon; I have promised, nay, am under oath," she said, gravely, "to marry a man who would make trouble, did he hear your words."

"For heaven's sake, Elaine, don't be mad! you would be wretched, chained to a man like that; for the light has all left your dear face, even when you name him."

"Beg pardon, luncheon is served, ma'am," said Thomas.

"I must hasten to the dining-room, and I fear I don't look very calm. Good-bye; remember and be brave; others there are who have no more a bed of roses than yourself."

"God bless you, good-bye; and I implore you, say *No* to him. I speak, as you know, from experience," he whispers, with a tight hand-clasp.

CHAPTER XV.

THE TREE OF KNOWLEDGE.

"OUR visitor is a strikingly handsome man, Mrs. Gower," said Mr. Dale, coming from the window to the table; "we shall be losing you one of these days as—Mrs. Gower," he continued, noticing by her pallor and the light in her eyes that she had been feeling intensely.

"He is wondrously so; and as well, what is more

perilous to the hearts of our sex, he possesses a. rare fascination of manner."

"I have been telling Henry not to jump at conclusions, for, perhaps Mr. King is married," said Mrs. Dale, curiously.

"He is, dear; but your husband is not one of those absurd beings who imagine all one's men friends to be possible suitors."

"Far from it, Mrs. Gower: I am a believer in men and women friendships, and if, in the numerous mistakes society makes, she would obliterate her opposition to such friendships, she would have fewer matrimonial blunders to chronicle."

"That is very true, Mr. Dale; I have frequently found it both mortifying, distressing and annoying to the last degree, at little social gatherings at Toronto, to find myself openly accused of flirtation, because some man friend and I dared to enjoy a *tête-à-tête* chat on some mutual topic of interest."

"But some women do flirt when they get a man in a corner, whether he is married or no," said Mrs. Dale.

"Yes; but because some do, we should not all drift as we are, into no conversation between the sexes," said Mrs. Gower.

"No, certainly not," said Dale; "Emerson says, 'I prize the mechanics of conversation, 'tis pulley, lever and screw;' and it is especially delightful between men and women—when it occurs."

"Yes, as you say—when it occurs—Mr. Dale; but why is it, that the more solid tone of conversation of men is so seldom blended with the, at times more refined, even if it be more frivolous, chit-chat of my sex? Simply because of our dread of gossip?"

"Then there is something 'rotten in the state of Denmark,'" said Mrs. Dale.

"There is, dear," said Mrs. Gower, gravely, rising from the table.

" Mr. Smyth is in the library, ma'am," said Thomas.

" Oh, ask him if he has lunched, Thomas."

" He has, ma'am."

" I am vulgar enough to have dined, Mrs. Gower,"
said Smyth, meeting them at the door of the library.

" As you please," she said, gaily, giving her hand;
let ilka ane gang their ain gait.' "

" Your son is acting on that motto, Mrs. Dale," he
said, looking from the window. " Don't stir, he is in
the back way ; and has evidently been wrestling with
our York mud."

At this juncture Garfield appeared, breathless ; and
his pretty Norfolk jacket and knickerbockers all be-
spattered.

" How did you come to grief, my son ?" asked his
father.

" Well, papa ; first, I knocked down a sparrow with
my catapult; it died game, falling on a foreign bird
perched on a lady's steeple bonnet. Well, she was
mad, phew ! called me names for killing birds. I told
her not to try to be funny, when she had stuffed ones
on her head-dress. Next, I saw a man down street
putting a mouth on his poor horse; man ! how he
sawed, tore the bit nearly through his head ; well, I
just let another lead fly, knocking his Christy stiff into
the mud; then, he out of his butcher waggon and
after me. I remembered some dimes in my pocket,
got 'em, threw 'em behind—he bit, and I took my
chance and distanced him," he said, panting for breath.

" That was sport," said Smyth, laughingly ; but I
have had to shut down on my boy's hunting, we swell
our city treasury by fining such fire-arms."

" Go to the kitchen, you poor little man," said Mrs.
Gower ; "and ask Thomas to brush you ; he will get
you some lunch, there is mud even in your curls ; here,
let me kiss you."

" Yes, you may," he said, condescendingly.

8

"Come along, son; mother will go with you."

"You don't ask what brought me in at this hour, Mrs. Gower," said Smyth.

"No, I have scarcely welcomed you, as yet."

"Well, I must out with it, even if it shortens my stay; for I have only a few moments. On my way up to dinner, I literally ran against King, he was in a brown study, and I in a hurry. 'Hello!' I cried, at which he stopped, and quite abruptly (so unlike him), said, 'Tell Mrs. Gower I have heard from Mr. Cole, senr., who has been ill at Montreal. His physician, Dr. Peake, ordered him to Florida, positively forbidding him to pass the cold season at Ottawa. He is extremely anxious about Charlie, who has not written him. A newspaper, with the announcement of his marriage, being the only communication from Bayswater direct;' and here it is, he gave it me for you. From some outside source he has heard that Charlie is ill, and wishes any of us to let him know immediately at his hotel, Jacksonville, if we have, or receive any news. He admits to King, that with the exception of the girl herself, the remaining members of the family Charlie has married into are a bad lot."

"Poor Charlie, he dreaded this marriage," she said, regretfully; "but seemed to be hemmed in by circumstances—a betrothal. Then she had five thousand pounds per annum, and his father wished him to carry it out; and Charlie is so yielding, altogether. When he told me about it, at the very last, I too advised him to go and carry out the arrangement. You see, as we know he was heart whole, and his salary was small, and he seemed born only to work the will of others, that it seemed a half natural sort of thing for him to drift into; still, if he is ill, and the family are horrid, and he over there alone, I feel sorry he went at all, poor fellow."

"A miserable marriage would break Charlie Cole up completely," said Smyth.

"Have you no mutual friend at London," said Dale, kindly, "to whom you could apply, and who might give you the facts of the case. Perhaps I can assist you. You told me before, Mrs. Gower, that it is to Bayswater suburb, your friend went; I knew a very prominent physician residing there, to whom I shall write, if you wish; a medical man is very often the very best medium in such cases."

"Oh, if you would, Mr. Dale; it would be a perfect relief to all of us," said Mrs. Gower.

"Here is the marriage insertion," said Smyth, reading: 'At Broadlawns, Bayswater, London, England, on September 28th, 1887, by the Rev. Claude Parks, Charles Babbington-Cole, Esq., of Toronto, Dominion of Canada, to Margaret, daughter of the late——"

"What's that! Miss Crew has fainted, poor girl," cried Mrs. Gower, "and hurt herself, I fear; there is water in the dining-room."

"I'll get it," cried Smyth.

Mrs. Dale, returning, said, "I wonder what caused it; she is delicate, I know, but I never knew her to faint before. My vinaigrette is on my dressing-table; would you get it, Henry, like a dear?"

"Thank you, Mr. Dale, she revives."

"Then I shall go, Mrs. Gower; and here, I shall leave the English newspaper with you; Lil wants you all to come over this evening, then we can talk over some plan—Mr. Dale's is a good one—to elicit information as to Charlie's position; Miss Crew is to come, too. Good-bye till evening."

"You had better go upstairs and lie down, Miss Crew; you look very white, and I fear you have hurt your head, poor girl," said Mrs. Gower, kindly.

"I did give it a knock, but you are all too kind; if it won't make any difference, I shall lie here for a few minutes."

"Very well, dear; and a glass of wine will be good for you."

"Oh, she never touches it, Elaine, she is rabid blue ribbon," said Mrs. Dale.

"And a very good color to wear, but when one is ill," said Mrs. Gower.

"Never mind the wine, Mrs. Gower, my head aches very badly, but all I want is to rest it a little; but shall feel very uncomfortable, though, if I delay your out-going ; do go now."

"Yes, I suppose we must."

"Garfield, you stay with Miss Crew, darling, while Mrs. Gower dresses, and I put on my wraps."

"All O. K., mamma." After a few moments spent with ' The Pansy,' he comes over to the sofa.

"Miss Crew, Miss Crew ; wake up."

"I was not sleeping, dear."

"But your brows were knit like this; and you looked so white. What did you faint for ? I wanted you to come with us."

"Oh, never mind, don't talk about me; I want you to give me your catapult."

"Yes, I reckon I will, as young Smyth had to give his up ; but I should like it if I get mad at a man for ill-treating his horse."

"But a better plan would be to read the name of the owner on the vehicle, and report him."

"Oh, that's too slow; when a fellow gets mad, he wants to let a lead fly right then," making a movement as if he was firing.

"Oh, but that is not the best way, my boy ; the wise men of old waited until they were out of their temper."

"We don't; we just go, bang ! but it was pretty good of them, I reckon. What did they say right at first, though ?"

"They said, when the evildoer was brought before them, having done them a great wrong, ' By the gods, were I *not* in wrath with thee, I would have thee slain.' "

" Well, I guess that was noble of them ; I reckon my catapult must go," he said, fondling it, " and here goes," he said, putting it into the fire ; but as I don't want to hear it hissing me, I'll put a finger in each ear."

Here Mrs. Gower, with Mr. and Mrs. Dale, entered, robed for the outer world, looking comely and comfortable. Mrs. Gower in blue, broken plaid skirt, with plain overskirt, and waist of same color, bonnet to suit, tight mantle, with fox boa and muff. Mrs. Dale in plum color, with seal mantle ; both women with the hue of health on cheek and lips, and with bright eyes."

" Come, Garfield, my son, into your overcoat with the speed of a New York despatch," said his mother.

" It seems too bad to leave you, Miss Crew," said Mrs. Gower, sympathetically ; " are you sure I can do nothing for you before we start ? "

" Quite sure, thank you ; my head aches a little, but I have some Dorcas work here, which will make me forget I have a head, I hope."

" Then you will be rewarded ; *au revoir*, dear."

" And now for the tree of knowledge," said Mrs. Dale.

After visiting the Wellesley and other city schools, the Church School for boys, the Collegiate Institute, Jarvis Street, and the Upper Canada College, they decided to place him at the latter, principally on account of the boarding school ; they being, at present, unsettled as to their future plans.

" Your city schools are admirable, and were we actual residents, housekeeping, I should ask nothing better for my boy. Some of your finest public men, I am told, Mrs. Gower, have sat at those desks."

" Yes, so I have always heard ; but I think, in Garfield's case, you have acted wisely. A boy coming from school to hotel life, has every incentive not to study."

" Yes, that's just it.   At the U. C. College, the example will be there in the other boys at their books,
and I consider it a great boon to be able to place him
under such management.   The masters are talented
gentlemen ; and if a boy does not make something of
himself under such guidance, mentally, morally and
physically, then he must be made of very poor stuff,
indeed."

" Garfield, dear," said his mother, " you will have to
be as starched as a Swiss laundry, minding your p's
and q's, like an Englishman."

" Oh, yes, I know; but they are the stuff, mamma.
You see they give a fellow cricket, and drill, as well
as book knowledge."

" Yes, they are wise ; you will study all the better.
See that you make a man of yourself while there,"
said his father."

" I shall never forget my goal, papa."

" And what is that ? "

" To be President Dale, of the United States of
America; and I reckon, when I run, my opponents
won't have any dirty stories to rake up about me, for
I'm going to begin right now."

" But they frequently coin falsehoods.   What would
you do in that case ? "

" Put mamma on their trail; have 'em up, and make
'em swallow or prove them."

" All right, my ten-year-old ; mother will be your
right hand man," she said, endearingly.

" I expect the lies men have to face in the arena of
public life are their worst foes," said Mrs. Gower.
" Beecher said, ' If the lies told about public men could
be materialized, they would roof in and cover over the
whole earth.' "

" He spoke feelingly," said Mr. Dale; Dames Rumor
and Grundy, with the newspapers, had him in a tight
place."

"Shall we go on further, Henry, and purchase the mattress, etc., for Garfield ?"

"No, I think not, Ella; I have to meet Dickson, from New York, at the Walker House, at six; can't you come in the morning, dear ?"

"Oh, yes."

"Do you dine with your friend, Mr. Dale ?"

"Yes ; so we arranged."

"Then you come back with me, Ella, and this wee man, of course ?"

"Yes, if we don't weary you."

"You know better, dear. Oh, Mr. Dale, will you kindly go into Mr. Smyth's office, and say we find it impossible to go over this evening, but will to-morrow —*sans ceremonie*, if agreeable."

"Consider your commission executed, dear Mrs. Gower." I shall drive up for you, Ella, this evening some time; *au revoir*," and, lifting his hat, he is gone.

After a delightful walk through the busy streets, from the Upper Canada College, by way of King Street West, thence north to Holmnest, they find Miss Crew a little quieter, perhaps, but apparently quite recovered from her recent swoon. Putting aside her Dorcas work, the three ladies sit in the firelight and gloaming, to chat until dinner hour.

"I regret you were not with us, Miss Crew; the schools would have interested you," said Mrs. Dale.

"Yes, I am sorry, too; for ever since our arrival I have heard so much in praise of the city schools, especially."

"Their praise is ever in our mouth," said Mrs. Gower; "but my views on the subject are somewhat contradictory. Though going with the progress of the age, I don't feel quite sure that this mixing up of the children of the rich and poor is to the ultimate good of either."

"Oh, I think it's better, Elaine, to bundle them all in together."

"I don't know, Ella; the Industrial School system recommends itself very much to me for the poorer classes, among whom, if there is any originality, it will out."

After dinner, to which Mr. Cobbe, coming in as it was announced, made one at, Miss Crew, not feeling quite herself, begging to be excused, retired to her room, and Garfield into the arms of morpheus on the lounge; when, during a temporary absence of Mrs. Dale, Mr. Cobbe said, quickly, while laying a hand on either shoulder of his hostess:

"What do you have that woman here all the time for? If she is going to spend the evening, I shall go."

"Were I Mrs. Ruggles, of Pickwick fame, I should object to my friend being called a woman," she said, half jokingly; "as it is, I——"

At this moment some pebbles were thrown against the window, cracking the glass. Mrs. Dale, now returning, said:

"What! is it the window fired at? Things are coming to a pretty pass," she said, with latent meaning; "We should have closed the shutters; don't, Elaine, I shall do it."

"I had better go out and frighten away the tramps," said Cobbe, his face flushing with angry impatience.

"Yes, Philip; if you will be so kind."

"You are a gentlemanly man, and a good looking one, Mr. Cobbe; but I don't love you," said Mrs. Dale, emphatically, shaking her clenched fist after his retreating form.

Mrs. Gower could not but smile at her little friend's vehemence, as she played with the bracelets on her shapely arms, her head bent in thought.

"Thomas is a good servant, Elaine; he has just fastened the hall door on the heels of Monsieur Cobbe; and now, *ma chere*, this is the time and place for confidence," she said, earnestly, while laying her jewelled fingers on her friend's brown locks.

CHAPTER XVI.

THE OATH IN THE TOWER OF TORONTO UNIVERSITY.

"YES, dear, draw over your rocker, he will not return, and since you are willing, I shall pour my griefs into the lap of your mind; seeking, as you say, to lessen the dead weight on my own.

"Just about this time last year, not so late though, for the trees were lovely in tints of deep orange and crimson, with the brown of the oak. Our beautiful suburbs, with the Queen's Park, looking like huge bouquets in the hands of Dame Nature; you know my passion for scenery, Ella. One day—a bright and glorious day, it had been—the blue sky, almost out of sight, it was so uplifted; a day sufficient to raise one's spirits as by some powerful stimulant, I was returning from town to my modest quarters (not here you know, dear), about four p.m., through the park; when, Mr. Cobbe overtaking me, suggested our going up into the tower of the Toronto University to enjoy the view. I consented, knowing that the slanting beams of the sinking sun would kiss good-night to the tree-tops, lighting them with additional loveliness. We entered the grandly beautiful building, the janitor, unlocking the door to the tower, reminding us of the rule, "keys turned at five." Up, and ever upwards, the spiral stairway, making one dizzy in the ascent; at length, the top is reached; and, oh! the view, Ella, was more than beautiful. My eyes only rested with a passing glance at the handsome villas skirting the park, ever returning to dwell on the superb mass of color in the trees; the sun seeming to linger lovingly while photographing their shadows upon the grass.

"I sat silent, or nearly so, for some time, when some-

how the very air seemed full of such quiet, solemn
grandeur, that thought becoming active, travelled in
and about bygone scenes and faces, bringing tears to
my eyes, as a strange fit of loneliness came upon me.

"I was just in the mood to say yes, to a proposal to
link my life with another, when Philip Cobbe pleaded
his suit, saying, 'In a home together we would be companions each for the other; that we would be happier
in a little home together than in the cold formality of
a boarding-house; that in our short acquaintance, we
knew each other as well as people who had a life-long
knowledge of each other; that we were each too warm-
hearted to be content alone; that the long, dark autumn
was coming on, in which we would be all in all to each
other; that his love for me filled his heart.'

"Then, Ella, he was really eloquent in his description of a little home together—a picture particularly
inviting to me in my loneliness and in my despondent
mood.

"I had been, as you know, under fortune's wheel, season after season, in the ice-bound winter, in the scorch-
ing sun of summer; sometimes in doubt in which I
suffered most. With a purse as 'trash,' society turned
a cold shoulder to me. Summer friends did not see
me; my real friends at a distance—yourselves among
the foremost—could not prevail upon me to visit them,
as I knew the only sin society refuses to pardon is an
out-at-elbows gown; and I was too proud to accept
gifts I could not repay.

"Yet, still I hesitated in accepting Philip's offer, which
seemed tempting in its home view; but would it be
wise for me to marry him, simply because my life was
a lonely one? I was in the act of telling him, 'I
would sleep on it, and give him his answer, to-morrow,'
when saying so, we were startled by the city clocks
and bells striking, ringing and chiming six o'clock!
Ella, Ella, my heart with fright seemed to stop beat-

ing; even yet a nervous tremor runs through me
when I recall that moment; it was too true, on Philip
consulting his watch, really, in the gloaming; for the
sun was then sinking to rest at about five-thirty.

"'Great Heavens!' I cried; 'the tower door will be
locked!' At this, can you credit it, Ella, the face of
my companion grew exultant, as he cried:

"'Then we shall be here together until morning, and
you will have to marry me!'

"At this, Ella, a shudder of repulsion ran through
me; all my liking for him seemed at once to leave my
heart, fear taking its place. 'What shall we do?' I
cried; 'there are no passers-by; God help me, for
truly, " vain is the help of man." Think of something,
do something, Mr. Cobbe—go to the foot of the stairs—
hammer on the door—anything—get me out some way,'
I said, almost in a frenzy. 'There is no one in the building,' he said. 'I would be no more heard than you hear
your dog Tyr whining for your return. You will have
to stay. We will be married, which some women would
not grieve at. Come, come, cheer up; we will be married quietly in the morning; say yes, with a kiss.'

"'Go away,' I said; 'you must have matches, I
have hit upon a plan. I am going to tie my bonnet
to the end of your cane, and set fire to it. Some one
will see it, and tell the janitor or steward, and we shall
be liberated; here, quick, the matches!'

"'I have not one about me,' he said; and which I now
feel sure was a falsehood.. 'Oh try, try; search every
pocket; if you will only free us I will promise anything,
only get us out of here,' I said, half beside myself.

"'You will promise anything,' he said, excitedly;
'then, down on your knees, and swear by all you hold
sacred, to become my wife.'

"'Oh, that is too awful an oath, ask me anything but
that,' for I was sure now I could not love him.

"'No, no; swear, or you stay here all night.' 'Half

my money, when I get it, instead, for pity's sake,' I said, distractedly.

" ' Nonsense ! I swear to liberate us from the tower and building, if you swear as I have dictated ; if not, take the consequences.' Again, he pleaded his suit, winding up by asking me 'How I thought I would look facing a crowd in the morning, emerging from such a midnight resting-place, and in his company ; of how the students would have food for jokes, for the remainder of the term ; of how the newspapers would get hold of it,' etc.

" Driven to desperation, I knelt and swore by all I held sacred, to become his wife—unless he himself set me free—the latter clause he allowed, laughing at the idea ; he then held me to his heart, telling me I would have a good husband in him, and never have cause to repent of my oath ; tying my bonnet on, for I trembled so, my hands were useless ; how I got down the steps on steps I don't know ; he must have carried me ; for what with the strain on my nerves from the whole scene, added to the spiral stairway, I felt dizzy and faint ; but we reached the bottom, and my astonishment and indignation is easier imagined than described, on seeing him coolly turn the handle and open the door ! The bells we had heard were fire-bells. The janitor, true to his trust, had locked the great door and gone to a lecture-room for a moment, intending after to mount for us.

" Philip seemed uplifted to a state of insane exultation at the success of his plan ; for, on my upbraiding him on such base means to attain his ends, he laughed, as he said, ' All is fair in love or war,' as turning the key in the oak door of the main entrance we were out in the free air. Free ! yes, but with my freedom gone. I looked at him with a sort of curiosity, as merely shutting the door, though I suggested burglars ; he for answer, taking me in his arms, saying thickly, to the accompaniment of the key turning, 'Make the best of me, love, it was only by stratagem I could win you; I am lonely, so are you; I will make you happy, so help me God!' and so it is, Ella, you find me engaged to wed Philip Cobbe."

"But, as you must see, there must be other reasons than my disinclination to have prevented our union, for, you see, he still haunts me, though not loving me so faithfully, perhaps," she said, gravely.

"Of course I see it, you poor dear," she said, coming nearer, and kissing her friend, "and you must *never* marry that man. What a romance of the tower it was; I have been fascinated listening to your recital. I now see what he meant by his—as he thought—strange manner, on Henry naming that we were going to the University with you. But, *mark my words*, there will be a tragedy if you wed this man; I know something."

A tremor ran through Mrs. Gower; she clasped her hands nervously, her lips quivered, and her dark eyes dilated, as she said, leaning towards her friend,

"You mean about a woman!"

Here Garfield awoke at the entrance of his father, whose ring his mother and Mrs. Gower had not heard. Miss Crew, entering, hat and mantle on, and carrying the out-door wraps of Mrs. Dale.

"Why, you both look startled!" said Mr. Dale; "have you been enjoying a spiritual seance?"

"No, Henry, but you had better avoid me, for I have been tasting of the tree of knowledge."

"We have had dogma, also, Mr. Dale; and your wife does not believe that the end justifies the means," said Mrs. Gower, as Thomas brought in a tray with delicious coffee and sandwiches.

"I hope such doctrine won't be forced down our throats some day, Mrs. Gower. Roman Catholicism seems to be coming upon you, wave by wave, and you in Ontario don't even seem to dream of a breakwater."

And so he talked on of city news, of the immense circulation of the newspapers, of the power of the press, etc., seeing there had been grave talk, and giving each time to bury gravity in heart's casket.

"Good night, little man; and so you get your feet on life's first rung, at Upper Canada College, on Monday morning."

"Yes, Mrs. Gower, and I mean to show them what a New York boy can do."

"That's right; defy circumstance and fate, and mount."

"Good night, and good-bye, dear Mrs. Gower, for I leave, as you are aware, for a run north-east, to look at some mines with our friend Buckingham."

"Yes, so I hear; what birds of passage you men are; but you don't leave until Monday, when your good little wife and Miss Crew come to me during your absence."

"I really don't know what Ella would do without Holmnest and—you."

"Take care of yourself, Elaine," said Mrs. Dale, with a meaning pressure of the hand.

"What for?" she said, rather sadly.

"Oh, for somebody!"

CHAPTER XVII.

BIRDS OF PREY.

IN the neat little parlor, with flowering plants in the window, its walls adorned with old-time Scripture prints and modern play-bills in droll blending, back of the shop-room for stationery, at Bayswater, on an evening late in October, sits Silas Jones, listless, and, with idle hands, apparently staring into vacancy, in reality wandering in busy thought into dim prison-houses and private asylums at London, in search of Sarah Kane, who, on his calling to see at Mrs. Mansfield's some weeks ago, as arranged, was informed by a housekeeper in charge that her mistress had gone south for the winter, and had told Mr. Stone some months ago she would like Sarah Kane to go with her as companion. When he sent her word she refused the offer, and that as to Mr. Stone bringing her, neither of them had been near the place.

On this, Silas Jones had racked his brain to discover her, advertising time and again; sure of foul play. One day he thought of seeing what the detectives could do, another of consulting a lawyer; he had, though knowing it would be useless, gone to Broadlawns, and interviewed Mr. Stone, who had answered carelessly:

"I never even try to keep track of servants we discharge. Why of Sarah Kane, who was a viper on our hands?"

"As to that, Mr. Stone, I shall not allow you to blacken the best woman in God's world. She went with you to London; where is she now?"

"I tell you again I don't know, even whether she be alive or dead, and if you come about Broadlawns again, I shall have you up for trespass. An Englishman's house is his castle, sir."

"Oh, Silas Jones, Silas Jones, she has grown tired of you," said Mrs. Cole, vengefully. "We found her in Mr. Cole's bedroom at midnight. What can an old man like you expect?"

"I don't mind your wicked words, they can't hurt Sarah; it's your deeds; and I implore you, if you have any of the woman nature in you, tell me where I can find her."

"And I answer, as Mr. Stone did, I never bother myself as to the whereabouts of discharged servants, so consider yourself dismissed," she said, calling Simon.

" Yes, ma'am."

" Open the door for Silas Jones, bookseller, Bays-water." And so had he been answered in harsh, un-feeling tones, as almost broken-hearted he had wended his lonely way mechanically back to the little parlor.

It is well he has sold out his business to the young man Mary has married, for he cannot give his mind to anything other than the loss of the one woman, in his simple loyalty, he has ever loved, and of how again to find her.

"Silas," said his sister, " I just now asked Dr. Mac-Neil, as he came up the street, how poor Mr. Cole is, and he says he is in for a bad attack of that nasty rheumatic fever; just think, brother, of him only out of brain fever and into this; it's out and out too bad."

" Does he ask for Sarah, still ? "

" Yes; doctor says it's most pitiful to hear him; and he (doctor) says, but it's 'cause he doesn't know the truth, that, of course, they are not to be blamed for the not bringing her, since she be so bad."

" Sister, I can't stand this suspense and trouble any longer; it's killing me. If it costs me every penny I have in the world, I *must* find my Sarah. I shall go into the city to-morrow, and put the detectives to work."

At this juncture the shop door was hurriedly thrown open, when Sarah Kane, cold, pale, and trembling, fol-lowed by the driver of a hansom, came in quickly into their midst.

" Now, Missis, you'll be as good as your word, I 'ope, and gim me my fare."

But she is in the close embrace of Silas, while Mary pays, dismisses him, and locks the front door, her hus-band being in the great city.

" Silas, it's my belief you are demented; let our Sarah go. I want to hear where the old de'il took her to, and how she comes in like this, with no bonnet or shawl, and her hair blown about like that. There, that's more like it," she said, kissing Sarah, as Silas, not speaking a word, only keeping his gaze fixed on Sarah's face, leads her to a chair, when, dropping on his knees, says earnestly,

" Thank God; thank God."

Now seating himself beside her, and holding her hand in his, Sarah says, her lips quivering:

" Yes, God be thanked, I am at home, home! Oh dears, you will never know the sweetness of home as I do, after the awful life I have had since 1 last saw your dear faces; and only that I ran away, leastwise, bribed the boy with my watch and chain—"

" You did!" cried Mary, in astonishment.

" Freedom is sweeter than jewels, Mary dear; but I must begin at the beginning. Yes, Silas, the tea has warmed me; I must tell you all now. You know how suspicious the people at Broadlawns are? Well, you can imagine the scene I went through when, running back from you that early morn, I found them waiting for me; they had got into my room with another key; they called me all the foul names in the spelling-books in England, I do believe. My heart, but it was fearful; and poor Mr. Cole calling me, and they not letting me near him; but I can't go on till I hear of him. How is he, and was it brain fever?"

" Yes, Sarah," said Mary, hurriedly, " and he could not bear Mrs. Cole near him; raving more even when out of his head, if she was in the room."

" Poor, poor young gentleman, and how is he now?"

" Well, he's just out, like, of brain fever, and into rheumatism."

" Dear, dear!" she said, in troubled tones; " Silas, I feel, dear, that I must endeavor to bring some speck of comfort into his life, for I blame myself now for not long ago going and talking it over with Dr.

9

Annesley; will you come up to the city with me, to-morrow, and try to see him?"

"Anywhere, so I am with you; for I do believe, Sarah, I shall never be brave enough to lose sight of your dear face again," he said, tenderly, still holding her hand.

"And, now, go on Sarah, and tell us where that old sneak thief took you to," said Mary, curiously.

"Yes, I must. Mr. Stone bid me only take my Gladstone bag, for he was not going to spoil the phæton with my trunks. So, merely putting in a few necessary articles, thinking, as you remember, to be back in a day or two; well, we drove into town; but not in the direction, as I remembered, of Mrs. Mansfield's; we went a long, long way east; and when I wondered, he answered, shortly, that he had business that required immediate attention, first; well, on we drove into streets and localities unknown to me. At last, after a two hours' drive, we stopped at the end house in a terrace; it was a gloomy street, though some of the houses were well-looking enough. In one of the windows of the house at which we stopped, was a card, 'Lodgings for single gentlemen;' but that was a blind, Silas, to cover the real state of affairs.

On Mr. Stone knocking, a bolt and chain were drawn and unfastened, and a big, strong, coarse-looking boy, large mouthed, and with cross eyes, opened the door.

"'Is your master in?' inquired Mr. Stone. 'Yes, sir.' 'Come in, Sarah Kane,' said the wicked master of Broadlawns. 'I have a good deal to say here, and you may as well come in doors, after your early morning walk' (that was here, you know, Silas) 'and your visit to a gentleman's bedroom last night.' It might have been Mrs. Cole; he spoke in such cold, hard tones.

"We were shown into the front room first flat; the

room with the notice in the window; it was extremely dirty and untidy; with a single bed in one corner; and what furniture there was looked like odds and ends picked up at sales; three chairs, one of brown leather, the others faded red and blue rep. On a table were pipes, tobacco, burnt matches, ale mugs, and cards, with copies of *Bell's Life*, in different stages of dirtiness; the room was littered with a man's clothing, and altogether unsavory. I was reluctant to enter, and stood on the door-mat.

"'Just go in ma'am; here's the master,' said the boy grinning.

"If the room was unsavory, the man was. Oh, Mary, if you saw him," she said, shudderingly; "he looked like a bully or prize fighter; a heavily-built man, short of stature, with bull-dog head and face; he wore no coat, and his shirt was unclean."

"Well, Lang, how are you getting along?"

"Do you mean as to funds, Mr. Stone; are you going to say the word, 'forego the back rents, take that lump sum for the house, and cry quits, that's the question?'" he said, with a wink. "Come in, Missis; I'm quite a dude, you see; but ladies don't mind that."

"I prefer to wait for Mr. Stone, out in the phæton," I said, with latent disgust.

"Here they exchanged what I now know was a meaning glance, Mr. Stone saying, 'Sarah Kane is a most particular young woman, as you shall hear, Lang; come this way, Sarah.'

"I protested that I preferred waiting outside, to no purpose. 'This way, Sarah Kane.' 'Yes, this way, Missis,' they said, one going before and one behind me up a stairway, covered with a common carpet, but thickly padded; there were five doors opening into a square hall; all doors shut. Turning the handle of one, Mr. Stone said, smiling grimly, 'Another lodger.'

'Yes; he's out airing; you bet, they keep me busy,' he answered, with another of his odious winks, saying, 'Here, Missis, just step in 'ere while the Squire and me square accounts;' this time he winked at me; and I began to think it a mechanical way he had of winding up a remark."

"Nasty beast," said Mary.

"I was no sooner in, than the key was turned, and I knew myself a prisoner; I called, hammered on the door, did every conceivable thing to make a noise; finally I sat down on the one greasy chair of green rep, and cried as if my heart would break. I thought of you, Silas, and you too, Mary, of poor Mr. Cole; and hope vanished, knowing by whom I had been trapped. From time to time I could hear a murmur of voices; then Mr. Stone's unmusical laugh; and the unfastening and fastening of the door. Then I gave myself up to despair; I could make no sign to the outside busy London world, for my small room was only lit from the hall by a curious window, up near the ceiling. A single bed, wash-stand, and tiny looking glass, hanging to the wall, too small and cracked to be of any use; every article being stale and dirty. Mr. Lang brought me a cup of tea, and some bread and cheese, telling me to make myself at home; and 'that even though I was in a single gentleman's house, no matter,'- with another odious wink; 'that Mr. Stone had told him I would not be sorry there were no ladies,' etc.; but to make a long story short, Silas and Mary, the people at Broadlawns imprisoned me to get me out of the way, so I should not speak of this fraud of a marriage."

"That's it, my poor Sarah."

"Days passed into weeks; and had it not been for my pocket Bible, the Pickwick papers, and a long strip of muslin embroidery and housewife I had put in my bag, I don't know what would have become of

me; I tried to keep calm, if only to devise a scheme
of escape. One day was much the same as another,
Mr. Lang trying in many ways to get private information of Broadlawns, telling me, to raise my wrath,.
that Mr. Stone had told him I was demented, and
nothing I said was reliable ; but I could not trust such
a man, so left him no wiser. Every day, for fifteen
minutes, I was compelled to go up two flights of stairs
to a room with an open skylight, and where I was
made, willingly though, to walk up and down ; sometimes Lang, sometimes another man, whom I loathed
even worse, or the cross-eyed boy, accompanying me
as jailer; this they called a pleasure airing. Yesterday, growing desperate, I offered my watch and chain
to the cross-eyed boy, to liberate me. He listened,
eyeing them greedily, saying to my delight,

"'Well, I'll try, Missis ; for I'm a bit tired of airing
of you and the three men, and a doing of other
chores.' 'Are there three other prisoners beside myself,' I cried. 'Oh, no, ma'am ; they be just a lodging
'ere on the quiet, loike you be.' 'You will free me,
then, and gain my watch and chain ; see how pretty
it is, and pure gold.' 'Yes, the first chance I gets ;
but ye're not lying ; ye'll give it all square ?'

"But to hasten, for I feel tired and weak, though
oh! so much better in mind ; the middle man gave me
my airing to-day, to whom I never spoke, though he
laughed and jeered at me continually. I worried myself by thinking that, perhaps, the boy was only a spy,
when this evening, after Mr. Lang had brought me my
tea, and I was again locked in, to my joy, in a few
minutes, the key turned, and the boy said, hurriedly,
'Come along, Missis ; don't wait to take nothing ;
master's out, and Bill's run to the gin-palace, telling of
me to keep guard.' Even as he spoke, we were downstairs, the bolt and chain undone, and, thank God,
with the free air of heaven about us. 'Give us your

'and, Missis, ye're goin' the wrong way;' and on we
sped with flying feet. 'Good-bye, Missis; now for the
timer. It's a dandy,' he said, pocketing it; 'there's a
'ansum; you'd better take it, you are out of breath;'
and with a shrill whistle, the man stopped; when the
boy flew, and I took the hansom; and here I am home
at last, thank God."

"What wretches!" cried Mary.

"You leave me no more, Sarah; you are evermore
my care; go to bed now, dear, and rest, for we will go
up to London to-morrow, to ask Dr. Annesley's advice.
I shall go now to Broadlawns for your trunks; good
night. Oh, how light my heart is now I have found
you again, Sarah," he said, tenderly kissing her.

"We will be an old couple, Silas, dear," she said,
quietly; "do you know, to-morrow will be our joint
birthday; this is the eve of All Saints."

"Yes; and we shall be married to-morrow, when
we are in the city; age doesn't count; our hearts are
young, Sarah."

"Yes, Silas; I feel so happy I could sing,

> "'Now we maun totter doon, John;
> But hand in hand we'll go;
> And we'll sleep thegither at the foot,
> John Anderson, my jo.'"

"Our lives have been ever hand in hand, Sarah, for
we exchanged hearts long, long ago; but here is
George; I shall go now with an easy mind, for he will
guard you safely; good night."

"I have only time, to-night, to wish you joy, George,
for I require rest," she said, going upstairs.

"Well, this is good," he said, rubbing his hands;
"but, good night, sister, that is to be; my little wife
here has her mouth open to give me your story."

When Silas Jones, with the light waggon, drove up
the carriage drive to Broadlawns, the family were at

supper; so Simon, glad of the chance, got the trunks down and into the waggon, without words; but as Silas Jones was thanking him for his assistance; telling him of Sarah Kane's escape, and inquiring for Mr. Cole, Mr. Stone, leaving the dining-room, encountered him, when he said,

"I am taking Sarah Kane's trunks away, Mr. Stone."

" And who has authorized you to do anything in the matter?" he inquired, haughtily.

" My future wife, Sarah Kane."

For once, he was non-plussed; when Miss Stone, passing through the hall, said, stiffly:

"I am sorry I cannot congratulate you, Mr. Jones, on winning a Christian woman."

" What can it mean," thought Mrs. Cole; " she is in tight keeping; safe enough." As a feeler, she says,

" You must have the faith of Abraham to trust her still; someone said she is living with a bachelor at London."

"Mrs. Cole, let me tell you there is such a thing as British justice, which we mean to have, when you shall eat your words in a court of law," he said, indignantly turning on his heel, and out into the night.

Simon, at his post in the sick room, told the good news of Sarah Kane's escape.

Turning suddenly, in his eagerness to face Simon, and hear more, the sufferer groaned in rheumatic pain.

" Can you not manage to bring her to see me, when *they* are *all* out; the once you did bring Mr. Jones, he said, when he found Sarah, they would go out to New York or Canada; I particularly wish to see them. Jove! the pain; the liniment, Simon; rub me, please, and close the door; if I could only escape, like Sarah; you will do what you can, I beg of you, to bring them to see me?"

"I will, sir, if I loses my situation by it."

Below stairs the birds of prey held council with closed doors.

"What the devil did that man Jones mean by daring to throw threats in our faces, Margaret?" said Stone, with seeming bravado, though, in reality, in dismay.

"Impudent bluster, perhaps, but I shall put my ears to their proper use," and slipping off her shoes, she crept noiselessly up to the door of the gloomy east chamber, which had been closed so they could talk privately, thus playing into the ear of the enemy.

"Well," said her uncle grimly, as she returned. "Well?" she answered, in the same tones, her eagle nose . more prominent, her awful eyes more stony than ever.   "She has escaped! and is even now at the bookseller's."

"The devil!"

"You may well say so. Thomas Lang has sold you. Simon does not know particulars, for our friend Cole was earnest in inquiries."

"Is it too late to go into the city now?" he said nervously.

"Yes, and you are too cowardly to face 'ills you know not off' alone. Let me see; the lower class are awed by pomp and show. We will drive into Windsor Terrace in the morning in the carriage and pair. If Lang has sold you, you must buy him, by letting him have the house at his own figure. Again, should she have escaped without his connivance, be prepared by selling everything you can. You, as guardian to my sweet step-sister, have unlimited powers until our pet is of age, which interesting event, they don't seem to know, has taken place. Rake in all the gold you can, uncle, as the United States looks inviting at present; to-morrow will be a busy day, Aunt Elizabeth, so you might tell cook to have breakfast an hour earlier. Good night."

As she left the room, her uncle said :

" She is every inch a Stone, Elizabeth, and not a bit like her chicken-hearted father."

" That's true, Timothy, but she grows plainer every day, and looks nearly as old as I do."

" Yes, she is no Hebe ; but had the blooming goddess been possessed of her wits, she would have blindfolded Jupiter."

CHAPTER XVIII.

THE ISLET-GEMMED ST. LAWRENCE.

N a morning late in December Mrs. Gower sat alone in her pretty restful library, with its olive-green velvet cushions and hangings, its water-lilies, like the beauties in our bay, with their green stalks and leaves painted on the panelled walls, its English ivy trained up and around the Queen Anne mantel, with graceful palms standing on either side of the floral blossoms on the stand. The occupant looks well in a close-fitting gown of navy blue flannel, embroidered in rose silk ; there is a halfsmile on the lips, and the dreaminess of some tender thought in the dark eyes, as she idly opens and closes a black lace fan, with a spray of honeysuckle painted thereon. A gentleman's card lay beside her work-basket on the table.

" So Alexander Blair is his name," she thought ; " how very, very long," with a sigh, " it has taken to come to me—his name, of course, I mean." She thought, with a smile, putting the card to her lips, " how foolish of me, but I have always had that way. I remember travelling to Port Elgin, from Toronto, and on my arrival, my trunk, containing my dearest treasures, was not forthcoming. I was wild with grief, when, after enriching the telegraph offices, at the expense of my purse, in three days it was again in my possession; and what did I do, why kissed and fondled both trunk and key. Elaine Gower, you are a foolish, impressionable woman. And so I dropped my fan at the Grand, last night. His card says, 'With compliments, dropped at the theatre.' He scarcely seemed a stranger seated beside me at 'Erminie,' and I feel sure he felt likewise. How handsome he is, or rather how essentially manly, with the look of strength in his broad shoulders, and of honesty of purpose in his fearless, blue eyes. He is iron-grey, and slightly bald, I noticed, when he stooped to pick up my handkerchief, but his beard and moustache are brown. He is decidedly dark; I wonder if Highland Scotch; for dark, and true, and tender are the North. His name suits him. I like them both for old association's sake, one being the maiden name of one whose memory is sacred, the other, the Christian name of my loved dead. I wonder what poor Charlie Cole would think of my having made his acquaintance in this romantic fashion. I remember, he also had had instantaneous photographs, as we laughingly called them, of a young lady who had interested him."

At this moment Miss Crew, entering, in walking costume, said:

"I met the letter-carrier as I came in, Mrs. Gower, and here is your share."

"Thank you. You look better for your walk; but did you walk?"

"Only from the Spadina Avenue car terminus, but I had some little walking in my district, but the College Street Mission is worth fatiguing oneself for. Oh, Mrs. Gower, have you heard how Mayor Howland purposes raising building funds for the cottage in connection with the Industrial Home at Mimico?"

"Yes, I read it in some newspaper, the *Globe* of yesterday, I think."

"Won't it be something to be proud of, if the children carry it out."

"Yes, and I believe they will; children are very much in earnest, when the heart is touched; and now for our correspondence; take off your hat and mantle here by the grate, though Gurney's furnace does keep us very comfortable all over the house."

"Pardon my interrupting you, Mrs. Gower; but I am reading a letter from Mrs. Dale, in which she says, to be sure and remind you to write her some description of your yachting on the St. Lawrence; those English friends of theirs would so much like to get some idea of the life, as they purpose purchasing an island."

"Yes, I must do so; but I fear any poor words of mine, will fail in doing justice to its many delights;" and on finishing reading her letters, seating herself at her *escretoire*, she wrote as follows:

"The Islet-Gemmed St. Lawrence.

"DEAR MR. AND MRS. DALE,—It has never been my lot to read anything descriptive of river-life, on our loveliest of streams, that I have considered did justice to its varied charms; so you may imagine how powerless I feel, in the task you have assigned me; but when I tell you that that martyr to *ennui*, Jack Halton, this summer owned to myself that he had, at last, found something worth living for, you will therefore not be surprised that I, loving nature as I do, should have gone into raptures.

"In the first place, our steam-yacht, the *Ino*, was the trimmest little craft, the daintiest little beauty on the river; and we had the perfection of host and hostess, each in their respective niche, leaving nothing to be desired. I told them they must have had ' Aladdin's lamp' stowed away somewhere; for we had but to clap our hands, and our will was done.

"Day after day, never tiring, ever with renewed zest we boarded the *Ino*, to dream away the hours in the most ravishing bits of scenery my eyes ever beheld. With hampers full of dainties and substantials, we wandered in and about the islands; sometimes meeting other idlers like ourselves, and pic-nicking at some chosen spot; sometimes the guests at one or other of our acquaintances having summer homes in this our Canadian fairyland. Truly, if all the year were June, the world in woods would roam; for our gay little *Ino* was a spirit of the waters, and though we had no spiritualists on board, still we had table rappings on some good story by our witty host; neither were we so spiritual as to despise the material, which we proved as we sat to dinner; and such dinners, Ambrosia! Yea, and for our goddesses; though with sunburnt faces we women did not much resemble the latter, our men looking handsomer the browner they grew; but as for dinner, we had from dishes to tickle the palate of our club epicures to— hodge-podge, which we relished.

"Yes, from morn till eve, and often late, late, in the white moonlight, we lived an ideal life on our pet yacht, the *Ino*.

"One will sometimes say, in meteing out great praise to some favored spot, that one would live and die there; but here, who talks of dying? One would fain live forever; for, every moment one lives, one breathes a new life; for on the luxuriously appointed *Ino*, we gazed out from curtained windows, or from under a canopied arch, while we reclined on softest of cushioned seats, and literally drank in the 'Elixir of Life.' The air of the pine groves as we passed, the air of the grandly dark and dashing river, full of ozone, is the air to inflate one's lungs with, and carry back with one to our crowded cities, which seemed so far away in that land of beauty.

"Some delightful evenings, we would tread a measure on the green sward, to music of flute and violin; for, had one or more of our group not been innate musicians, the scene was enough to inspire one, and so, in songs, merry laughter or sentiment, our days passed as a dream.

> " For we stem the shining river,
> The river of the isles,
> On our fairy yacht, the *Ino*,
> With our love beside our side.

For I there met a sorcerer, who robbed me of my heart, and whose spells I could not break until I fled from this scene of enchantment. And again we board our trim yacht, and what varied scenes of beauty met the eye, whenever and wherever we gazed. Such lights, such shadows, such artist bits, such trees, such rocks, such everything! Surely we were in fairyland, and not in plain, practical Canada.

" On some of the islands are ideal summer homes; now we came upon a fairy-like structure, in Italian villa style; now, upon a palatial mansion; now, upon a camp all alive, and signalling *Ino* the fair.

" The only specks in my sun were, that the American islands were made more beautiful by their owners than our own; and that uneuphonious names had been given to some of these charming islets. Fancy one ' Pitch Pine Point '—I failed to see the point of christening it so.

"The rocks take most fantastic shapes in the shadowed moonlight. By and under the rock-bound shore, I used to fancy I saw nymphs dancing on the rippling waters, which was to them music; and, dreaming on, as we lazily stemmed the tide, it all came to me, that in days of yore, the youths from the shore, coming to row and sport in the waves at eve, saw the water-sprites, and fell in love; when the sea-gods, for revenge, fell upon them, transforming them into some of the most fantastic-shaped rocks we see; and, the sea-nymphs, pitying the sons of men for their fatal love, prayed the gods to transform themselves into trees, to grow into the clefts of the rocks; and so protect their would-be lovers from old Sol's fiery beams, and their wish was granted.

"But we invariably turned ere a bend in the river robbed it from our sight, to take a last loving glance at the beauteous Isle Manhattan, where we had been most hospitably entertained by its charming American inmates. It is beautifully wooded, and an elegant mansion thereon, with one of the most hospitable of verandas, stretching long and wide, with many American rockers and pillowed rattan sofas, on which we have reclined or sat while partaking of iced claret and, for those who liked it, champagne *carte blanche*, and where we had one of the most perfect views from the commanding tower of the villa.

"A view that wants a Lett, an Imrie, or an Awde to sing of, a Longfellow to immortalize—my pen is lifeless in describing its beauty; a beauty that would ravish the soul of a poet, and send an artist wild; a view which brought to my mind the remark of a dear old Scotchman, whom a party of tourists came upon, lost in admiration of the Falls of Niagara. On one of the party asking him what he thought of the Falls, he said, 'Eh, man, I just feel like takin' aff my bonnet til't.'

"In the far-stretching scene of loveliness here, in the heart of the Islands, one should go to the Tower, at Manhattan alone, leaving the merry, madding crowd on board the yacht, or on the veranda; one should go alone, or in dual solitude, where a clasp of the hand, or a look, is sympathy enough; for one should carry with one one's fill of such a scene of perfect beauty, to brighten darker days and drearier times."

CHAPTER XIX.

EYE-OPENERS.

ON the morning of All Saints' Day, and while numerous bells, in tuneful voices, reminded London of souls departed, and souls to be saved, Silas Jones and his twin spirit, Sarah Kane, having arrayed themselves in best bib and tucker, had taken the underground rail from Bayswater, and with the multitude were trying not to lose one another in the London fog—a regular pea-souper, in which the coat-pocket of Silas had been picked of pipe, tobacco and handkerchief.

"Mercy me, Silas, look well that they don't steal the license."

"You are right, Sarah; which the thieves would not ask for leave or license to take; 'tis a big world our London; and it's my belief the thieves' quarter is the biggest half."

"We should have made sure of the license, Silas, by being married at first."

"That we should, dear; but you have always let a fancied duty come between us. And now for Picca-dilly and Dr. Annesley, in this fog."

"Hello, Missis; a feller can't see in this 'ere yeller fog; 'ere, get into my barrow; it's clean, and I'll run yer through," said a boy's voice, running against them; and which Sarah Kane recognized as that of her liberator, the cross-eyed boy.

His offer was hurriedly declined by Silas, who dreaded Sarah taking her hand from his arm. On ascertaining from the boy that he had hired to peddle fruit for a huckster and that he had pawned the watch and chain they offered to redeem them, and give him a sovereign and-a-half for them; which offer he joyfully accepted; they also, giving him their address, told him, if at any time he wanted advice or assistance, to come.

A policeman now directed them to the residence of Dr. Annesley—a genial, kindly old gentleman, who was at home, and pleased to see them. On their relating the doings at Broadlawns, he was both astonished and indignant, disgusted and outrageous.

"As to any sharp tricks in money matters, I am not surprised," he said, impatiently; "but that they should have dared to perpetrate such an outrage as the marriage of Mr. C. Babbington-Cole, to that intensely disagreeable, ugly, cruel, Miss Villiers, is monstrous, monstrous!"

"You may well say so, sir," said Sarah Kane, sadly.

"How is it you had no suspicions, Mistress Kane, and you under the same roof?"

"I only overheard a word now and again, as to a marriage; but I never suspected this horror; I supposed it meant Miss Pearl, and that they were going to bring her back, when of age."

"Nothing can be done for Babbington-Cole; he is tied for life; but how he could ever have fallen into their net, is more than I can imagine," he said, in disgusted tones.

"You know, I told you they took him by surprise, sir; and his father lay ill; and cablegrams came telling him to wed Margaret Villiers, and hasten with her to his bedside; and he was just demented-like, between it all, and brain fever coming on."

"Well, well, it is a bad, very bad business. I confess to the having been so disgusted, on Villiers making Stone guardian to Miss Pearl, until she attained her majority, that I, metaphorically speaking, washed my hands of the whole affair; especially on Miss Pearl herself telling Brookes & Davidson, her mother's lawyers, that she agreed to it; this she said, on their telling her that, as her father had had softening of the brain at the time, nothing he said was worth considering."

"Depend upon it, doctor, Mr. Stone had used coercion to induce Miss Pearl to agree," said Silas Jones.

"Yes, I see, he must have," he answered, thoughtfully.

"And you don't know anything of poor Miss Pearl's whereabouts, do you, sir?" asked Sarah Kane, anxiously.

"Yes, I can give you a clue, for I love her for her own and her mother's sake; and as time went on, and I heard or saw nothing of her, I wrote T. L. Brookes, the senior partner, for I have had nothing to do with the hypocrites at Broadlawns, since Villiers' death; and he sent me an address at New York. Here it is, 'Mrs. Kent, The Maples, Murray Hill;' but, it is only a clue, for I have written, and have not, as yet, received a reply."

"Oh, please copy it for me, sir, for Silas and I are going to be married, and go out and find her. I promised her mother to look after her; and I have not heard from Miss Pearl; but she has written, for she said she would; but they have read and destroyed them, the same as they did to some that came for Mr. Cole just before and after he arrived."

"Horrible! horrible! How is he now; you just come from there, I presume?"

On Sarah Kane relating her late enforced retirement under Tom Lang's roof, and her escape therefrom, he opened his eyes in astonishment, saying, indignantly:

"The rascal! and you know nothing of the locality?"

"Nothing whatever, sir."

"Even if she did, Dr. Annesley, Stone would coin some plausible reason for placing her there."

"Yes, yes, Jones; he is as cunning as the arch-fiend; people would believe him, too, as he is a good churchman."

10

"But, you know, Silas; he has his falsehood ready. Sir, he told /my jailer that I was demented, and—worse."

"Ah, his plots have no flaw; poor creature, after the kindness and respect Mrs. Villiers showed you, and which you deserved; too bad, too bad."

"The poison of their lying tongues has already done Sarah harm in Bayswater, Doctor. People pass her without a nod; they at Broadlawns say they found her in the bedroom of a gentleman guest at midnight, and that she stole out of the house at three in the morning to meet another."

"Shocking! you can have them up for defamation," he said, sternly.

"But, sir, I must tell you, it was to poor Mr. Cole's bedroom I went, and he with brain-fever coming on, to do what I could to comfort the unfortunate. gentleman; and it was to Silas and his sister I went at night to tell them of the awful marriage; that I was turned out, and going to Mrs. Mansfield's, which I was foolish enough to believe," she said, with tears.

"Well, well, Mistress Kane, there, there, don't recall it; go off to a clergyman's and marry this good man; and here are five pounds to buy some trifle in Cheapside, to remember the day by. And now, let me see, there was something I wished to see Jones about," he said, kindly, rubbing his forehead. "Yes, I have it; did they give you all the wearing apparel of the late Mrs. Villiers, Mistress Kane?"

"Oh, no, sir! I would not expect such beautiful things. I thought Miss Pearl should have them, whenever I see Miss Stone wearing the lovely furs and satins."

"Did you ever receive five hundred pounds sterling, Mistress Kane, left you, by the will of the late Mrs. Villiers?" he asked, slowly, and with emphasis.

"Sir, you take my breath away. Silas, tell him, no,

sir. I! I! receive such a sum. No, nor one penny since Mrs. Villiers' death; but that, I cannot claim, for I have staid on willingly, to watch dear Miss Pearl's interests, and this is the end. Come Silas, let us go now to the parson; it will be our first step out of Old England, to find Miss Pearl," she said, nervously, her tears flowing apace, partly with the troubled excitement of the words of Dr. Annesley, partly at the having, at last, a clue to the whereabouts of Pearl Villiers. Not so, Silas, who loved her too well to allow the words of Dr. Annesley to pass unnoticed.

"Do you really mean that the late Mrs. Villiers left Sarah a legacy, Doctor?" he said, in some excitement.

"I do; and infer from your united words that that rascal has pocketed it; I must see to it," and going to the telephone, ringing up Brookes & Davidson, ascertaining that they were both at their offices, said:

"Hello! Have been interviewed *re* Villiers' estate, am now sending the persons to you; they are quite reliable; shall see you to-morrow."

"All right, send them on."

"This is all I can do for you at present," he said; "and I advise you to make oath as to your not having received the legacy; it will save time.

"I am selfish enough to be glad you are going out to New York; something tells me you will trace Miss Pearl; and I can assure you both, you have my fullest sympathy in your dealings with Stone; I can scarcely restrain myself from taking the law into my own hands, going out, and charging them with their villainy."

"Thank God for your friendship, Doctor," said Silas Jones fervently, as he smoothed Sarah's bonnet-strings, and gave her her satchel.

"Good-bye, sir, and heaven bless you for your kindnesses," said Sarah Kane, with feeling.

"O, pshaw; my only regret is that you have only

found me out to say farewell; but you must both come back, and bring Miss Pearl, to see an old man."

On reaching the offices of the law-firm, Sarah Kane made oath as to the not having received either money or wearing apparel.

W. Davidson, Q. C., saying:

"My eyes are being opened every day by the revelations of my clients; but what you say confirms my suspicion, that the schemes of some *certain* people are such cunningly devised fables, as to make it next to impossible for all the law courts in the kingdom to convict them."

On leaving Temple Bar, they dined comfortably at a restaurant, talking faster than they ate. Afterwards, by the words of a clergyman, they were at last made one, at which, with hearts full of thankfulness and quiet content, they took a Bayswater omnibus.

Again in the little back parlor, where Mary had a table groaning under its good things, with a bright fire to welcome them, to which they had scarcely done justice, and beginning to relate their adventures in the city, when Simon, the man from Broadlawns, entered, saying, hurriedly:

"I gave my word to the young gent up to the house that I'd fetch you folks up to see him when they, over there, were out; so, come along, please, if you be in a mind to give the poor gentleman his way."

"Yes, indeed, we will, Simon," said Sarah Kane, readily tying on her bonnet. "Come, Silas, dear."

He rose, somewhat reluctantly, for the neat little parlor is doubly home to him now, with the sweet, gentle face of Sarah looking at him with the loving eyes of a wife.

"But are you sure, Simon, that they are all out, and for the evening, for I cannot answer for myself if I come across them?"

"Sure as the Bank of England, Mr. Jones, they be

at the parson's. He's a showing of them off to a big missionary from foreign parts as his best angels."

"The Rev. Mr. Parks is so good," said Sarah, "that I always regret that his eyes are closed to the color of his angels."

"The trouble be, Mistress Kane, that they blindfold more nor parson," said Simon, as they hurriedly made their exit.

"Mistress Kane no longer, Simon, for I am glad to tell you we were married in the city to-day."

"Lawk-a-day! you don't tell me; but I am mighty glad to hear it. You will have a man of your own now, to take your name out of the gossips' mouth."

On arriving at Broadlawns, they went at once to the gloomy east chamber, when Sarah could scarcely repress an exclamation of intense pity at the change for the worse in the appearance of the long-suffering inmate. He was wasted to a shadow, and his brown locks had been shaved during brain fever, his kindly blue eyes looked black in the transparent paleness of his face, as did his whiskers and moustache, but in which many grey hairs had come. Holding out a thin, white hand, he welcomed Sarah warmly, saying:

"Oh, it *is* good to see your face again. I expect I look like a galvanized corpse, Sarah. What with the horror of my forced union with Medusa (a pet name I have for Mrs. Cole), and then brain fever, which, I don't wonder, caught me, and which, having that woman about me, aggravated. You banished, and maligned, at which I stuffed the bedclothes into my ears, and now my old enemy, inflammatory rheumatism, I have had a pretty tough time of it."

"Yes, indeed, you have, poor fellow," said Sarah, restraining her tears, and scarcely able to look at the wreck before her; "but you are on the mend now, and we must trust in God to bring you around soon.

It has been a heartbreak to me, Mr. Cole, that I was not allowed to nurse you."

"Only another piece of their cruelty, Sarah. But tell me about yourself. Where did that old sinner incarcerate you? tell me everything," he said, with feeble eagerness, for sometimes the pain was intense, causing him to set his teeth, or catch his breath.

But Silas Jones, seeing how much she was affected, and wishing to give her time to recover, himself gave the sick man a vivid picture of her imprisonment and release.

"Jove! what a wretch—I mean Stone; for the man Lang was simply his tool. Gad! I shall exercise a treble amount of will-power to get well, and out of their clutches, and back to dear old Toronto. 'Out of every evil comes some good,' they say; though, in my case, not much; in Sarah's, yes, for you have given me a tonic, Jones. From this moment I am determined to recover."

"That's right; be brave, sir, and you'll pull through right smart," said Silas Jones; for Sarah is swallowing a lump in her throat."

"Yes, bear up, Mr. Cole," she said, trying to smile, as she seated herself on the bedside, taking his poor, worn hands into her own, warm with vitality. "But Silas has not given you a bit of good news—that the happiest part of our lives is to come, for from to-day, we pass them together!"

"Yes," said Silas, coming beside her, laying his hands on her shoulders; "yes, I have nothing more to wish for, with Sarah beside me. I cannot remember the time, sir, that I did not want Sarah."

Two tears rolled down the sick man's cheeks, as he thought of his own wretched fate; but, by a visible effort, controlling self, he said, simply:

"I am glad you are together, and happy. Yours is a blessed union. God help me to health and strength, that I can free myself of *her* presence," he cried imploringly. "Sarah, I have a fancy—it may be a dying one, heaven knows—it is to see a likeness of Pearl Villiers, the girl I was, by right, to have married."

"Here she is, poor dear," she said with alacrity, unfastening a locket suspended to her chain.

"How strange! how like her! only older, and more careworn. Sarah, I have seen a face like this three or four times on the other side of the water; the face, too, strange to say, haunted me; a nice, good face, rather than pretty; but if the careworn, troubled look was gone it would have been pretty. Yes, the same features; small, pale, and regular."

"And with fair hair and slight figure?" cried Sarah, clasping her hands.

"Yes," but with the restlessness of the invalid he changed the subject, saying:

"You and your husband are going to America, you say. I am going, too; *when* I get well. You might meet me there, if you can't wait for me," he said, wearily; "and, yes, there is something else I must hasten to say before those people return. I have received no letters since my arrival, only a few newspapers; here they are. I love them because they come from dear Toronto," he said, in nervous haste, taking from beneath his pillow a copy of the *Mail*, two of *Grip*, with a *Globe*.

"Letters were here to meet you, sir?"

"Then the sneaks have read and kept them," he cried, angrily.

"Perhaps I should not have told you, sir; but I don't like you to think your friends have forgotten you."

"You do me no harm, Sarah, by your eye-openers. Wrath is a good tonic; tell me if you know what postmark was on them."

"Here are some envelopes I picked up from the grate the morning they sent me away."

" Yes, they said their letters would be here to meet me. This is quite plain, from Will Smith; this I can scarcely decipher; but it's—yes, it's Mrs. Gower's writing; and this from a namesake of yours, Mr. Jones. Ah, it's good to see even these scraps. I could preach sermons on the wickedness of my jailers," he said, weakly, " but now, at once, before they come back, take my address here, on——"

"How dare you enter my roof! it is more than flesh and blood can stand," said Mrs. Cole, entering stealthily, her face in a flame with rage—a virago, from the crown of her head to the sole of her foot, and arrayed, with her usual contempt for harmonious coloring, in pea-green satin, jet trimmings, with crimson bows.

" Calm yourself, Mrs. Cole; we are in the presence of a sick man," said Silas, with intense pity for the invalid, and endeavoring to curb his own tongue.

" Don't dare to address me, but get out of my house immediately; there, follow your bonnet, Sarah Kane," she said, furiously, pitching her bonnet and satchel into the hall, on which some change rolling therefrom, she was the richer by a half a sovereign, which, stealthily picking up, with an inward chuckle, she slipped into her boot.

" What's all the racket about upstairs? Wait a few moments, Lang," said Stone, who, on returning, ascertained he had been waiting for him in the kitchen for a full hour, they having missed each other in the morning.

Sarah Jones, in nervous haste to be gone, picked up her bonnet and satchel, taking the hand of Mr. Cole in good night.

" Remember! and here is my address," he whispered nervously.

But the woman he has married is too sharp for them; for, on Sarah turning from the bedside, she snatched the paper, tearing it into fragments.

"Good night, Mr. Cole. I am truly sorry for you; you are too good for the inmates of this house."

"Again you dare to trespass," said Stone, meeting them on the stairs, turning and following them down.

"I warned you before that I should make you pay for this. I am master here, and I tell you I shall kick you out if you ever show your ugly faces here again," he said, choking with passion.

"Good evening, Mistress Kane," winked Lang, as they passed him. "It was not square of you to skip off from me without paying your board. I'm dead broke, so you or your follower better pay up now; it's only five sovereigns, and save law expenses."

"You are unwise, Mr. Lang, to add insult to injury," she said, quietly, as she went out into a serener night.

"Provide yourselves with plasters, and we shall provide ourselves with copper toes, the next time you trespass," shouted Mrs. Cole, over the banisters.

"We shall only trouble you once more," said Silas Jones, curbing himself, "when Mrs. Jones will give you her signature in exchange for five hundred pounds, with interest on same, left her by the will of the late Mrs. Villiers."

CHAPTER XX.

"YOUR EEN WERE LIKE A SPELL."

THE silver chimes of the mantel clock rang four p.m., as Mrs. Gower descended from her sewing-room on the last day of the old year. She looked well in a gown of soft, grey silk, hanging in full, straight folds, unrelieved by ornament, save a few sprays of sweet heliotrope at her collar-fastening.

She stood at the library door, unseen by Miss Crew

the only occupant, who made a pretty picture, the last
beams of the setting sun coming in through a west
window, lighting up her fair hair and pretty brown
gown, the firelight lending color to her pale cheeks; a
cabinet photo is in her hand, at which she is gazing so
earnestly, and with such a troubled expression, that
she has not heard Mrs. Gower, though singing softly,
as she descended the stairs,

> " Your een were like a spell, Jeanie ;
> Mair sweet than I can tell, lassie,
> That ilka day bewitched me sae
> I couldna help mysel', lassie."

" Who are you trying to read, Miss Crew ? "

" Your friend, Mr. Babbington-Cole, Mrs. Gower,"
she said, with a start, placing the photo back in its
frame.

" And has it told you its name was Babbington-Cole,
ma chere ; we only give the latter ? "

" Yes; but you know his name is Babbington-Cole,
Mrs. Gower," she answered, evading the question.

" We do. Do you like his face? "

" Yes, very much ; he looks so kind and sweet-
tempered."

" Poor Charlie Cole, he is all of that ; excessively
amiable people so often wed the reverse. I do hope
it is not so in his case." " It is a dreadful fate," said
the girl, absently. "But we must hope for the best,
Miss Crew; but his long silence makes me fanciful;
however, if we don't receive news direct very soon—as
I have had some queer dreams of him lately—I shall
write the clergyman at Bayswater."

" The reverend—I mean, how will you address it;
just to the clergyman, or how ? " she said, intent upon
her work.

" Yes, that's very true, I don't know his name. Oh,
I have it; Mr. Smyth left the paper with the marriage

insertion; I do hope it has not been destroyed;" and
going to the rack, to look over its contents, Miss Crew,
excusing herself, left the room to get into her wraps, as
she was due to tea at the Tremaine's.   Mrs. Gower,
looking in vain for the English newspaper, seated
herself comfortably to read the report of the Board of
Trade dinner to the Honorable Joseph Chamberlain.

Miss Crew entered, robed for the winter streets.
"Good-bye, Mrs. Gower; I shall not be late."

"*Au revoir;* give Mrs. Tremaine my love; and say,
as the Dales may return from New York this evening,
I found it impossible to leave; and be sure and wear
your overshoes : our streets are in their usual winter
break-neck condition.   I do hope the new Council
will enforce the by-law."

"I hope so, too; I had an awful fall the other day;
the city treasury would be overflowing did they collect
the fines," she said, going out; when, at the hall door,
she returned, saying hurriedly, "Oh, here is the English newspaper you were looking for, Mrs. Gower; it
was upstairs."

"Thank you, good-bye."

"Having made a note of the clergyman's name at
Bayswater, and become conversant with the news in
the city papers, she gave herself up, in the gloaming,
to quiet thought.

"Yes, I like him very much, there is a manly,
straightforwardness in his words; a steadfastness of
purpose in his honest blue eyes; a firmness in the
lines of the mouth, with a kindliness of manner; all
stamping him as a man whose friendship would be
true, whose love faithful; how strange, that at last I
should meet him at the house of a mutual friend.   Mr.
St. Clair tells me he has known him for years, and
the Tremaines since summer; had any one told me
two weeks ago, that I should sing 'Hunting Tower'
with him in ten days, at the St. Clairs', I should have

thought them romancing.   He has a sweet tenor voice,
he asked me if he might call; how pleasant it would
be if he were here now.   I used to wonder and wonder,
in meeting him so frequently at lectures, concerts, or in
the cars, and walking about, what his name was.   Now,
Alexander Blair has come to me; and his tenderness
to the little veiled lady, who was, I suppose, consump-
tive, by the slow way they walked.   I wonder where
she is, I never see her now: his care for her touched
my heart.

I am so glad he has come into my life: I feel lonely
at times; and he is so companionable, I know.   What
dependent creatures we are, after all—houses and
lands, robes *a la mode*, even, don't suffice.   Intercourse
we must have.

"But," and a shudder ran through her, "what a
desolate fate mine will be if Philip Cobbe will persist
in keeping me to my oath.   We have not much in
common: he is kind, but neither firm nor steadfast,
and now this woman comes between us; and what
would she not do were I his wife?   As it is, I live in
daily dread of her doing something desperate.   It was
enough to terrify any woman similarly situated, the
way in which she acted that Sunday evening, coming
from church; and again, that night at the Rogers'
meeting in the Pavilion.   A ring!   Can it be the
Dales?   No, it is Philip; I wonder what mood he is
in."

"Alone! for a wonder," he said, warmly.   "Leave
the gas alone, Thomas, the firelight is sufficient."
"And thinking of me, and wishing for me," he said,
as the servant left the room.   "Yes, I can tell by your
eyes."

"There Philip, that will do, I am actually afraid to
have you in my house.   Remember that woman last
night! if looks could kill, then would I have been
slain," she said, tremblingly.

"She can't harm you, and I'll put a stop to her tricks. You see, Elaine, she is so infatuated with me, she can't keep away," he said, personal vanity uppermost.

"But, that's just what I want you to see, Philip; it would be running too great a risk to marry you."

"'Pon honor, love, I don't know how to shake her off."

"You did not seem to exert yourself last night. When I looked over my shoulder to speak to you in the crowd, coming out, she had her hand on your arm; and you were bending down listening to her."

"I know; and when you looked, she clutched her hold of my arm all the tighter," he said, with the eagerness of a child.

"What did she say?"

"She said, you *shan't* go home with her to-night."

"Exactly the same words she used that Sunday evening. Words and an act that will ever be stamped on my memory. That act came between my heart and yours, Philip, for all time," she said, sadly thinking of his foolish flightiness in allowing anything of the kind to break up their friendship, if no more. "You must see, Philip, that you should set me free."

"No, no; don't talk like that; you should want me all the more when you witness her infatuation," he said, with his juvenile air, attempting to kiss her.

"No, Philip; I cannot let you come near me with the occurrence of last evening so fresh in my memory."

"Oh, nonsense; when I am your husband you will be just as infatuated about me as she is."

"Do you know, Philip, you are as vain as a girl."

"Well, yes; I suppose I am vain; but so would any man be who was as successful with the fair sex as I am," he said, drawing himself up to his full height of five feet nine, a look of pleasure in his large bright eyes.

"I can assure you, Philip, I felt anything but vain at the Pavilion, or coming out of church, with the spiteful eyes of that tall, common-looking, over-dressed Mrs. Snob full upon me, as social astronomer; she took in the situation at once."

"A fig for what such like see or think; I thought you were above valuing the opinion of our wealthy plebeians."

"But we were so conspicuously placed; I shrink from giving such women food for gossip."

"Hang them all; our east-ender, Mrs. Snob, Ragsel, and the whole tribe, or anyone that bothers you, Elaine."

"But, Philip, do be rational; release me from my oath; give me my freedom; we will never be happy married, or with our engagement still on; for she will grow bolder, and more persistent with each advance; do, for pity's sake, free me."

"No, no; you ask too much," he said, angrily, thinking of these comfortable quarters of which he should be master, and of the woman beside him also.

"But see how you left me for her last night; you *must* be fond of her."

"I am *not*, so help me God; but I could not shake her off without making a scene."

"But just fancy, Philip; if we were married she would prowl about the place even more than she does at present."

"It is all your own fault, Elaine, that she gives you those scares in the evening; for she only comes when she knows I am about; if you lived more to yourself, and did not have all these women about you, I would come in the afternoon, like to-day; and she would be none the wiser, for she is at work in the day and can't come."

"It is a fearful life for me."

"Be reasonable, Elaine: any man as fascinating to

your sex as I am must, of necessity, have women breaking their necks for them."

"How you amuse me," she said, smiling ironically, comparing him with someone else.

"I don't see why; you know I speak truth," he said, innocently; "let me come in the afternoon; don't have any one else; than, pet, she will not see me watching to see you when your guests are gone at night; and so you will not be troubled with her."

"But just think what a proposition you are making; she is to control our actions."

"Yes; but only for a time, pet; she will, perhaps, tire of pursuing me; if she had me, and you were out in the cold, I feel sure she would agree to my proposition."

"You certainly have a most amusing way of putting things."

"I know I have; it's my large, kind heart and wish to please; and when we are married I will both charm and amuse you."

"No, no; it will not be safe for me to marry you; for how about this other woman; would you charm and amuse her also?"

"Just as I was in the humor; if she angered me, I would not think twice of setting Tyr on her."

"Dinner is served, ma'am."

On repairing to the dining-room; and having done ample justice to a substantial dinner, prepared with a view to the possible advent of the Dales; and when the oyster soup, roast beef, with delicious vegetables, had been removed, dessert on, and Thomas dismissed, Mr. Cobbe said, in pleased tones:

"I must congratulate you on your cook, Elaine."

"Then you congratulate myself, Philip; for my seraph of the frying-pan knows next to nothing of the art; I devote two hours of each day to my culinary department."

"For which you have the thanks of your guests, and for which Bridget will make you pay."

"Yes; I know; but they all do it; when they feel their wings, they demand higher wages, or fly.

"When will you marry me, Elaine?" he said, lightly, as they entered the drawing-room.

"*After all I have said, you still ask this,*" she said, freeing herself, and at her wits' end to know what to do with him, remembering her oath; but this woman, and what revenge she may take, terrifies her. Mr. Cobbe lights the gas; but the inside shutters must be shut; and as she closes them, he assists her, standing so near that his cheek touches hers.

"Don't speak to me like that, Elaine; we love each other; and hang her for coming between us; come here, pet, and sit beside me; it is a treat to have you all to myself."

"No; I am in no humor for a *tête-à-tête;* and the Dales may arrive at any moment."

"Hang them; can't they go to a hotel; I dislike them; and surely you had enough of them, and that doleful Miss Crew, while Dale went north."

"Tastes differ, Philip; I have a sincere friendship for them; as to their coming now, most of my little friends' wardrobe is——"

Here a sharp ring at the hall door startled them.

"What! a ring; that woman will be the death of me; I tremble now, once evening comes, at every peal of that bell."

"Beg pardon, sir; a person—a—a lady, says she is waiting to speak to you, sir."

"Go, Philip, quick, for heaven's sake; this is dreadful," she said, in a gasp, holding her hand to her side.

"Mr. Blair," said Thomas; and the old gold *portière* hangings are again closed, and they are alone.

"Forget I am with you; don't try to speak yet," he said, kindly leading her to a seat; "you will breathe naturally in a few minutes, you have been startled; but it is all quiet now; your servant carefully fastened the door; lean your head back to this cushion; there is something, after all, in material comforts. Ah, now your color comes, and your eyes—well," he said, smiling, yet with a grave tenderness, "your eyes have lost their startled look, and may again weave their spells." For she had now opened her eyes, keeping them closed so she could better listen to his voice as he talked on, giving her time to recover that self which in alarm had fled.

But with her nerves more quiet comes a thought which she must set at rest. So intent on her question is she, that self-consciousness is altogether absent, as, looking into his face, she says,

"You must be a married man; you are so good a nurse, knowing exactly what is best for one; are you?"

"No; I was," he said, indicating, by a gesture, a mourning ring on the third finger of his left hand.

"Forgive me; I should not have asked you so abruptly."

"I don't mind you, you don't seem a stranger; and my poor wife was an invalid, so that her death, thirteen months ago, was not unexpected."

"No; under those circumstances, you would be more or less prepared."

"Tell me, did you deem me impertinent to turn my eyes to your face when we have so frequently met, before our introduction?"

"No; else I should have to share in your blame; for I should not have seen you had I not been guilty of like fault," she said, drooping her eyes.

"Believe me, I couldna help mysel', lassie, no more than I now can help myself coming to your house, and feeling so at home with you, as though I had known you for years, instead of for days. Do you

11

feel a little as I do," he said, in his eager earnestness, turning his blue eyes full on her face.

"I do; you will never be a stranger to me," she said, simply.

"Thank you; do you know that evening coming from the Grand, after 'Erminie;' I was in the seventh heaven after having been so near you."

"'So near, and yet so far,'" she said, smiling; "for the frowning battlements of the conventionalities were still between us."

"Yes; but I dreamed that your pretty lace fan would waft them away, being a woman (though, by your eyes, I feel sure a warm-hearted one); still, you cannot know how my heart leaped when I saw that you had forgotten your fan; my first impulse led me to follow you with it, but Scotch second-sight suggested the means I adopted, to tell you my name. How did you like it?"

"Very much, indeed," she said, smiling, as looking into his face half shyly, remembering how she had pressed his card to her lips; "I love both your names, for reasons I may tell you another time. Are you Highland Scotch?"

"Yes; and from fair Dunkeld."

"Indeed! you must be proud of your birthplace; the scenery must be beautiful, were it only in among your groves of trees. I love the giants of the forest so, that I wonder in the Pagan world they have not been as gods; now we sing,

> "'Ye groves that wave in Spring,
> And glorious forests sing,
>   Alleluia.'"

"You have a passion for trees, I see, and would surely like Dunkeld; 30,000,000 alone are said to have been planted by a Duke of Athol; we father on to the scenery a spice of romance running through us."

" Don't try to excuse it by fathering it on to other
than your own nature ; our age is too practical ; but
Emerson expresses my thoughts exactly when he says
' everything but cyphering is hustled out of sight ;
man asks for a novel, that is, asks leave for a few
hours to be a poet.' But, perhaps, you don't agree
with me ? "

" I do, or I should have a larger account at my
bankers ; I fear I am not a canny Scotchman, for I
have spent a good deal in giving my poor wife and
self a glimpse of the poetry of other lands."

" That was right, and kind. Do you know I think
the world would be a better place to live in if, after
one had made a sufficiency, one was compelled to give
place to others, and if no credit was given in any case."

" That, without doubt, would settle a good deal, and
do away with communism," he said, laughingly ; " for
there would be no large fortunes to grab. As to no
credit, I fear, until we reach Elysian fields, we shall
have failures, duns, and other fruits of the credit
system," he said, gravely.

" Do you intend remaining in Toronto ? " she said,
intent upon her embroidery.

" That depends," he said, trying to read her ; " don't
go away ; that old gold chair, with its crimson arms,
becomes you (in woman's parlance), and brings out
your warm tints."

" I should think you would admire a woman like
pretty Mrs. St. Clair, as you yourself are dark."

" Yes ; she is a pretty little thing ; a triumph of art
though ; but, if you will allow me to say so, I admire
your style ; usually there is more force of character
in dark women rather than in fair."

" Yes ; do you think so ? "

" I do ; now, for instance, there is St. Clair, miserable at the aimless existence of his wife : she is either
in hysterics or in—cosmetics."

" We hear he is insanely jealous of her."

"Rumor, as you know, dear Mrs. Gower, says more than her prayers. He tells me he is not jealous; for he does not believe any man would be silly enough to give him cause; but that by he or his son going about with her, her quest for admiration is held in check."

"Oh, I see; that is the reason they attend her so closely; what a pity we are so foolish as to throw away life happiness, and the passing of our time in rest and quietness for the evanescent soap bubbles of a passing hour; but it is growing late; come and see my palms in my pet room, the library, before you go."

" Thank you;" the mere words were naught, but he looked so quietly happy, as he drew the hangings for their exit, that the color came to her cheeks as she remembered her oath, to as quickly fade on the clock striking ten, and the hall bell ringing simultaneously, as a man outside stamped the snow off his boots, impatiently saying, hurriedly, the startled look again in her face:

" Ten o'clock ; I fear I must postpone your visit to the library."

"Is there any trouble I can shield you from ? if so, you have only to command me," he said, quickly, taking her hand in good night. " No, no, not now," she said, with a troubled look.

"Think, and tell me on New Year's Day," he said, buttoning his overcoat.

" I shook her off, Elaine," he said, impulsively, not seeing Mr. Blair, who was rather back of the door. " Oh, I beg pardon," he continued, sulkily. "I thought you were alone, and watching for my return."

" It is so late," she said, as Mr Blair made his exit.

" Nonsense, who was the man; I don't think it's right of you to have gentleman visitors," he said, in aggrieved tones.

" Now, Philip, does not that sound rather absurd ?

and, as I have before told you, I wish you would not come here at such a late hour; I don't like it," she said, gravely, as they went into the dining-room, where the usual little supper stood on a tray.

"But we are engaged, it's you who are absurd," he said, pettishly; "but don't let us bother about it, my frosty walk has been quite an appetizer. Did you find it long, pet, while I was away? but I forget, you had that man here. A ring! bother."

"It is Miss Crew, who is, you know, visiting me. Excuse me a moment, I hear Captain Tremaine's voice."

"Hang all her visitors," he muttered.

"I am glad to see you back, dear; come into the dining-room, both of you."

"Thanks, 1 believe if you only had potato and point, you would offer some one the potato."

"If so, they should thank you; for, from admiration of your hospitality, to imitation, was but one step."

"Blarney, blarney, you might only say that to the Chinese. These oysters are very fine, nothing like eating them off the shell."

"Just my taste; these were sent me by a friend."

"I never saw a man look more at home, than you, Cobbe; if all bachelors looked as contentedly jolly, we would not pity you so."

"No pity for me, Tremaine, thanks. I have given many of you cause for envy."

"He is not at all vain, Captain Tremaine," said Mrs. Gower, amusedly.

"Not for him," said Tremaine, jokingly.

"What is to be our color for 1888?"

"Orange or blue, Mrs. Gower; half the men I have met to-day say one, half the other; opinions are divided."

"Had the other man been a green Reformer, though, I would have bet on him," said Mr. Cobbe, buttoning on his overcoat.

"There is something in that," she said; "for some would say he would have the Ontario Government at his back."

"So he would, and good backers they would be, too. Good night, Elaine; shall I see you at St. John's Church, to-morrow?" he said, in an undertone.

"Don't ask me, after my last experience; I am going all the way to Holy Trinity Church, with Miss Crew; but shall be at home Monday, excepting while at the polls."

"All right, *au revoir.*"

On his exit, Tremaine said, laughingly,

"Good night. If the candidates were as sure of their election as our friend Cobbe is of his, they would sleep till Tuesday without a narcotic or a charm from the good fairies."

CHAPTER XXI.

A HAPPY NEW YEAR.

"HAPPY New Year! A Happy New Year!" is on every tongue, and how exhilarating is the cry uttered by thousands. From the weakly voice of our aged loved ones, to the bird-like notes of the wee children, mingling with the merry sleigh-bells, do our politicians take up the refrain; and our manly men, and ambitious women, sing out in various chords, as they swarm to the polls, "A Happy New Year! A Happy New Year!"

And Old Boreas takes up the refrain, and blows till his cheeks crack, down Yonge street, from his northern realm. Yea, forty miles distant, does he send his cold breath. A Happy New Year! A Happy New Year.

And our young men and maidens, our girls and our

boys, laugh till the air rings. Hurrah for the north wind, we'll go to the Granite and have a good skate.

And one gathers from the merry medley that our King Coal, and the *Sentinel*, are this year's favorites; but those who have put money up, and those who have not, must even wait with bated breath till midnight, or till dawn; and in dreamland, see their pet schemes forwarded, their own man in the Mayor's chair.

It was a busy day at Holmnest, a bee-hive with no drones, by eleven a.m. Mrs. Gower has polled her vote; afterwards, with Miss Crew, drove through snow-mantled Rosedale, down villa-lined Jarvis street, through those stores of wealth, Yonge and King streets, along the margin of the silver lake, ere turning the horses' heads to the north-west and Holmnest; visiting, also, some of the poorer streets, in which quarters Miss Crew has found God's poor, many cases having touched her heart, she now leaves little parcels of good things to gladden these homes.

"You will become bankrupt, Miss Crew," said Mrs. Gower, as they are driven home.

"I am almost so, now; and if it will not bother you, I should like to tell you of a plan I have in view."

"Bother me? I should say not. You should know I take too much interest in you for that." "Thank you; some connections, until recently, have remitted to me a sum amply sufficient for my needs; I know not why," she said, in troubled tones, "they have discontinued it; but they have, and it remains for me to face the difficulty, now that Garfield has outgrown my tuition, I cannot remain dependent on the Dale's kindness; and of Mr. Dale's generous, good treatment of me, a stranger, I cannot say too much; but I must exert myself to get a new situation," she said, nervously. "And will you, dear Mrs. Gower, do what you can in advising me; I have been looking in the newspapers, but have seen nothing suitable."

" Excuse me, Miss Crew, " but are you entitled by
law to receive this remittance you speak of ? if so, you
should not quietly relinquish it, but should consult a
lawyer. We, at Toronto, are blessed with several
honest, as well as clever, law firms. I will accompany
you readily, or do anything I can for you."

" You are very kind, but I shrink from lawyers,
they ask so many questions," she said, timidly.

" You must not mind that, dear ; if you were ill,
what would you do, send for a medical man ? and the
more questions he asked, the better he would understand your case."

" I wish I was braver ; but I am only a girl, and
have had much trouble, which has made me very
nervous and timid."

For one so extremely reticent, this was quite a confidence.

" Yes, it would have that effect on one of your temperament ; but with me, my troubles have made me
more self-reliant ; finding few to trust, I have leaned
on myself."

" Yes, you seem to me very brave ; but don't you
think I should advertise for a situation at once ?"

" No, decidedly not. You should ask Mr. Dale to advise, and I shall be very pleased to have you with me
all winter."

" How very kind you are, Mrs. Gower," and the
tears came to her eyes, " but I should be more satisfied, adding to my purse."

" Very well, dear ; I commend your decision, but remember the bed-room you occupy is Miss Crew's own,
and your little home-nest will be ever ready for you ;
but do not forget my advice, which is to confide in Mr.
Dale, fully and entirely ; he can, and will, give you the
very best advice."

" Oh, I don't see how I can. If you only knew ; but

how selfish I am, spoiling your drive, and on New Year's Day, too."

Here a small sleigh, in which were seated a comfortable-looking couple; the man a mass of grey tints—complexion, hair, whiskers, over-coat, and fur cap—looking like a man who had led a sedentary life; the woman, fresh of color, partly bent by the breath of old Boreas, both looking quietly happy, but so intent on turning their heads, as if on a pivot, first on this side, now on that, as they drove down handsome Saint George street, as to be oblivious of the approach of the sleigh in which were seated Mrs. Gower and Miss Crew.

"Look out, there," shouted the driver. At this, the man, giving his whole attention to his horse, turned him out of the way just in time to save a collision; the woman, as they passed, looking at the occupants. She gave a great cry to stop them, but the driver had given his horses the whip, and on they dashed. Miss Crew had leaned forward, pale as death, her lips blue and parted, she tried to frame the word, "Stop," but failed. Mrs. Gower, in sympathy, defining her meaning, cried:

"Stop, driver, please."

On his doing so:

"Is the sleigh we just passed out of sight?"

"No, ma'am; the gentleman has turned, and is a following of us. Would you, ladies, like a New Year's race? if so, I'm your man," he said, grinning.

But Miss Crew, white as the snow, and looking whiter by contrast with the pretty red hat, has leaped out of the cutter.

"My dog-skin coat is very warm, Mrs. Gower; don't wait; I must speak to them," she said, in the greatest excitement, her eyes glistening, her color coming and going.

"But you will take cold, dear; get in beside me again until they come up."

"No, no, I beg; I wish to meet them *alone*, she whispered.

"On one condition; are they friends?"

"Yes; oh, yes, she is one of my best."

Mrs. Gower, seeing them almost close, wishing her an affectionate good-bye, bade the man drive on, and, as was natural, fell into a reverie over the strange occurrence happening to a girl of Miss Crew's remarkably reticent character. She seemed pleased, but so intensely excited, one could scarcely tell her real feelings. She thought, "But I sincerely hope it will be a bright incident for her to begin 1888 with; for a more truly pious, gentle, amiable girl I have never met."

On the driver drawing in his horses, to allow a gentlemanly-looking man to pass, who was crossing Bloor West, at the head of St. George street, Mrs. Gower waking from her reverie, sees Mr. Buckingham.

"The compliments of the season, Mrs. Gower," he said, lifting his hat.

"The same to you. Whither bound?"

"To Holmnest."

"Then you had better come into the sleigh; 'there's room enough for twa.'"

"Thanks; with pleasure."

"Driver, you see the young lady ahead of us. I expect she is coming to my place. Just pick her up, please."

"All right, ma'am."

"I suppose you will think our sleighing a make-believe, after Lindsay and locality."

"You will be surprised to hear I now come from New York. Dale telegraphed me to meet some railway men, so I have been there ever since."

"But won't your interests north-east suffer by your absence?"

"Oh, not materially, I hope; still I am anxious to

be on the spot. There is a splendid mine out that way I should like to get hold of."

"Iron, I suppose?"

"Oh, yes; it is, you know, to be the great industry of the future."

"But you only mean if we get Commercial Union?"

"Yes, as far as Canada is concerned."

"What is the name of this special mine you covet? I have heard Mr. Dale speak of several; this may be one."

"It is the Snowden, in Victoria county; the ore is a fine grained magnetite; the mine is favorably situated, having a railway running into it."

"Indeed! all very favorable; do you think you will succeed in becoming a purchaser?"

"Of that, I regret to say, I am somewhat doubtful, as I am told there are several obstructionists connected with it; but I am not going to worry about it," he said, quietly; "if I don't get it, there are others."

"What an easy temperament you have," she said, looking into his quiet unmoved countenance.

"My dear Mrs. Gower, I hold that a man should have himself under such perfect control as to be able to look at himself, in a manner of speaking, with other eyes; sit in judgment upon himself; dissect his motives, reward or punish. I look upon one who lets loose the reins of reason, giving blind passion or impulse full swing, as only an animal of the swine family, whatever his name may be," he said, smiling.

"What must he think of me," she thought; I am as impulsive as a Celt. "What a superior race of beings man would be were his convictions your convictions."

"I think he would be happier, for he would not give way to excitement, which is, in my opinion, a sort of insanity; and also in its reaction, which is melancholy."

"That reaction, after excitement, is one of the

strongest blue ribbon arguments; we had a 'chalk talk' thereon at the Pavilion on last Sunday afternoon; what do you think of the Prohibition movement?"

"I go with it, to the letter, for the mass of humanity cannot, or will not, control themselves; how do you go?"

"I believe in temperance in all things. Professor Blackie says, 'We have too much of everything in our day; too much eating, too much drinking, too much preaching, etc;' and I am so far at one with him, that I believe in temperance, and coffee, even on New Year's Day," she added, smiling. "Stop, driver, please."

"Come, get in, Miss O'Sullivan, and a Happy New Year to you, dear; this is my friend, Mr. Buckingham."

"I was on my way to your place, Mrs. Gower, to ask Miss Crew to come and spend the day."

"She is out with some friends; but you must lunch with me, and wait for her."

"Whose is that large, hospitable house, Mrs. Gower, at the head of St. George Street?" asked Miss O'Sullivan.

"A Colonel Sweeney's, dear, who, I was going to say, has a heart as large as his house, he is so kindly hospitable."

Here they overtook Mr. Blair, whose handsome face lit with pleasure, as he lifted his hat; and, somehow, Mrs. Gower was glad of the advent of the young lady, though, before seeing him, she had not minded her *tête-à-tête* with Mr. Buckingham, with whom she likes to talk.

In a few minutes Holmnest is reached, when Mrs. Gower, telling Mr. Buckingham to make himself at home, he must stay for luncheon, and until it is time to take the Midland rail, went upstairs to make her toilette for the day.

Mr. Buckingham looks and feels at home ensconced

in a deep, softly padded chair, near the blazing grate, in the restful library; he is soon lost in the *Iron Age.*

On Miss O'Sullivan, a sweet-faced, blue-eyed girl, entering, looking bright as the morning in her pretty red woollen frock, the occupant, with the innate courtesy of his countrymen, laying aside his news-paper ,adapted himself to her girlish chit-chat in a manner that charmed her, until the entrance of Mrs. Gower, in a very becoming gown of brown silk, with old gold plush trimming, ecru lace chemisette, and elbow sleeves—for she dressed for all day, and any friends who may come to wish her a glad New Year; she first goes to the kitchen to see that the machinery is actively in motion, as she had set it before going to the polls; one servant maid, with the boy, Thomas, being sufficient for the requirements of her cosy little home.

"Well, you both do look comfortable," she said, entering the library.

"Yes; I think we do," said Miss O'Sullivan.

"We only want you to want nothing more," he said, in pleased tones, placing a rattan chair, with its dark green velvet cushioned back and seat, and turn-ing the fire screen to protect her face.

"Not yet, thanks; my poor palms have had no water to-day. How do you think my plants are look-ing, Mr. Buckingham?"

"Very fine; but if you kept them more moist they would do still better; but most amateur gardeners make a like mistake," he said, cutting some bits of scarlet geranium; "this bit of color will make your costume perfect."

"The costume! but what about the woman?"

"Oh, the woman knows right well," he said, lead-ing her to the mirror.

"Give me the good taste of an American gentleman, in preference to a mirror, which is frequently untrue."

"Luncheon is served, ma'am."

CHAPTER XXII.

"BETTER LO'ED YE CANNA BE."

FTER a substantial luncheon, to which they bring good appetites, given by their exhilarating outing in the frosty air, they cross the hall to the drawing-room, when Thomas opened the door to Miss Crew and Mr. Cobbe.

"Ah, here is our truant," said Mrs. Gower.

" Me!" laughed Cobbe, wishing her the compliments of the season.

Mr. Buckingham thought he detected a slight cloud of dissatisfaction pass over her face, even as she welcomed him.

"I have made fifteen calls already; the fair sex like to be remembered, Buckingham."

" Man is too selfish to forget what he could not do without, Cobbe."

" Give me an American for a due appreciation of our sex," said Mrs. Gower, gaily.

" No, no; you are wrong. *You* ought to know an Irishman to be the most gallant man that lives," Mr. Cobbe said, sulkily.

" Well, yes, perhaps you are the most gallant," she said, thoughtfully, "but in the bearing of an American man towards my sex there is a something more— there is a gentle courtesy, a deference, a grave tenderness."

" Tut, tut," said Mr. Cobbe, turning over the leaves of an album impatiently.

"I fear you flatter us," said Buckingham.

" No, I think not; simply because your great Republic is so highly civilized and progressive, the outcome of which is our enthronement with you; while, in other

countries, we are still midway between our footstool of
the dark ages and our throne with you."

Here Mr. St. Clair, Captain Tremaine, and a young
barrister, a Mr. McCullogh, made their *entrée.*

" Your drawing-room is looking very pretty, Mrs.
Gower," said Tremaine; " the holly and mistletoe brings
me home again."

" Yes, it looks so well against the blue and tan panels, that I am tempted to let it stay."

" Where did you get it; it is very fine and healthy ?"
asked St. Clair, admiringly.

"Well, thereby hangs a tale ; it is a Christmas gift
from Santa Claus. All I know about it is, it came
(Thomas thinks) from Slight's."

" It was no slight to you, Elaine," said Cobbe, jokingly.

On the mention, before so many, of her Christian
name she made an expressive *moue* at Tremaine, unseen by the others, whose attention was momentarily
given to several booklets and cards which lay on a
pretty gilt stand, and while Miss O'Sullivan and Mc-
Cullogh turned the pages of " Erminie " for Miss Crew
at the piano.

" Wait until Monday, Buckingham. I take the Midland then, in your direction," said St. Clair.

"Impossible, St. Clair. I should have been as far as
Lindsay yesterday."

On the clock striking three, St. Clair started to his
feet, buttoning his coat.

"Good-bye, Mrs. Gower. 'Time and tide,' you
know."

" Oh, yes ; but Time is not such a churl as to bid
you away before I have had even a look at you."

" But we men come to look at you, to-day, and, as
usual, gratify ourselves. *Au revoir.* I promised
Noah to be back at three, to let him off for a skate,"

" ' What's in a name ?' " said Tremaine.   " I wonder
what relation he of the Ark was to that boy."

" But fancy !   I heard a clergyman in this city bap-
tize an unoffending infant Shadrach, Meshach and
Abednego."

" Did he throw in the ' and ' ?" laughed Tremaine.

" Oh, no.   Did I give it ?"

" Yes. Well, I just call my boy plain Paddy."

" Do you throw in the ' plain ' ?"

" Oh, come, now ; you ladies are having the best of
it all through to-day," he said, making his adieux.

" At the polls too ?" she said gaily.

Several callers now came in in rapid succession, Mr.
Cobbe rising as the last made their exit.

"Think of me, Elaine. I shall come in and cheer
you up when I get through," he said, in a loud whisper, as she was having a last quiet word with Buckingham.

" Here Mr. Blair entered, and both men thought
they saw a something in her smile that had not been
given them.

" Good-bye has come again, Mrs. Gower," said Buckingham.   " One must always regret leaving Holmnest ;
but I have only time to catch my train."

" Good-bye, and may all your wishes be granted."

Miss O'Sullivan, saying she must really go, took Miss
Crew (who had a new light in her face), Mr. McCullogh accompanying them.

" I am fortunate," said Mr. Blair, as the *portière*
hangings closed after them ; Mrs. Gower smiled.

" Rest, after running about ; though I think the
fashion of New Year's calls is fast dying out."

" It is, undoubtedly ; this is my third and last. You
are looking well after your frosty drive," he said, seating himself at the gilt stand beside her.

" Don't you think my friends have good taste ?" she
said, directing his attention to the cards and booklets ;

" this white ivory card is pretty, with its golden edge, white roses, and snowdrops, and gold bells, as they ring,

> " May every Christmas chime awaken in your heart
>   Each bliss of by-gone years in which your life had part."

"Yes," he said, thoughtfully, "if one could only drink a good bumper of the waters of Lethe, and forget the pain, remembering only the bliss."

"But 'tis the memory of the bliss that brings the pain ; at least I have found it so," she said gravely.

" Yes, you are right ; I have not thought of putting it to myself in that way; but I must not give you a sad train of thought. Ah, this is original," he said, picking up a large card, on which was painted a bunch of scarlet poppies, with the lines :

> "O! sleep; O! gentle sleep, how have I frighted thee,
>   That thou no more will weigh my eyelids down,
>   And steep my senses in forgetfulness ?"

" All the way from Ottawa; he evidently sees your eyes, which keep his open," he said, trying to read her.

" You are fanciful, Mr. Blair ;" but her color deepens under his gaze ; " but, be it as you say, he should close his eyes, possess his soul with honor, and clasp the hand of duty."

" You give him a hard task, still I would lay any wager on your kindliness of heart, on your strong sense of honor. I don't think you would fool with a man's affections," he said, earnestly.

In spite of herself she trembles, for she feels that he is more to her than any living man ; and as he sits, his elbows on the table, his fingers ran through his iron-grey hair, looking at her, her eyes droop, her hands nervously play with the cards, her sensitive lips showing her emotion, as she thinks of Mr. St. Clair's words to her the evening of their introduction, of the no-

12

bility of this man's character, of his devotion to his
late wife, of his clean record among men as to his
truth and honor in all business transactions; and now
she knows, intuitively, in fact, did at their first meeting, that his heart is seeking hers.

"I am right, you would not play with a man's affections; you have had sorrow yourself; tell me."

In spite of herself, a tear glistened in her eyes as
she looked into his face, as she thought of her oath.

"No; do I look so faulty, frivolous and foolishly
wicked?"

"No, you have a sweet, kind, womanly face," he
said, smiling gravely; "and were I to tell you of my
lonely life, and how I long for just such a womanly
presence, just such companionship to gladden a home,
to make my broken life complete, with a sweet sense
of peace and rest, would you send me from you desolate?" and his voice thrilled with intense feeling.

"If so, and that my act left me also desolate, would
you not forgive me?" she said, brokenly.

"I would forgive you, yes; for I could not live with
enmity in my heart towards you; but, why do you
speak so?" he said, earnestly, her words giving him
the key to her heart, as he came over beside her, and
with an arm around her, drew her head to his chest.
"Don't resist me; you know I love you, and you will
be my ain bonnie wife." He felt her tremble, though
she yielded to him. "Better lo'ed ye canna be," and
stooping, he kissed her on the lips: "those lips, a
thread of scarlet," and he looked at her tenderly.

At this her color deepened, and, with a sigh, she
said, her voice trembling with emotion: "Release me,
dear, it can never be; I am promised to another. Go
now, and leave me to my fate," she said, tearfully.

"Never! You *shall* be my wife, and that before the
next moon wanes. Whoever this man is, he has not won
your heart. Yes, *my* heart twin, *my* own companion

every day for our journey through life, my Elaine, not
his;" and, again and again, for a few blissful moments
that she is strained to his heart, do his kisses come to
her lips. "Look up, dear wife, and tell me by one look
that I am in your heart. Yes, love, your eyes tell me
that our lives will be again worth living, again complete. No, I will not let you go; and I just want to
see this man who thinks he will rob me of you."

At this juncture the hall-bell rings, just as the clock
was striking seven, the hour Mrs. Gower had ordered
dinner; and, as quick as her hastened heart-beats
would allow, donning society's mask, she is playing
Chopin's music, while Mr. Blair is intent on "The
Miniature Golden Floral Series;" when Mr. Cobbe
enters, evidently by his manner having done more than
"look upon the wine when it is red."

"Well, Elaine, don't scold me, I could not come back
any sooner," he said, with a jovial air; "but, hang it,
I never see you alone these days."

"Can it be possible, she has promised herself to this
swaggering fool!" thought Blair.

"What's the matter, Elaine?" he continued, leaning
on the piano, and looking into her face, "you have a
tragedy face."

"Sometimes I seem to be taking part in one," she
said, gravely; hoping he would remember the woman.

"Oh, I see; you have been playing 'Faust;' if you
want something devilish, try French opera; German
is horns and hoof, and no fun."

Seeing his mood, she abandoned all hope of fixing
his attention on any quieting thought, glancing at Mr.
Blair for sympathy; one look told her his opinion of
her friend. "How he must despise me," she thought,
introducing them. "And now, you must both dine
with a lone woman."

"It will give me great pleasure to begin the year
so," said Mr. Blair, with the determined air of a man

who could and would hold his ground, as he put her hand through his arm, whispering, "Courage!"

"You look very much like a lone woman, I must say," said Cobbe, sulkily. "I told you before, Elaine, that I don't think it's right of you," he said, recklessly.

As they crossed the hall to dine, the geraniums dropped from her gown.

"Oh, my poor flowers," Mr. Blair picking them up. Mr. Cobbe said, jealously, "Poor flowers, indeed; I should just like to know who gave them you."

Fearing he would think it had been Mr. Blair, and not feeling equal to a scene, she said, hurriedly:

"A friend who has left town; but you are too sensible to allow such a trifle to spoil your dinner."

From the moment of their passing through the *portière* hangings into the hall, Blair had seen the face of a woman peering through the vestibule door, Thomas having neglected fastening the outer door on letting in Mr. Cobbe. On entering the dining-room, Mrs. Gower, in looking over her shoulder in making the above remark, saw the face. Not so Cobbe, who was wholly absorbed in rage at the present state of affairs.

Mr. Blair felt his companion tremble as she said to herself, "That woman!" At that, pressing her closely to his side, he again whispered, "Courage!"

"Thomas, go quickly to the vestibule door."

"Yes, ma'am."

"Why, what's the matter now, Elaine; do you expect another gentleman?"

"Go and see." "No, no; if he comes I'll see him soon enough, and the soup smells too tempting."

Thomas returned and waited, when Mrs. Gower said, nervously, "Are both doors securely fastened, Thomas?"

"They are, ma'am."

"Queer time for a visitor to call, just at dinner hour," said Cobbe, in aggrieved tones.

This was more than Thomas could stand, who had

more than once confided to the kitchen his opinion of
Mr. Cobbe for doing likewise, so he said, respectfully:

"Beg pardon, sir; but it was *that* lady for you, sir."

"Hang it! you told her I wasn't here, I hope."

"No, sir; I said you was at dinner, and I couldn't
disturb you, sir; so she said she would wait outside."

"It's very cold for her," faltered Mrs. Gower.

Here the merry sleigh-bells jingled and stopped at
the gate; voices are nearing; and now the hall-bell
again rings, when Mr. and Mrs. Dale are heard in the
hall stamping the snow off their boots, and divesting
themselves of their wraps.

"Thomas, get plates, etc."

They enter looking as if Jack Frost has given them
a chilly embrace, for they have had a cold drive from
town.

"Welcome! this is a glad surprise, though I half
expected you yesterday. Mrs. Dale, allow me to introduce Mr. Blair; Mr. Dale, Mr. Blair; and now be
seated; I am so glad to have you back again, Ella; I
have missed you much."

"Thank you, Elaine; we both wished you were with
us; Henry's English friends, the Elliotts, are delightful, and were charmed with your description of river
life on the St. Lawrence."

"They will think I have scarcely done it justice, on
their revelling in it themselves."

"We have Ella Wheeler Wilcox and Rose Elizabeth
Cleveland, at New York, this winter, Mrs. Gower,"
said Dale, in gratified tones.

"What a treat it would be to meet them; they will
give new life to the women's literary circles."

"Oh, where is Miss Crew?" asked Mrs. Dale.

"Out spending the day at the O'Sullivans."

"I am glad of that," said Dale, kindly. "Miss
O'Sullivan has the brightness our little friend lacks,

and will, perhaps, win her confidence, which we have been unable to do."

"That is very true," said Mrs. Gower, who now related the incident of the morning, regarding the couple they had met while out sleigh-driving; at which Mrs. Dale was all eyes and ears, her pretty little face aglow with excitement.

"How strange! and she persisted in seeing them alone! did she seem glad?"

"Oh, yes; for such a quiet, self-contained little creature, very much so."

"And did she tell you nothing on her return?"

"No; she had no opportunity; we had callers, and Miss O'Sullivan was here; but she looked happier, poor, lonely, wee lassie."

"She is likely to remain lonely, too," said Cobbe; "a man does not want to marry a girl as stiff as his beaver, and as prim as its band."

"Poor girl; one cannot expect her to show that careless joy in living our girls show, who have happy homes and ties of kin."

"In my opinion," said Dale, "the women and girls who take life easiest, and seem to feel that the good things of life are their heritage, are the American women."

"I don't go with you, Dale," said Mr. Cobbe; "I'll back up some of our own women against them for monopoly of that sort."

"I am at one with you, Mr. Dale," said Mrs. Gower, "for this reason : from the time an American woman can lisp, she is taught the cardinal ideas of the country, viz., liberty and equality."

"From your standpoint, Mrs. Gower, your sex should be all Republicans," said Mr. Dale. "What countryman are you, Mr. Blair?"

"A pure and unadulterated Scotchman ; and I hope you like the land o' bagpipes, heather and oatcakes sufficiently as to like me none the less."

"No; for was I not English, I would be Scotch."

"And I," said Mrs. Dale, " would have liked you better were you Irish-American."

"You are candid, at all events," he said, smiling.

".You had better live as near perfection as possible, by remaining in Canada, Mr. Blair," said his hostess, rising from the table. "Come, Ella, we shall leave them to their cigarettes and the subjects nearest their hearts."

"You are one of the most thoughtful women I have ever met," said Dale, drawing the hangings for their exit; " but our smoke will be but a passing cloud; we shall soon sun ourselves in your presence."

"Listen to him," said his wife, merrily; "don't I bring him up well."

As the two friends sipped their coffee from dainty Japanese china, the red silk gown of Mrs. Dale contrasting prettily with the brown and old gold in the dress of her friend, they made a sweet, home-like picture, in this tasteful little drawing-room, with its gaily painted walls, hangings in artistic blending, its softly padded furniture, not extravagant—for Mrs. Gower's income is but $600 per annum—now that house and furniture are paid for, but Roger's bill was very reasonable, for all is in good taste; and with two or three good pictures, a handsome bronze or two, with a few bits of choice bric-a-brac, all the latter gifts from friends; with the glowing grate, the colored lights, the holly and mistletoe, all make an attractive scene.

"And now about yourself, Elaine; I hoped on my return to have found your mercurial friend out in the cold."

"No, Ella; I can do nothing with him," she said, gravely.

"Can't he get it into his head that no woman would marry a man with another woman dangling after him. I have no patience with him. Does she haunt your place still?"

"Yes; she is certainly most constant. Did I tell you of a fright she gave me at two public meetings?"

"No; you wrote me that you must do so on my return."

"Just fancy coming from the Rodgers' mass meeting, before the mayoralty election. I went with Philip, and she must have followed us, for she managed to get near us, and in the crush making our exit, took hold of his arm, and *would not let him see me home;* picture me in that crowd, having to fight my way through, and alone! I think I shall never forget that night; fortunately the cars were running; so taking the Carlton, College and Spadina Avenue car, I managed to reach home. Ella, it was awful, the lonely home-coming," she said tearfully; "the cowardly (I suppose it was) fear of meeting acquaintances; but the feeling that I was engaged, nay, under oath to marry a man who could allow this, was worse than had I met dozens of acquaintances; the late hour; then after I had left the Spadina Avenue terminus, the lonely walk up here—all together made me so nervous I was not myself for a day or two."

"I should say you would be; it was dreadful; and as you say, dear, the feeling that you were engaged to such," she said, contemptuously, "added bitterness to the act; oath or no oath, he must release you."

"He won't."

"He *shall;* and I am determined to stay with you until I can interview that woman. What a horrid man he is, any way."

Here the gentlemen entered, and a truce to confidentials.

"Has my little wife told you, Mrs. Gower, that I have tickets for 'Faust,' and we hope you will care to accompany us?"

"No; she had not told me, though we were speaking tragedy."

" Well, yours was the .prologue; now for ' Faust;'
you will come ?"

" Yes, with pleasure," she said, feeling that her
tête-à-tête with Mr. Blair is over, for Mr. Cobbe would
remain; feeling also that such *tête-à-tête* was too full
of quiet content for her to indulge in, engaged as she
is to another.

Mr. Blair .very reluctantly rises to depart, seeing
that the evening he has promised himself, in dual
solitude with the woman he determines shall be his
wife, is broken in upon.

"Good-night, Mrs. Gower; the walk to town will
seem doubly cold by contrast with the warmth of your
hospitalities," he said, holding her hand, a look of
regret in his blue eyes.

"Button up well, then, to ensure my being remembered for so long," she said, quietly.

" Good-night, Elaine; expect me to-morrow, at five
p.m.," said Mr. Cobbe, with an important air.

Outside, to Mr. Blair, he said, " Fine woman, Mrs.
Gower; I am in luck, but she has too much freedom,"
he said, pointedly.

"How do you mean ?" asked Blair, by an effort
controlling himself to speak quietly.

"Oh, too many gentlemen coming and going; I
must arrange for our marriage at once."

" You are honored by a promise from her to marry
you, then ?"

"Yes; but by more than a promise; by an oath,"
he said, flightily; "and she is not the only woman
who is infatuated with me," he added, chuckling at
his companion's discomfiture

"You are fortunate," said the canny Scotchman,
hating him for his words; but aware that there is
some mystery in the case, knowing Mrs. Gower to
shrink from fulfilling her engagement; having recognized the face of the woman at the vestibule as the

woman he has seen prowling about Holmnest at night-
fall, he affects a friendly air to draw his companion out,
trusting that his intense vanity will lead him to com-
mit himself insomuch as to give him a hold upon him,
which he will use as a means of freeing Mrs. Gower.

Hearing steps behind them, he looks, and lo ! the
light of the street lamp shows the face of the woman
of the vestibule

"By George, you are a lucky fellow ; here is this
poor little woman at your heels ; you are too gallant
to allow her to walk alone ; step back and introduce
me," he said, with the vague hope that he might in
this way find the hold she has on Cobbe ; but *l'homme
propose, Dieu dispose,* for he said importantly :

"So she is ; between you and I, the more faithless
I am, the tighter she hugs ;" and, turning on his heel,
the woman with him, they go at a run down Major
Street, leaving Blair, in blank dismay, standing in the
cold of the snow-mantled night.

After seeing talented Modjeska at the Grand, in
"Faust," Mrs. Gower, having wished her friends a
warm good-night, as she sleeps, dreams of a manly,
handsome face bending over her, while the light in his
eyes give point to his words of "Better lo'ed ye canna
be."

CHAPTER XXIII.

THE THREE LINKS.

N a cold afternoon, in January's third week,
when fair Toronto's children wore the colors
of Old Boreas ; when the spirits of the air
floated on the frozen breaths of humanity,
and when imagination held that the giant
cyclone of the North-west had hurled into our midst a
bit of the North Pole, on such a day Holmnest is a

snug spot; not one of those mansions with a small coal account that some of our moneyed citizens exist in in cold grandeur during winter's reign; but small, warm and homelike. So thought Mrs. Dale, who is again spending a few days with her friend, and who is now seated with Mr. Blair beside the glowing grate in the drawing-room; he cannot keep away, and having confided his hopes and fears to her, they have become warm friends.

Mrs. Gower and Miss Crew are down town shopping, the latter having abandoned her intention to seek employment other than her voluntary deeds of good as a city missioner, she having received a bill of exchange from the mother country on the Bank of British North America; whether from this cause or from the fact of her constant visits to the quietly happy-looking couple she had met on New Year's Day, her friends can only guess; but she is certainly looking happier, though still reticent as to her private history, merely telling Mrs. Gower, to whom she has become much attached, that before long she will ask their advice, and tell them all.

Mr. Cobbe has just called, but had not gone in, ascertaining from Thomas that his mistress was not at home, but that Mrs. Dale and Mr. Blair were in the drawing-room—he volunteering the latter information, instinct telling him it would not be agreeable; for the kitchen did not approve of him as the coming master at Holmnest, saying. one to the other, "Pretty fly he is, to think of dividing up of the likes of he between our missis and that bold hussy as follows him."

At this moment, in the drawing-room, Mrs. Dale, as she alternately pats Tyr's head, or, with deft fingers, embroiders a cushion, says, with a curl on her scarlet lips, her Irish eyes flashing:

"I am glad Elaine was out. You see, he knew enough not to come in and be entertained by us."

"Yes, he knows enough for that," he said, mechanically, waking from a reverie. "I wish to heaven we could interview the woman. I am convinced we would elicit information sufficient to absolve our dear friend from her oath. I am driven to my wit's end, I am in such misery. I can assure you, Mrs. Dale, this matter has taken such hold of me that I neither eat, drink, sleep, nor even think naturally."

And the ring of truth is in his words, as he starts up, and paces up and down the room like a caged lion, eager for action, yet compelled to inactivity. Papers and magazines strew the carpet where he had been seated, on which he had in vain tried to fix his thought. Now he again flings himself into his chair, she sees his brows knit, his eyes small with the intentness of inward musing; his manly, independent bearing is crushed, his firm, determined mouth is still set with a fixed purpose, but his face has lost its glow of happiness.

He haunts Holmnest some hours of each day, his eyes following her every movement as she goes about her home duties, or sits quietly reading, or holding book or newspaper, under pretence of doing so, giving herself a few moments' silent thought, ever and anon lifting her eyes to his face, as quickly to withdraw them, lest sympathy lead her to betray a grief akin to his. One day he asked her how it was she had come in the first place to allow Mr. Cobbe the privilege of friendly intercourse, when she told him all. Of the deaths of loved ones, of her long and tedious law suits, of her losses through the wrong-doings of others, of the flight of summer friends, of her difficulty in earning a sufficiency to eke out her small income, and of Philip Cobbe being introduced; when his jovial, free-from-care nature diverting her attention from her many cares, she and he gradually drifted into a very friendly acquaintance, which resulted in their walk through the Queen's Park. Of her oath she had already told him on the 3rd of January, on his relating to her the boastful words of Mr. Cobbe on the evening previous. At which he had been driven nearly desperate, as also on her resolve that, in honor bound, she must be true to her oath.

She had never allowed him to kiss her since those few blissful moments that lived in the memory of each, in which he had asked her to become his wife on Monday, the 2nd of January, and when he had read her heart.

"It's a miserable fix for Elaine," said Mrs. Dale, picking out a few false stitches she had made in giving her attention to him as he paced the floor in his agony of mind. "She cares for you, but will remain true to her oath; she will go on in this wretched way, Mr. Cobbe coming and going, boasting of his engagement, to keep rivals at bay, and that woman haunting the place until a tragedy ends the whole farce. Elaine will postpone and postpone her union with that man until she dies broken-hearted, poor thing. She has had no end of trouble in the past, and now this must all crop up. Nasty Cobbe; I *hate* you," she said, emphatically.

"So do I," he said, moodily; "but what availeth it? We, with our strong natures, are as wax in the hands of this vain, foolish, empty-headed fellow; he has the whip-hand of us. I never felt small, impotent, powerless in my life until now. You don't know what mad thoughts come to me sometimes, when I see her going about in her sweet womanliness with a pretence of gaiety lest I feel for her, making this truly home, sweet home; now going to her kitchen, now sewing quietly; again singing, though in unsteady tones, the songs of my own land."

"Perhaps it would be better for you; easier, I mean, if you kept away from her."

"Kept away! that's what she tells me. No; come I must. I am not fit to attend to business, to face the busy hive of men down town. I have not as yet rented an office, or put out my shingle as broker and estate agent, so the world which knows me not does not miss me. Did I not come, I should be tortured by the thought that Cobbe had persuaded her to marry him, and that with the false hope of making me forget her, and the woman to give up her game' as lost, she would consent. No; I shall come in the seemingly aimless way; but not aimless, for I am her bodyguard. Already my being here, and holding my ground, has more than once prevented a *tête-à-tête*, and saved her from (I make no doubt) his hateful caresses. He hates me, and would revenge himself upon me if he could; and, insomuch as he can, he does do so—by using her Christian name, leaning familiarly over her shoulder as she reads or sews, following her even to the kitchen. Once he dared to kiss her good-bye, but I don't think he will try that again; for, on his looking at me maliciously, to note my jealousy, I gave him one look, at which he made a hasty exit."

"So far so good, Mr. Blair; but you and myself are really doing nothing to free Elaine. We *must* get a hold of the woman; she is not very well clad; is, I dare say, poor; I shall try if the dollar will grease the wheels of her tongue. Now, how shall we manage it? This evening I shall express a wish to telegraph Henry. You must offer to accompany me; this will allow of time to work on Mr. Cobbe's Mary Ann. We shall walk up and down on the other side of the street (thus putting ourselves in Grundy's mouth) until she appears, when, pouncing upon her, we will *make* her tell her relations to Cobbe. You understand?"

"Yes, but he will be here alone with Elaine."

"Just like a man: as jealous as a rooster in a barn-yard. Miss Crew will be here, and chance callers."

"Very well; it shall be as you say, though I mortally hate not being present when he is here; but here she comes, her cheeks like roses, and eyes bright from the frosty air," he said, brightening.

"Oh, you pair of fire-worshippers!" she exclaimed, giving her hand to Mr. Blair. "I have had a glorious walk from Yonge, through Bloor west, and up here. We took the Yonge up-cars, when Miss O'Sullivan, who was one of us, carried off Miss Crew till to-morrow."

"I suppose King Street wore its usual afternoon dress of dudes and sealskin sacques," he said, drawing her wrap from her shoulders.

"I suppose so; but we only went as far as Roche's. What a world of a place it is. Mrs. Francis says, 'One can buy everything but butcher's meat there,' and she is about right. The up-cars were, as usual, over-crowded; we were to blame for taking one, I suppose, as so many poor fatigued-looking men were obliged to stand. However, we were sorry for them in a practical way, for we only occupied one seat by turns; the company should run extra cars about six, or label them, 'For men only.'"

"On the other side," said Mrs. Dale, "men say it's a poor rule that won't work both ways, so, as we advocate equal rights, they, as a rule, don't yield their seats."

"Is that so?" said Blair. "I wonder at that, for Mrs. Gower tells me there is a shrine to woman in every house."

"Oh, never mind her, she is our champion, fights and wins our battles. I used to hope she would marry among us, and strut under our big bird; but alas, she sees more beauty in a common Scotch thistle," she says, teasingly.

Blair smiled, gravely, saying with his eyes on Mrs. Gower, in her pretty, dark blue gown, with broken plaid over-skirt,

"I fear not; to the shamrock she plights her troth."

At this the color rushes to the roots of her hair, to as quickly recede, leaving her like marble, and, gathering up her wraps, saying, in unsteady tones,

"Excuse me a moment, I must see what the kitchen is about: it is near dinner time."

Blair, drawing the hangings, said, wistfully following her into the hall:

"Forgive me, dear."

"I must, when you look so sorry; but, that compulsory oath is killing me, Alec; driving me into heart disease," she said, tremblingly.

"My darling! is it possible? but I can see it. Your heart is fairly jumping, your hands cold, your nails blue; come in here for a few minutes' quiet," he said, sorrowfully, leading her into the library, taking her wraps from her, seating himself quietly beside her, simply taking her hands, while whispering soothing words. His own heart breaking the while, that he may not take her in his arms; but with her breath coming in gasps, the excitement would have killed her, even did she permit any demonstration of feeling from him, which indeed, she had unconditionally forbidden.

On the dinner-bell ringing, she said, in low tones:

"You are nice, and good, and kind to have talked to me so quietly until I recovered the use of my tongue. You see, dear, I can give it a rest sometimes; now come for Ella, to our dish of roast beef and Yorkshire pudding. Don't look so grave, Alec; 'Richard is himself again.' I wish you would go away for a time, leave the city; as you have not commenced business actively, really got into harness, you could easily do so; it would be easier for me, I think, if I did not see you," she said, almost breaking down.

"I cannot," he said, looking into her face gravely; and it would not help you; all I can manage, is to keep to the conditions you made: that in coming I must not speak of my love for you; and you must own, dear, that I fulfil those conditions; holding myself continually in check, curbing my feelings, never outwardly letting loose the reins of passion, even when I see that man hanging about you."

"Yes, you are very good; but still, I—oh, I don't know what to say or do," she said, in anguish, covering her face with her hands; then, by a violent effort controlling herself, took her place at table.

During dinner, she was pale and flushed, talkative and silent, by turns; her companion keeping the ball moving to give her a rest.

On their returning to the drawing-room, Mrs. Dale gave them some music, thus giving each time for quiet thought. The sweet sounds suddenly ceasing, she wheels round on the piano-stool, saying, energetically,

"I feel restless this evening, active exercise will cure me; a brisk walk down street, or even the toboggan-slide."

But Mr. Blair does not take her up, and sits with averted eyes, not thinking Mrs. Gower well enough to be left with Mr. Cobbe.

"Well, Ella, Mr. Blair is too gallant not to accompany you. You will both go; when I tell you that I wish to see Philip *alone*, I am going to again appeal to him."

"I am afraid it will be too much for you, Elaine, perhaps," she said, hesitatingly, for she does not like to give up her plan; "perhaps Mr. Blair ought to stay, he need not be in the very same room with you."

"Yes, that is a good idea; I shall go to the library," he said, in relieved tones.

"No, dears, you will both do as I wish. With the knowledge that I am alone, I shall doubly nerve myself to the task."

For she dreads that Mr. Cobbe's excitable temper will give way, causing a scene.

13

"Well, if you are going to talk to him, Elaine, tell him everything; and that Mr. Blair and I say he is breaking your heart."

"I fear. Ella, your united opinions would have little weight with him," she said, with the ghost of a smile; "but I shall tell him *all*, never fear," she said, earnestly feeling that Mr. Blair was, as usual, following her every word. "Never fear, I shall be a good pleader, for I have my life's happiness at stake; away with you at once, and don't come back with broken bones from the slide."

CHAPTER XXIV.

A HAND OF ICE LAY ON HER HEART.

T is a cold, frosty night, the moon and clouds seeming to have a game of hide-and-go-seek across the sky, when Mrs. Dale is already enveloped in her warm dark blue blanket suit and Tam-o-Shanter, with Mr. Blair, in heavy brown overcoat and Christy hat, not having been in our land long enough for his blood to have lost its warmth and to feel the need of furs.

Before they start Mr. Cobbe rings the bell, and is admitted to the library, Mr. Blair turning out the gas in the drawing-room, and Thomas receiving orders that "no one is at home."

"Suppose she should not come this evening," said Mrs. Dale, as she and her companion returned from a brisk walk to a post box, and reared Holmnest. "You know, she misses his trail; at all events, does not watch for him here every evening."

"Hush! she is in the shade of that pile of lumber and bricks in front of the house that is being built next to Holmnest," he whispered, hurriedly.

"So she is; that is lucky; and now to follow our plan. We shall not see her for some minutes, but endeavor to interest her by our talk about that scallawag and poor Elaine."

"I don't think, on second thought, that that would be our best plan; we had better go up to her and demand to know her relations to him," he said, quickly, in an undertone.

"No, no; I know best."

As they neared, the tall, slight figure, clad in a brown ulster and small round hat, disappeared to the other side of the lumber, almost out of sight, but well within earshot.

"Stand here a minute, Mr. Blair; before we go in I want to tell you what I fear will be the result of Mr. Cobbe's determination to marry Mrs. Gower against her will," she said, in clear tones. On this they could hear that the woman took a step nearer in the deep snow on the boulevard, that had drifted in the recent storm to the lumber. "You must see yourself," she continued, "that the compulsory oath he compelled her to take is killing her; and none know better than you do yourself that her love is not his; almost all friendly feeling even she had for him prior to that oath, has fled; yet still he will keep her to it; and she will marry him some day, in a fit of desperation to get rid of him, and to show you that you are free to marry some more fortunate woman. It's my belief he is a mere fortune-hunter, and cares no more for her than we Americans care for you, in annexation; we only care for the loaves and fishes (especially the latter). I simply hate to go in to the house; it makes me double my fists to see him making love to her." The last words she said to rouse the woman's wrath; she knows her sex well, for, ploughing through the snow a few steps, she faces them.

"Mrs. Dale gives a little scream.   Mr. Blair, turning quickly, says, in decided tones,

"Oh! you are here again; well, I am not sorry, for I had determined to put a detective on your track to-morrow, and am glad to have an opportunity of warning you first."

"Any woman would do no more nor I do, just standing here when I please," she said, doggedly, her teeth chattering, partly from nervousness, partly from cold.

"Poor thing; you are half frozen," said Mrs. Dale, to show she was not unfriendly.

"We shall not detain you long, young woman," said Mr. Blair, quickly, as he thinks of the woman he loves worried by the man he hates; "all we want to know is your name and address, and what hold you have on Mr. Cobbe; for a woman of your respectable appearance would not follow a man about unless she had some hold on him—some real right to watch his movements.   You have overheard this lady and myself talking over this matter, and I can assure you it would add materially to our peace of mind could we compel Mr. Cobbe to do right by you; come now, no delay, no beating about the bush; tell the truth and shame the devil; out with it."

"Gentlemen lie quicker than a working girl, like myself," she said, suspiciously.   "I have heard what this lady said, but how do I know that it's all square? Phil. said if you caught me hanging around after him, you'd get me took up, and here is a peeler coming; I see what you're after."

And she tries to run, but Mr. Blair holds her firmly until the policeman passes.

"I tell you I mean you no harm; but you *must* tell your connection with Mr. Cobbe, *and at once.*"

"Give me till to-morrow night, sir, for the love of heaven, and I will try again if Phil. will give your lady up, that I have wished to kill for coming between

us; aye, and would have fired Holmnest on her some
night, but for this lady's words that she don't want
my man. My name is Beatrice Hill, and I live at 910,
Seaton Street; I will tell you the rest to-morrow
night, if he will not give her up," she said, bursting
into tears.

Mr. Blair made a note of the address, Mrs. Dale
saying kindly, "You had better come around to the
kitchen and get thawed; you are——" when, turning
suddenly to Mr. Blair, who has his back to a couple
coming down the street, she says, quickly,

"Here are the Smyths; stand where you are; and
you too, Beatrice Hill."

"Hello!" cried Smyth, coming upon them suddenly
(that is Toronto's pass-word). "How do you do, Mrs.
Dale; how do, Blair?"

"How happy would I be with either," said his lively
wife, aside to Mr. Blair; oh, I beg pardon," she continued, seeing the other is not one of them. "How is
Mrs. Gower?"

"She is not very well this evening, and is, I hope,
resting. How is it your little son is out when he
ought to be under the bedclothes? That's one thing I
am glad my boy is at boarding-school for.

"Oh, this young man has been to a party at the
Halls, and we had to trot up for him. Give Elaine my
love, and tell her one look at handsome Doctor Mills,
on our street, will cure her; he cured my baby. So,
come around to-morrow, all of you. Oh, Will, we had
better go in to Holmnest for a minute. I want to tell
Elaine you have heard from Charlie."

"Oh, no; go in to-morrow. This little chap is nearly
asleep."

"All right. Mrs. Dale, please tell Mrs. Gower that
Charlie Cole is at New York, and she may expect to
see them any day. Good night."

"Good night."

" Come, Mrs. Dale, we had better go in at once ; you must be very cold."

" Yes, I am. You had better come round and get thawed out in the kitchen, Beatrice Hill, I will bring you."

" No, thanks ; I am used to it. I'll just walk up and down, to keep from freezing."

" Perhaps you had better not try to see him to-night, it is so cold."

" Not try to see him !" she exclaimed. " I see him too seldom, and love him too much for that," she said, pathetically, " and I must see if he will promise me to come no more where neither of us is wanted."

" Remember ! you are to be here to-morrow night to tell us your hold on him, unless he gives Mrs. Gower up," he said, firmly.

" I will, sir ; thank you both," she said tearfully, as, turning towards the gate of Holmnest, they each slip a five dollar bill into her hand.

" Poor thing, I think she is hard up," said Mrs. Dale, as they ring the bell ; " see her examining the bills by the lamp."

" Yes, so she is, to see if they are 'Central'; had she not been sold by my *béte noir*, I should say she was a canny Scotchwoman."

" On Thomas opening the door, they see Mr. Cobbe draw close the *portière* hangings of the library, as if to say, no admittance.

" Have you a match, Thomas ?"

" Yes, ma'am."

" Then light one jet in the drawing-room, please."

Here they sit quietly talking for half an hour, during which, at times, Mr. Cobbe talked loud and excitedly, while sometimes Mrs. Gower's voice came to them in pleading, or quieting tones.

At last he goes into the dining-room, asks Thomas for some sherry, drinks two glasses; is again in the

hall, his over-shoes, coat, and fur cap on, in his excitement picking up Mr. Blair's gloves, which, when in the
street, finding his mistake, he dashes into the road.

Angry and troubled by Mrs. Gower's words, he is
kinder to Beatrice Hill than he has been for some time.

" You here again, Betty. *You* are infatuated with
me, anyway."

"Indeed, I am, sweetheart, but my love doesn't
content you. You bet, I'd sooner have a black look
from you than a kiss from any man living. The
saints forgive me, when I think of the holy Father
and cardinals, and how I worship you, Phil."

" Yes, you are wild about me, I know, Betty, but we
men are different to you, you know; we have so
many adorers, we can't go mooning forever around
one woman."

"And you are not angry with me to-night, Phil, for
coming again to get a sight of your dear face ?"

" No, I am not angry with you to-night ; but you
must not come again ; they don't like it," he said,
importantly.

"If I don't see you, I may as well die," she says
despondently. " I love you better than any of them
ladies do," she says, feeling her way.

"Hang her, she is as fickle as her clime," he says,
half aloud, thinking of Mrs. Gower.

His companion made no response, knowing who he
meant, but her heart is lighter at his words.

" Hang it, Bet, it's a freezer ; if you have any
money about you, I'll hail this sleigh if it's empty."

" Yes, sweetheart, here it is," giving him one of the
fives.

In a minute they are under the buffalo robe, when,
according to promise, she coaxes, entreats, and implores
him to give Mrs. Gower up, but he angrily refuses
to listen to anything on the subject ; entertaining
her, instead, with recitals of all the girls on King

street who, he is sure, are dying for an introduction
to him, and of several women of his acquaintance
being infatuated about him, his companion assenting
to all he said; getting out at his own quarters,
paying the driver to 910 Seaton street, pocketing the
change. Beatrice Hill alone, thinks out her plan for
the following evening with tears, which she brushes
away with bare hands, having given her mits to her
fickle swain to keep his hands from the frost.

"Yes, I must tell them all," she thought, weeping
silently, "else Phil will make her marry him. Father
Nolan would tell me to do so, to save him from
guilt. He will turn to his faithful Betty again when
he sees how they sit on him, when they know all."

As the hall door had closed on Mr. Cobbe making his exit, Mr. Blair said, turning out the gas:

"Let us go to her."

Mrs. Gower meets them in the hall, looking pale
and agitated, her eyes larger and darker in her pale
face, her sensitive mouth quivering.

"I was just coming for you," she said, and on her
eyes meeting Mr. Blair's, in answer to his loving, steadfast gaze, her's told him that her appeal has been in
vain.

"He would not free you?" he said, compassionately.

"No."

"Well, then, he must be compelled to," said Mrs.
Dale, energetically; "we are not going to stand by
with folded hands, and see the remainder of your life
made wretched by a weak, vain, frivolous thing like
that. You have had trouble enough in the past,
heaven knows."

"Yes, we must act; we must endeavor to interview the woman," he said sympathetically, preparing
her for what might occur.

"I fear your kind efforts in my behalf will prove
useless, Alec. You would only ascertain that she is

some poor creature whose heart he has gained, but who is not bound to him in any way. She is faithful, where he is false," she says, gravely, "and is breaking her heart for him—a way we have—that is all. No, 'Blessed are they who expect nothing,' I must keep well in my mind for the future. I scarcely deserve this from Fate, for I have been pretty brave hitherto through troubles, that at the time were sufficient to crush all hope, leaving not the faintest gleam; but I struggled through the clouds in my sky, which, finally parting, I saw the sunbeams once more. My plan now is, to close up this my home, sweet home, or ask you, Ella, or Mr. Cole, to take it off my hands for a year. It would please me best to know some one I care for was among my little treasured belongings."

"Mr. Cole, Charlie's father is at the Tremont Hotel, Jacksonville, Florida. My place is to ask Miss Crew (as you don't require her services, and her mind is easier as to money matters), to accompany me for the remainder of the winter to same place as my friend Charlie's father; he is a most worthy man and a gentleman. At the close of winter we would cross to the British Isles. To myself, a Canadian, it would be a complete distraction, as I have never been across; and I pray fervently, will take me out of self," she said sadly. "We would visit London and some pretty rural spots, the Devonshire lanes, perhaps; and then the Emerald Isle, thence to bonnie Scotia's shores; taking, perhaps, more than a peep at fair Dunkeld," she says, trying to smile in the grave face of Mr. Blair. "I have foreseen the result of my appeal to Philip, and so have been laying my plans for some days."

As she spoke, trying vainly to hide her emotion, more than one tear had been stealthily brushed away by her sympathetic little friend, who, seeing that Mr. Blair is suffering intensely, from suppressed feeling, says bravely, though rather doubtful at heart:

"Mark my words, Elaine, that woman will free you; say good night to us, Mr. Blair, I am medical attendant *pro tem.*, and Elaine must take a sedative, and room with me to-night."

"You are right, Mrs. Dale; be brave, Elaine, he says, holding her hand in his firm grasp, "to-morrow your clouds must again pass, I shall come in after luncheon.

CHAPTER XXV.

"HERE AWA', THERE AWA'."

THE following is an ideal Canadian winter day; the sky, a far-off canopy of brightest blue, with no clouds to obscure the sunbeams, which pour down on fair Toronto, melting the icicles when his smiles are warmest, and gladdening the hearts of the million. There is just enough of frost in the air to make a walk to town pleasant, cheering and exhilarating, so that Mrs. Dale is glad when Mrs. Gower proposes their going. The whole city seems to have turned out, and the streets are alive with the busy hum of life, and the tinkling music of the merry sleigh-bells

Mrs. Gower, who had slept little, arose with the determination to appear reconciled to her fate, not wishing to add to the sorrow of Mr. Blair and Mrs. Dale, on her account; feeling that there will be time enough to give way, when "large lengths of miles" divide them. She cannot bear to dwell upon the separation, she has decided, is for the best, and dreads to think of her heart loneliness, with Mr. Blair gone out of her life, and the sympathy of Mrs. Dale, not beside her. How she will miss her quiet talks with him, his manly advice and interest in all her acts, the

oneness of their views on many questions of the day—
religious, social, and in part political.   The Tremaines
and Smyths also; with her many favorite walks and
resorts, the public library, and other places of interest.
Yes, to leave them all and her snug Holmnest, is hard;
but to go on in the way events have shaped themselves—Mr. Cobbe, a privileged visitor, as her future
husband; the woman haunting her home; her misery,
seeing daily the grief telling on Mr. Blair would be
harder still; so, nerving herself for the parting, she
determines on making her preparations at once.

No one meeting the friends, as they walk into town,
would imagine that the dusky shadow of sorrow sits
in each heart; the pretty little face of Mrs. Dale
being set off by a bonnet, with pink feathers, her
seal coat and muff making her warm and comfortable.
Mrs. Gower, in a heavy dark blue gown, short dolman
boa and muff of the bear; a pretty little bonnet
blending with her gown, the glow of heat from exercise lending color to her cheeks.   Down busy Yonge
street to Eaton's; Trowern's, with Mrs. Dale's watch;
thence to gay King Street, to Murray's, Nordheimer's,
the Public Library, back again West, and to Coleman's
for a cup of coffee, are all done; at the latter place
they run across Mrs. St. Clair with Miss Hall.

"Oh, you two dear pets, I am so awfully glad to
have met you," says pretty Mrs. St. Clair, effusively;
"I want to know when you can talk over a programme
with me—tableaux, readings, etc., in aid of the debt on
our church.   Say when?"

"I really cannot, Mrs. St. Clair," said Mrs. Gower;
just at present I am very busy, and am daily expecting a small house party."

"Dear, dear! that is too bad; what shall I do; you
are so smart, and would know just what would take.
You will talk it over with me, Mrs. Dale," she said,
beseechingly.

"No, thank you ; on principle, I object."

"How funny! might I ask why ?"

"Certainly. I think offerings to such an object as a church debt,should be voluntary."

"But, Mrs. Dale, people expect a little treat for their money."

"They have, or we have, the church service, and the ministrations of the clergyman."

"That's just the way Mr. St. Clair damps my ardor," she says, poutingly ; I do so want to pose as Mary Stuart. Mr. Cobbe says I'd look too sweet for anything ; you won't be jealous, Mrs. Gower."

"Oh, fearfully so ; but joking apart ; how do you think he would pose as Bunthorn ?"

"I see you are laughing at him, Mrs. Gower?"

"Not at all ; the twenty forlorn ones would keep him in good humor, and the bee in his crown would be a safety valve for his restlessness."

"No, no ; I would not like that, and I wonder you, above all, would propose it ; for the whole twenty would fall in love with him, he is so fascinating ; don't you think so, Miss Hall ?"

"Yes ; but.it would be good fun ; you cawn't do bettah, Mrs. St. Clair."

"It has my vote, too," said Mrs. Dale, as she and her friend wish them good morning.

"What a well-matched couple Mrs. St. Clair and Philip would have made," says Mrs. Gower, as they go east to Yonge street.

"Yes, I have thought that before to-day, Elaine ; it's a pity to spoil two houses with them."

Here they come across Mrs. Smyth waiting for a Spadina Avenue car.

"Oh, Mrs. Gower, who do you think I have just seen ?"

"Perhaps our mutual friend Charlie Cole," she answered, smiling.

" Well, you are smart, to guess exactly; have you seen them? Isn't she frightfully ugly?" she says, in one breath.

" No, I have not seen them. What a pity she is not pretty. I received a letter from Charlie, saying to expect them."

" Oh, you sly thing; why didn't you let us know? Oh, how ugly she is! May we come round this evening? Here is my car."

" Certainly. We have been to your husband's office to invite you."

" Thanks. O!" she cried, stepping on to the car. " Will gave me a new piano yesterday."

" Whose make?"

" Ruse's, Temple of Music, over there."

"I congratulate you." As they walked on she continued, absently, " What a pity she is plain looking."

" Who; not Mrs. Smyth?"

" Oh, no, Ella; her animation will always make her pretty. I was thinking of Charlie Cole's wife. I wonder where she saw them?"

" Oh, somewhere in town, I suppose. So you expected them to-day."

"Yes, and I would have told you, but I want their advent to be a surprise for Miss Crew, whom I have frequently found secretly studying Charlie Cole's photo. She is so guardedly reticent, that I am curious to see if suddenly confronting him will cause her to show any interest in the original of the photo."

" But you should make sure of her, Elaine. She may remain at the O'Sullivans; and as I own to taking an interest in human bric-a-brac, I hope you will call for her."

" I fancy she will return for certain, as she tells me the couple we met on New Year's Day are coming to Holmnest this afternoon; the woman, quite a lady-like looking person, is to alter her black silk ; but we shall call on our way home for her."

" Yes, that will be best, and here is our car; but it is too crowded. As members of the Humane Society we had better wait for the next."

As they wait in front of the Dominion Bank, Mr. Cobbe joins them.

" Good morning, ladies ; won't you turn west, and have a promenade, Elaine ?"

" No, thank you. Time has gone too fast for us already."

" O, pshaw ! I want to speak to you. When do you return to New York, Mrs. Dale ?" he says pointedly; disliking her, and feeling freer at Holmnest in her absence.

" I have not the remotest idea, Mr. Cobbe, indeed," she added, in return for his ; " we may take dear little Holmnest off Mrs. Gower's hands if she carries out her present intention to leave Canada for a time."

" Leave Canada !" he exclaims, flushing.

" Please, stop the car, Philip, quick."

" What does it mean, Elaine ?" he whispers, seeing them on board; but the bell rings, and off they go. Two yards distant, and he calls out, " I shall be up after office hours."

" Talk of cruelty to animals. I gave him a blow, but he richly deserves it. But I do believe, Elaine, you are sorry for him," she says in amazement, and under cover of the noise of travel.

" I am. He is his worst enemy. Yes, I am sorry for his weak, vain nature. A man without stability of character, in our stirring times, is of no more account than are the soap-bubbles blown by a little child."

Getting out of the car at Webb's, to leave an order, they there meet Miss O'Sullivan, who, with her own bright smile, comes forward quickly to shake hands.

" Oh, Mrs. Gower, I am so glad to see you. I have

something to tell you. Miss Crew left our place for
Holmnest at ten this a. m., and I have her promise to
tell Mr. Dale her history, and ask his advice."

"I am glad of that, dear,"

"Oh, so am I, she is such a darling; but I was not
satisfied to have her without some good gentleman
friend to advise her."

"Has she confided in yourself ?"

"Yes, Mrs. Dale; but not until last night."

"Was it sensational enough to keep you awake, or,
as I suppose, of no more interest than 'little Johnny
Horner sitting in the corner eating his Christmas
pie ?'"

"You see, dear, Mrs. Dale is disgusted with Mother
Goose for not telling us of his bilious attack," laughed
Mrs. Gower. "Good bye, dear, here is our car, College
and Spadina Avenue."

"You will not be disappointed in Miss Crew's story,
Mrs. Dale. The bilious part is not omitted; poor dear,
I am so sorry for her."

On reaching Holmnest they find Mr. Dale, who has
returned from the North-West, and Miss Crew, in the
library.

Mrs. Gower, not pretending to notice that the latter
has been in tears, and to give her an excuse to make
her exit, asks her to carry her wraps upstairs for her;
and then to go and give them some music during the
few minutes before luncheon.

"Mrs. Gower is taking better care of you, little wife,
than you are of her, now that the roses from the frosty
air are fading. I notice she is paler and thinner."

"Don't blame me, Henry," she answered, stroking
his whiskers; "blame Mr. Cobbe. I declare to you
both, I never name him without doubling my fists."

"My impression has always been, dear Mrs. Gower,
that he will be no companion for you in the hand-in-
hand journey through life."

"Yes; but you are not cognizant of certain facts which has led to our being in our present relation towards each other," she says, gravely; "and of which we must tell you, perhaps to-morrow. We have enough on for to-day, and there is the luncheon bell, come."

"Oh, Henry, do you know that the Coles are expected here to-day, and have you told Miss Crew? because, don't," she whispered hurriedly.

"No; I thought it as well not to," he said, in constrained tones, adding, "she has been telling me her sad story, poor girl; which you and Mrs. Gower will know shortly, little woman."

CHAPTER XXVI.

ELECTRIC TIPS AMONG THE ROSES.

DURING luncheon, Mrs. Gower, seeing that her companions seem too full of busy thought to be talkative, exerts herself keeping up a constant flow of little nothings, requiring no replies; her spirits became less depressed by the effort to keep sorrow at bay, her pleasant walk to town has really been a tonic to her. And now the knowledge that the Coles may come in at any moment; that a handsome face, so full of power and sympathy with herself, will be here also; with the meeting by the Smyths and herself of the wife of their old friend Charlie Cole; all this is a powerful stimulant to her, as well as the little surprise and excitement for the quiet, fair-haired girl, with tear-stained cheeks, on her left.

"Would you like a trip down to Florida with me, Miss Crew. Orange groves and outdoor blossoms would be as a glimpse of Paradise, with one's eyes full of snow flakes.

" Yes ; I should like to go anywhere with you, Mrs.
Gower ; that is," she adds, glancing, timidly, at Mr.
Dale, already now he knows her history, turning to
him as a child to a parent ; "that is, if it would be
best for me."

" Do you really contemplate this trip ; if so, and
you do not leave for a few days, I think it would be
the very thing for Miss—, for this little lady," he
says; thinking she is merely running away to escape
the remainder of the winter.

" I do really intend going," she said, slowly, and
with an unconscious sigh.

He looks at her earnestly, thinking there is some
latent reason, when his wife, making a *moue* at him,
accompanied by an almost imperceptible shake of the
head, when, Mrs. Gower, changing the subject, says :
" Did you see how Professor Herkomer has been lauding the Americans, Mr. Dale ? "

" I did ; but I only agree with him in part."

" Not so with me ; I am at one with him, to the
echo ; but I should tell you I have only seen extracts
from his expressed views, in which he says, 'he was
impressed by their keen, nervous temperament, keen
intelligence and ambition to excel ; ' and when he says
America will become a leader of art in the nations as
of nearly everything else."

" I don't go with him that length," he said, shaking
his head ; " give me the Old World for art in the present, as well as in the future."

" In the present, I agree with you, I think ; but
their very ambition to excel, their-go-ahead-ness, to
coin a word, will, I feel convinced, gain them first
place in the future."

" That's right, Elaine ; give it him, he is too conser-
vative, this dear old hubby of mine ; the stars and
stripes float over the smartest people on earth."

At this a general laugh makes them all feel less

14

blue, Mrs. Gower saying, as they leave the dining-room :

"Well, let us see which of us, England, United States or Canada, will be the smartest in taking a few minutes' rest, and getting into a dinner gown," Wending her way to the kitchen, she meets Miss Crew, bringing water and seeds for the birds.

"Thank you, dear; that saves my time; when you have done that, run away up to your room, and put on your pretty heliotrope frock; the Smyths may dine with us."

"Very well, I shall ; and oh, Mrs. Gower, may I tell Thomas when my friends come (you know I told you I am going to have my black silk altered), he is to show them into the dining-room; though, perhaps, they would not be called gentlefolk, still, they are not servants, and they are *so* good."

"The highest recommendation you can give them, dear ; I shall tell Thomas myself."

Closeted in their bedroom, seated side by side, upon a lounge, Mrs. Dale tells her husband of Mrs. Gower's troubles, and the stratagem by which Mr. Cobbe has obtained her oath to marry him; of the woman who haunts Holmnest ; of how for long months Mrs. Gower has been imploring him to release her from her compulsory promise. Also of Mr. Blair's love for Elaine ; and of how he has surprised her into a confessing of her own for him; but of how in no way has she allowed him any demonstration of that love since those few moments on New Year's Day. Of her own and Mr. Blair's plan to induce the woman to speak."

"You astonish me, Ella !" he exclaimed ; but I agree with her ; she cannot break her oath, *she belongs to him;* does she know of your plan to interview the woman ? "

"Yes ; but thinks we shall elicit no item of importance ; but, Henry, dear, say nothing to her of our plan for this evening; I only tell you, so that should you miss Mr. Blair and myself, you will not remark on it."

"I see. How do you like this Mr. Blair; you know, I have only met him once?"

"I like him very much; you should hear that reticent Mr. St. Clair praise him. He is though, really, a manly, generous, straight-forward, determined fellow; just the reverse of Mr. Cobbe."

"Yes; well I hope it will come out all right for poor Mrs. Gower, though I had hoped that she and Buckingham would have made a match," he said musingly.

"So have I; but he has been too deliberate, a trait his German mother is to blame for; and he may have imagined there has been something between her and Mr. Cobbe Now, hubby, I am just dying to know if Miss Crew has confided in you, and if there is anything worth a snap in her story."

"I cannot tell you just yet, dear; and, besides, we have not time; it is three-thirty, time for my little wife to dress."

On descending at four p.m., to her cheerful drawing-room, Mrs. Gower has so far conquered her feelings as to cause a casual observer to say, she is quite happy, and at ease; for her dark red gown is becoming, and she has compelled her mind to dwell only on the pleasurable excitement of a re-union with her old friend, Mr. Cole; wondering also what he will think of her new friend, Mr. Blair. The air, redolent of hyacinths and roses, tells her he is in the drawing-room; and the color deepens in her cheeks as her heart throbs faster.

"He comes to meet her, from a table, piled with blossoms, which he is placing in Japanese and glass bowls.

"You will become bankrupt, Alec."

"Not while there are blossoms in the market, and you to accept them; I am a canny Scotchman, you know; you should always wear this gown," he says, quietly, pinning some roses near her chin."

" You said so of my old gold dress, you fickle man:" and, as she speaks, her eyes rest for a moment on his.

With a sigh, he returns to his task.

" Don't, Alec, it breaks my heart to hear you sigh like that, and I am trying so hard to keep up."

" I sigh that I am forbidden to take you in my arms," he said, gravely, as their fingers meet in arranging the flowers.

" But, you know, I am acting for the best."

" Do you allow him ?" he said, with a steadfast look.

" Never, when I can prevent it."

" These flowers remind me of an incident I have often thought to tell you, Elaine. · Do you remember one time, about a year and a half ago, going to make a call upon some people who were transient guests at the Walker House ? they had left town ; and while you waited, while this fact was being ascertained, a wee lady, an invalid, was carried in by an attendant, and placed on a sofa ; she was emaciated and fair complexioned. On your leaving the parlor you asked her to accept a bouquet you carried ; it was composed almost entirely of roses. Passionately fond of flowers, she was very pleased, telling you so ; do you remember ? but your face tells me you do. That poor little lady was she whom you had frequently met in the street with me, before she became too weak to walk ; that was my poor little wife."

" And I met you as I was entering the hotel," she said, softly.

" Yes ; I was going to Brown's livery stables for a cab ; I generally went myself, instead of using the telephone, as Jessie thought I got an easier one."

" Poor little creature ; I did not recognize her, because meeting her with you, she had always been veiled. I remember how pleased she was with the flowers ; my kind friend, Mrs. Tremaine, had given them to me to brighten my room ; I could not afford such luxuries then," she said, sadly. "Your wee wife had a sweet little face, and I frequently thought of her again. Meeting the manager, Mr. Wright, one day, I asked him about her, when he said 'she and her husband had left town.' It was all very sad for you, Alec."

"It was, she told me, a winsome lady, bonnie, and sae strong-looking, had given them to her, and from her description, I knew it must be you. I endeavored, even then, to ascertain your name, but failed," he said, gravely, holding her hands among the roses for a moment in his own; when Miss Crew entered, with her work-basket, followed by the Dales, Mr. Dale carrying some open letters, with newspapers, which he placed carefully on a table beside him, as he shook hands with Mr. Blair.

"Talk about the sunny south," cried Mrs. Dale; "one sighs for nothing in this atmosphere; what with the sun streaming in all day from south and west, the perfume of flowers, the Christmas decorations not yet down, the glowing grate, even with the snow outside, we are pretty snug."

"I am glad you feel so, dear; I suppose with my small income, I am recklessly extravagant in not shutting out the sunbeams; but my furniture must fade, rather than that my flowers, birds and self, live in gloom."

"I think you said real estate is your business, Mr. Blair; have you opened an office yet?" inquired Mr. Dale.

"Broker and real estate is what I have been engaged in; but I have not as yet rented an office; there will be some good rooms over the Bank of Commerce, when completed; but that is a long look."

"Three years! a life-time, from a business standpoint; at least, as we look at things on the other side," said Dale.

"I wonder what the Central Bank will be converted

into; it, I should say, is a good location, if the public wouldn't fight shy of a man hanging out his shingle from such walls," said Blair.

"The owners should give it a man rent free for a term of years, who would paint it white," said Mrs. Gower, half in joke.

"They have it black enough now," said Dale; "its career is a disgrace to the city."

"It is indeed," said Mrs. Gower; "and one of the worst features of the case is, that we have lost confidence; men are daily asking, who is to be trusted?"

"Here is the *North-Ender*, taking up the refrain; it says," said Mr. Blair, reading, "'other bank failures have been bad enough, but in sheer, utter, unadulterated baseness, this excelleth them all;' and here, in another newspaper, they say, 'whole families are beggared by it, having nothing to buy bread.'"

"How terrible!" cried Miss Crew, clasping her hands; "if I only had money," and she glanced timidly at Mr. Dale, "how much I should like to assist them."

Here Mrs. Smyth enters, full of excitement.

"Oh, I am here before them; I am so glad," she said, untying her bonnet.

"Allow me to take your things upstairs for you, Mrs. Smyth."

"Oh, thank you, Miss Crew; but it's too much trouble for you."

"Not at all."

"How lovely your flowers are, Elaine; you cause me to break the tenth commandment."

"Cease, then, and help yourself; as you love them."

"Thanks; oh, I just met Emily Tudor and her mother, on Huron street, on my way up; and what do you think; they have lost every cent by the Central. Emily and Mary have left school, and are looking for situations; the mother seemed just heart broken."

"How dreadful!" cried Mrs. Gower, "they are such

a worthy, honorable family, and the delinquents! are rolling away in parlor cars to luxury in fairer climes."

Here Miss Crew returns, and Mrs. Gower, asking her to give them some music, in the midst of Leybach's "Fifth Nocturne," the Coles drive up, ring, are admitted, and announced by Thomas.

CHAPTER XXVII.

A SERPENT IN PARADISE.

AD a bombshell exploded in their midst there could not have been more pity, astonishment, and dismay, than was felt by the group of friends in the pretty little drawing-room, at the sad change in poor Charlie Cole, and the shock experienced at their first sight of the extremely plain woman beside him with the stony eyes and termagant written on her brow. But horror-struck as they are, all wear society's mark, excepting the fair-haired girl, who still sits transfixed to the piano stool; in the introductions ner back is turned, though she had had one glimpse on their *entrée*, she having wheeled around for one instant; but now it is her turn, and Mrs. Gower, stepping towards her, laying her hand kindly on her shoulder, says, "Turn round, dear." Turning her small, clear-cut features, white as a statue, standing up, but not lifting her eyelids, she acknowledges the introduction in conventional form.

The face of Mrs. Cole, a dull red, with a redder spot marking the high cheek bones, took a momentary grey hue, while Charlie Cole, with a violent start, and a half-formed " oh !' dropped his heavy cane, for rheumatism still troubling him, he was obliged to use it as a support; Miss Crew made an involuntary step to reach it, but Mr. Blair is before her. On raising her head, her eyes meet the stony gaze of Mrs. Cole, at which, in spite of a visible effort to control herself, she trembles almost to falling.

"The piano stool is uncomfortable; take this chair," said Mr. Dale, kindly placing one beside his own, and giving her her work-basket. Oh, how grateful she is to him, as she bends over her wools and flosses.

"Allow me to take your wraps, Mrs. Cole, or will you come upstairs at once?"

"Never mind me, Mrs. Gower, I shall just unbutton my mantle."

"But you are going to stay with me, so may as well make yourself comfortable at once."

"Oh, I don't know, Mrs. Gower, Mr. Babbington-Cole requires such an amount of attendance, that, on second thought, it is best we should return to the hotel," she said, doggedly.

"But, Margaret, you told them at the Palmer House you——"

"It does not signify what I told them; that is past; perhaps your hearing has become impaired. I said, on *second* thought," now thinking—goodness, how they stare; think I am not spooney, I suppose; says, "You see, Mrs. Gower, I have to think for us both. A man's mind is not good for much after a long illness.'"

"My poor friend, you do look as if you had had a hard time of it," said Mrs. Gower, with latent meaning; "but you must know it would be a real pleasure to have you stay with me, and Mrs. Cole also. Do take off your muffler, Charlie, the room is warm. Excuse me calling your husband by his Christian name, Mrs. Cole, but it is a habit I must break myself off now."

"Yes, I suppose so, now he is a married man," she said, showing her teeth; "but he'd better keep muffled up."

"How did you stand the voyage, Mr. Cole?" inquired Dale.

"Very badly. You see I am pretty well battered out, and could not get about much. A stick is a shaky leg in mid-ocean."

"You are right. Did your uncle and aunt come out with you, Mrs. Cole ?" continued Dale.

"What the mischief does that grey-haired, weasel-eyed man know, I wonder," she thought, saying, briefly, "Yes."

"Poor Charlie, you had nurses enough," said Mrs. Smyth ; who felt so badly at seeing her old favorite so carelessly dressed, his last season's overcoat, and a purple and white muffler; looking feeble, emaciated, and unhappy, and with such a wife, that she is almost silent, and nearly in tears.

"Are you acquainted with Mr. and Miss Stone, Mr. Dale ?" asked Mr. Cole, wiping the perspiration from his brow.

"No, not personally, but by reputation," he says, pointedly. "A friend of this little lady here," indicating Miss Crew, "who is also a friend of my own at London, has written me the particulars of your marriage."

"Indeed!" said the invalid, brightening, feeling braced up by being at last with friends; not so the woman he has married, who mentally wishes herself back at New York, in the congenial companionship of her uncle and aunt. She hates this pretty, modern drawing-room, with its comely women becomingly attired, its bright flowers, its home-like air.

Here Thomas enters, telling Miss Crew some friends wish to see her, at which she leaves the room for five minutes, with Mr. Dale.

"Do you purpose settling at Toronto, Mrs. Cole ?" asks Mr. Blair, unconsciously referring to her as the best horse.

"I had some thoughts of doing so; but since seeing it, I rather think not."

While Mr Blair momentarily occupies her attention, Mrs. Gower, with Mrs. Smyth, one on each side of their old friend, pet and sympathize with him more by looks than words.

On Miss Crew and Mr. Dale returning, the face of the latter wearing a set, stern look, he said, on seeing Mrs. Cole, arising to depart:

"Mrs. Cole, might I ask what has caused you to change your mind about staying with Mrs. Gower? You entered with the intention of making her a visit, and one can see at a glance that the being here would be a panacea to your unfortunate husband; I again ask, why you have changed your mind?"

During his words her face was a study, in its various stages of wrath, culminating in the hissing of the following words:

"If yours are Canadian manners, I cannot congratulate you, Mr. Dale.   My reason for changing my mind is *my* reason, not yours."

"Your words and actions, Mrs. Cole, force me to act at once."

"Come," she said, with a sneer at the speaker, now turning to her husband, "Come, Charles, I regret to interrupt these ladies in their attentions, but you must button up your top-coat."

"I wish you'd stay even for dinner," he says, nervously.

"No, the night air is bad for ·you, come at once;" and she fixes him with her stony eyes.

"Sit down again, Mrs. Cole;" said Mr. Dale, firmly; and to the renewed astonishment of all, "I have something to say to you."

"No, I take no interest in the sayings of an ill-bred man.   Good-evening, Mrs. Gower."

"This won't do, Mrs. Cole; I regret your line of action, as it forces a disagreeable duty upon me in my friend's drawing-room, and not in a court of law, as I had intended. My friend Dr. Annesley, of London"—at this, she set her teeth in a determined way—"Dr. Annesley has written me the sad history of this little lady."

"You are a very rude man to detain me, while you prate of a perfect stranger," she says, her face blazing, and making a move to the hall, "Come, Charles."

Mr. Cole, instead of nearing her, hobbles across the room, seating himself beside Mr. Blair, whose face with its look of power, draws him unconsciously.

"In as few words as possible, Mrs. Cole, I affirm on oath, and from indisputable evidence, both from Messrs. Brookes & Davidson, barristers, London, England, and from parties now in this house, that you, with your uncle and aunt, Mr. and Miss Stone, late of Broadlawns, Bayswater, London, England, have," he said, sternly, consulting some English letters, "appropriated the income from the estate of your late step-mother, for the last ten years, to your own uses, merely sending a sum to pay expenses at school to your step-sister, who, to further your base ends, you had banished from her native land; which allowance, even, you cruelly stopped some three years ago; since which time she has been compelled to earn her own living. Not compelled, had she had the nerve to push her claims and assert her rights; but being a nervous, timid girl, the outcome of cruel treatment by you and yours, during her childhood, she, in fear of other evil deeds from you all, dropped her surname, and assumed the maiden name of her mother; and this poor girl, who by law and the will of her dead mother, the heiress of five thousand pounds sterling, per annum, was for two years, a mere drudge, as nursery governess, at New York City." Sensation! "By a wicked fraud, you also are married to the man to whom as a child she was betrothed; but I pass this over in consideration of the feelings of your unfortunate dupe, and of a lady now here also. To return to the servitude of the girl, your step-sister, whom you robbed of her birthright. A year ago, on my wife advertising in the columns of the New York *Herald*, for a governess for our little son, the girl you have wronged, answering our advertisement, was accepted; and since that time has been an honored member of our little circle."

Mrs. Cole, who has only remained in hopes he would show his hand as to what steps the prosecution will take, now in uncontrolled rage bursts forth:

"Mrs. Gower, I ask you, as my hostess, to order a servant get me a hansom, at once; I never was so insulted in my life before!" her reason for asking for a cab being, she sees now she will go away alone, and the driver will know the streets.

"My friend, Mr. Dale, does not mean his words as insults, Mrs. Cole; and I fear, I must ask you to remain until he has finished. However, my servant shall immediately telephone for a hack;" and giving the order, it was quickly flashed to Hubbard's.

Mr. Dale, now taking the trembling hand of Miss Crew, led her forward, saying deliberately:

"This, my friends, is the heiress of whom I have been speaking; who has been so basely defrauded of her fortune. This is Pearl, baptized by the family name of Margaret (her mother's name), her father was the late Edward Villiers, and she is step-sister to Mrs. Cole."

To describe the sensation his words caused, would be impossible, no one attempting to hide their horror at the wicked conduct of Mrs. Cole and her relations; or their joy at their quiet little friend's good fortune.

"It is a put-up job, a black lie from beginning to end," shouted Mrs. Cole, driven to frenzy at her defeat; and before the friends of the man whom she has married, and whom she has despised for falling into the net; "my half-sister behaved so badly, we sent her to your pious city of New York, where she would find kindred spirits," she sneered; "and she was drowned three years ago in the Niagara River."

Mr. Dale had left the room during the congratulations of Pearl Villiers, as we must now call her; and now returns with the quiet-looking couple Mrs. Gower had seen on New Year's Day; and who proved to be none other than our old friends, Silas Jones and his loved wife Sarah, who made oath to the truth of Mr. Dale's statements.

Insane at her defeat, at her loss of power, for which she had lived, for which she had sold her soul to Mephistopheles. In a rage at her humiliation before Silas Jones and his wife, whom she has hitherto walked over, whom she feels will rejoice with her victim over her discomfiture; and whom she feels will sing the *Te Deum Laudamus* over his freedom, which she knows he will grasp at as eagerly as the timely rope by the drowning man; and so, hissing forth many words of fierce invective and malicious threats, she takes the hack from Holmnest.

Mr. Dale's first expressive act on returning from escorting this amiable creature to the cab is to shake hands with Mr. Cole; then, crossing the room to Pearl Villiers, to congratulate her, he ascertains she has fainted.

"No wonder, poor girl," said Mrs. Gower, coming to her relief; "I expect, this is not the first time her terrible step-sister has caused her to find relief in unconsciousness."

"Do you remember, Elaine, she fainted once before, on Mr. Smyth announcing the marriage of Margaret Villiers with your poor friend here?"

"I do, distinctly."

"I wonder," continued Mrs. Dale, "was she aware of her mother's wish that she should marry Mr. Cole?"

"Yes, Miss Pearl knew it right well, poor, long-suffering darling," says Sarah Jones, who is supporting her, while whispering soothing words of comfort. She now recovers, and is able to sit up, smiling at the sight which meets her eye, of Mr. Cole shaking Silas Jones by the hand, as if it was to be perpetual motion. Then, hobbling to the mirror, tears off his unbecoming muffler, throwing it at Tyr; saying, half wild with joy at his deliverance:

"Away with her fetters; I shall begin to look like a Christian again; if I had a razor now, it would not be used on the jugular vein, but on my beard; but Mrs. Smyth, Mrs. Gower, see how grey I am, Jove!" and he gave a glance at the fair-haired girl, who withdrew her eyes, while both color. "Medusa was my pet name for her; oh, it was a den of villainy, eh, Sarah," he said, excitedly.

"It caps anything I have ever heard," said Dale, seeing how weak Cole looks, and making him take an easy chair.

"Dinner is served, ma'am."

After dining, Mr. and Mrs. Jones sitting down with them at the pressing invitation of Mrs. Gower, Mr. Dale read all the communications he had received relating to the fraud practised by Miss Villiers, and the Stones antagonistic to the interests of Pearl Villiers; Brookes & Davidson undertaking to prosecute in the interests of the latter, should she so decide. Before leaving England, some weeks previous, they had robbed and plundered the estate to such an extent as to reduce the actual income from five thousand pounds sterling per annum to three thousand.

These facts had been ascertained by Messrs. Brookes & Davidson, who said, as the delinquents had sheltered themselves beneath the stars and stripes, they were safe personally; but some of the properties could be wrested from parties to whom fraudulent sales had been made by Mrs. Cole. Her plea would of course be that she, Margaret Villiers, had wed Charles Babbington-Cole; but that had no weight, for a clause in the will would make such plea not worth a row of pins; they, the lawyers, only wishing they were in England, when they would indict them for fraud.

"You will prosecute the wretches, Pearl; for we are going to make you feel at home, and call you so," said Mrs. Dale, eagerly.

But the girl, saying in a low voice, though heard by all, that she will not go to law; that three thousand per annum is ample for her; that in most cases, perhaps, the lessees were not cognizant of the fraudulent sale, and so would be punished, while the guilty people were the gainers.

"They have a nice little nest egg," said Mr. Blair, indignantly; " so does the green bay tree flourish."

"Yes," said Mr. Dale; "and will likely pose as saints on the other side. Only that our little friend here would suffer much during a complicated law-suit, and that the enemy are hard to reach, I would advise her not to turn the other cheek, as she is doing but to fight; however," he says, smilingly, "for Canada, Miss Pearl, you are quite a little heiress."

"Ladies and gentlemen," said Silas Jones, as he and his happy wife bid them all good-night, " Sarah and I don't know how to thank you for your kindness to our Miss Pearl."

"Yes; may the blessings of heaven rest upon you for it," said Sarah, tearfully and reverently, as the girl kissed her, lovingly.

"Amen," said Silas; "and I would add that this poor gentleman has gone through a fiery furnace of affliction in his forced union with that vixen of the iron will and heart of stone; but she will trouble you no more, sir, it was only your name she wanted; it meant gold."

CHAPTER XXVIII.

SQUARING ACCOUNTS.

N the evening of the day on which the Coles' had arrived, and Miss Crew had come out in her true colors as Pearl Villiers, the heiress, in which her step-sister, Mrs. Cole, was branded with the name and character she has earned as devotee of the father of lies; there was so much to say, and so many to say it ; so many hand clasps for the poor victim, Charlie Cole, on the incoming for his wife of Will Smyth, the Tremaines. the A. Jones, and others, that the slipping out of Mrs. Dale and Mr. Blair, to meet the girl, Beatrice Hill, is unnoticed.

After waiting in the shadow of the house, building on the next lot, for a considerable time, and evening is fast waning into night, Mr. Cobbe appears in the distance, coming at a brisk pace; nears, opens the gate, is up the walk, rings, and is admitted.

"Now she will come, I fervently hope," said Mrs. Dale, impatiently; "horrid pair they are, interfering with our hearing the circus indoors. If our friend, Mr. Cobbe was mated to that hideous scold, Mrs. Cole, I reckon he would not get too much line. But she would never have trapped him, he knows too much ; unless, indeed, she had settled half the plunder on him to close his mouth with the bon-bons that his soul loveth."

"Your words, Mrs. Dale, give me an idea; I wonder if he would pose as 'Pooh Bah,' and pocket an insult, in the shape of a bribe, to give our dear friend her freedom."

"Yes ; I do believe he would," she answers, eagerly; "I wonder we have not thought of that before."

"But how can we work it; I cannot appear, though my bank notes are at his service; I wonder if your very philanthropic husband would undertake the delicate mission?"

"Indeed, he would; he just loves making rough places smooth for people."

"It is very good of him," he said, gratefully." I fear this girl, Hill, is as slippery as Cobbe himself; you had better return to the house, and I shall go to her address, Seaton street; and if I do not find her, shall see if I can elicit any item of importance from others in the house."

"But you will wish to come in and tell Elaine goodnight first; you will not sleep otherwise," she said, teasingly.

"You are right; but I must practise self-denial; indeed, it is my life just now, and endeavor to earn a blissful reward by gaining her release from Mr. Cobbe. Did you ever see such a contrast in faces and expression as that vixen, Cole's wife, presented, compared to our dear Elaine?"

"No; unless it was myself, which of course you did not see," she said, saucily; "but I like you all the better for it. I hate your men who are all things to all women; go now, and success attend you. Goodnight."

Walking rapidly, winged love buoying him up, he soon reaches the Spadina Avenue terminus, when, fortune smiling, he has not to wait the twenty minutes for the car, for the driver is in the act of turning the horses' heads south. Entering, wrapt in thought, he does not notice the numbers on this broad highway who make their ingress or egress. Pretty girls, peeping from cloud-like fascinators, attended by their chosen valentine, or by chaperon, evidently, by their gay trappings, bent on scoring a last dance before Lent, for this is St. Valentine's Day, and to-morrow will be Ash

15

Wednesday, and so good-bye for a season to the pleasures of Terpsichore. No, he is observant of nothing, excepting the many stoppages, at which he is impatient. Even electric lighted King street is passed through unnoticed ; men thinking, on seeing his bent head and knit brows, poor fellow, probably bit by the " Central." Girls whispering, "He has missed the ring in his Shrove Tuesday pancakes this evening, getting only the button What a pity, for he would be handsome if he would only see us."

At the crossing of his turn north, the driver calling Sherbourne street, he changes cars, and in due course leaves them, to walk up Seaton street. Reaching his number, he rings the bell of a small rough-cast house. A man in his shirt sleeves, and with the smell of fresh pine about him, opens the door.

"Does a young woman, named Hill, live here ?"

"Yes, sir ; just step in, please," and ushering him into a sitting-room, at one end there being a new pine table nearly finished, tools and shavings about. A woman, who is nursing a baby, says : "Take this chair, sir ; but I'm a'most feared Beatrice has too bad a head to see you."

"Tell her, please, that I must see her, if she is able to sit up at all," he says, decidedly.

"Very well, sir," and going to another room on same flat, he could hear half-angry words and sobs.

The woman returning, eyeing him suspiciously, said :

"No, sir ; she says as how she'll see you to-morrow."

"That won't do. I *must* have the information she has promised, otherwise the detectives will do the work for me at once," he said sternly.

"Detectives! oh!" she cries, quickly, in changed tones, leaving the room; when there is more parleying on the part of the woman. She now returns, saying :

"Please, step this way, sir."

Going into the girl's room, who is evidently a vest-maker, by the pile of said articles on a table, another on the sewing-machine. She gives a sulky nod, pointing him to a chair. She has a seedy gown on, untidy hair, and no collar, looking as if she cared for naught. There is an attempt at decoration on the flowered wall-paper, in shape of business cards pinned thereon, with the inevitable bow of ribbon; three cane chairs, a trunk, a bright rag carpet, two tables, and a small lounge, furnish the room. Conspicuous among the photos lying on a table, and the only one enthroned in a scarlet plush frame, is a smiling photograph of Mr. Cobbe.

Determined on showing nothing like feeling, in her half hysterical state, he says, briefly:

"Well, what have you to tell me, as you failed in keeping your appointment? I have come to hear."

"And suppose I go back on my word, and don't tell you?" she said, doggedly.

"Then you shall be made to speak," he says, with a brave front; though his heart is heavy at her words.

"Oh, I know what fine gentlemen's boasts add up to," she says, crossly and defiantly, dashing away her tears; "to just nothing."

"You shall be put in the lock-up if you are caught prowling about any one's residence after this."

"And what would you gain by that?" she says, cunningly.

While Blair, sighing for woman's tact, wishes Mrs. Dale was with him, when a sudden thought occurs to him; rising, as if to go, he says, with assumed carelessness:

"Very well; if you won't help yourself and me, by making a clean breast of it, things will have to take their own course, and that man," indicating by a gesture the photograph of Mr. Cobbe, "and that man will be lost to you, as the husband of a certain lady in the north-west end."

At this she is humble enough, her tears bursting afresh.

"Oh, no, no; I am just crazy to-night, that my Phil is with her; and I have been crying my eyes out, because I daren't go up, because of you coming out to make me tell on him; oh, oh, oh."

"But can't you see, girl, that this is the only way you will keep him to yourself, by telling what hold you have on him. If you don't, as sure as you are alive, he will marry yonder lady, and spurn you like a worm under his heel," he said, with angry impatience.

"Oh, never; oh, oh, oh, me! I suppose I had best tell, then." And going to the trunk, taking out a small box, which she unlocks with a key, suspended by a ribbon around her neck, she takes therefrom a few lines written on half a sheet of paper, handing it to him. It read:

"SIMCOE ST., March 16.

"DEAREST LOVE,—Be *sure* and be on time at the Union Depot. It's all nonsense your asking me to marry you before we start. It's not common sense of you. The other women who want me would tear your pretty eyes out. No, Betty, my petty. I will marry you when we get to Buffalo; not before; so do not make me angry, when you ought to be the happiest woman in Toronto at going away with your own

"PHILIP."

"Did he marry you?" asked Blair, placing the paper carefully in his pocket-book.

Coloring, as she hangs her head, she does not notice his act.

"What's that to you?" she said, doggedly.

"It's everything; speak, or take the consequences."

"He didn't, then; but he's not free to marry that

hussy, since I have his writ promise, where is my paper ? Give it me."

"Softly, softly, young woman; I want him to do right by you."

"But you'll only rouse the devil in him, sir; and he'll see me no more," she says, wringing her hands.

"Listen to reason, girl, I will borrow this paper, and on my honor; but pshaw, you won't credit me with so scarce a commodity," he says, half aside. "Lend me the letter until this time to-morrow, and here is ten dollars; when I return it you shall have ten more."

"Not much; you bet, it shan't leave my eye-sight for any money."

But after a weary talk she unwillingly consents; when he leaves the house.

During the next three days and nights Mr. Blair was half beside himself with anxieties, doubts and fears; for Mr. Dale, even with the letter to Beatrice Hill in his hand, could do nothing with Mr. Cobbe. As mulish as the girl Hill, he refused to release Mrs. Gower from her oath ; finally, in fiery wrath declaring there would be a heavy breach of promise case, did she break faith.

The result was, that with the Dales, Pearl Villiers and Mr. Cole, at Holmnest, a busy week was spent.

Mrs. Gower telling Mr. Cobbe, since he would have it so, she would wed him sometime or other, parting with him at the foot of the altar, henceforth to meet as strangers; that but for his own acts, they would have been friends; but she could never forget all she had already suffered in nervous fear of the girl Hill.

And so, as rapidly as possible she prepares, as before arranged, to leave Holmnest for some months. Charlie Cole was to join his father at Jacksonville, Florida, the following day; Pearl Villiers and herself following. The house to be left in care of the kitchen, the Dales making it their home when in the city; but in a day or two, they would be most likely summoned to New York on peremptory business for a few days.

Mrs. Dale and Mrs. Gower were amused in a sad sort of way, for their thoughts were gravely set, on the attitude taken by Mr. Cobbe. Still, it was a sort of distraction to note the manner of each toward the other; of Pearl Villiers and Charlie Cole, the latter demanding, and the former seeming to think it her duty to wait on him, humor him, go out for little sunlit walks on the veranda with him, play his favorite music, and endeavor to make up to him for her step-sister's wicked act, in coming between them.

"It's a rather dangerous game though, Elaine; they will trade hearts unconsciously."

"Yes, I have feared that, Ella; God spare her from that misery," she says, gravely, with hands pressed to her own aching heart.

"Pearl," said Charlie Cole, as throwing away his cane, he leans lightly on her arm, as they pace up and down the sun-warm veranda, half an hour before the hack arrives to convey him to the Union Depot, "Tell me, Pearl, dear; but for my wretched union with your wicked step-sister, would you have married me willingly, mark me, willingly?" he says, probing her.

"I would," she says, truthfully, blushing vividly; "but I don't think it's quite right to talk of it now, Charlie, is it? only, if we had known long ago when we have met as strangers, Margaret might have been spared this sin."

"How your eyes seemed to follow me, Pearl. Our friend, Mrs. Gower, and myself have been the foot-ball of circumstances, she used to have instantaneous photographs of Blair, and is doomed to Cobbe; same fate as mine."

"My heart is full of pity for you both, dear; but try and think of it as God's will, and it will come easier."

"I know all that; but it's confoundedly hard that those vultures should have it all their own way."

CHAPTER XXIX.

"MAIR SWEET THAN I CAN TELL."

N an evening at the close of February, when the mercury has risen so high that all nature is in a melting mood; the snowy mantle of winter disappearing fast on the warm bosom of dear old mother earth, while Holmnest is a very bower of love, a very haven of peace. . Upstairs, downstairs, and in my lady's chamber, everything is warm, home-like, sweet and fresh; with dreamy, turned down lights, showing the dainty sleeping apartment of its mistress, with its blue and white prevailing tints, its lace bed-spread and pillow shams; its pretty feminine adornments, with three or four pictures, and a vase of fresh flowers giving life to its repose. But we notice in the dim and shadowy light, a something unusual, a something different, a new element in this, the bed-chamber of Elaine Gower; a something that makes the heart throb faster, and a look of wonder, with a smile of content come to the face, a something which gives a tone of strength, of completeness to this bower of rest; it is, that here and there, one can dimly see a man's belongings, and one remembers to have read, "it is not good for man to be alone."

But; and we start with fear, for the inaminate cannot speak and tell us if Mr. Cobbe has had his way, and those manly belongings are his; if so, if so, alas!

But the kitchen says, no, as with a broad grin of content it sits over the *debris* of a late dinner; when, at the tinkle, tinkle of the library bell, Thomas is away like a flash; we follow, peep in and see Mr. Blair, reclining on a lounge, holding between his fingers a cigarette; he forgets to smoke, a look of ineffable content and happiness on his manly face. He has rolled the sofa over beside the Davenport, at which sits his twin-spirit, the mistress of Holmnest, who is within easy reach of his hand, as she sits writing. She wears a gown *couleur de rose*, and is looking very lovable, her face transfigured with quiet happiness. As Thomas appears, she says, in her sweet tones:

" No one is aware of our return, Thomas, so we don't expect visitors ; but in any case, we are not at home."

" Very well, ma'am."

" My bride of a week ; my ain wife, my other self," he says, his heart in his eyes, " bend down your sweet face and kiss me." Holding her in a close embrace, he says, " and so you are not sorry that a great, rough man like myself has crept into your bonnie Holmnest, and stolen your heart ? "

" Nay, not stolen, dearest ; mine has been a willing surrender ; and you must not call yourself names in my hearing. Mine has been a very lonely life, especially of late years ; and you don't know how humble I feel at this great happiness coming to me, or my restful content in leaning on this strong arm."

" There is one thing to be said for me, my own wife, and that is, that no other woman has a real or fancied right to lean on me. I have never been a flirting man, for which I may thank my father and mother, who aye were leal and true. What a picture they were in fair Dunkeld, going down life's hill together ; he only living after her to close her eyes. How I wish they could have seen you, my other better self."

" Yes ; it would have given me great joy to have met them ; your words of them remind me, Alec, of a dear old couple who reside in our sweet Rosedale. A day in their home is a living idyl ; to see his tender care of her crossing the bridge into Bloor street, is a life lesson ; I used to liken you and your wee lost wife to them, dear. I must tell you of an incident that attracted me to Mr. Smyth more than years of acquaintance. Prior to an illness of his wife, she had a photo taken at Gagen and Fraser's. On her recovery we were comparing it with a previous one, when he said, 'I like one I have better than either of them.' His wife, looking amazed, said, 'What one, Will?' while I said, 'Show it to us.' He answered, "This one,' encircling her in his arms."

"Only what he should have done, darling. Each for the other, shall be our motto; but must you write Mrs. Dale to-night?"

"Yes, dear; just fancy how eager she must be to hear, as they were called away so suddenly, and they are such faithful friends. Shall I hand you the evening papers to look at while I write, dearest?"

"No, thanks; I shall look at my wife's face instead."

"HOLMNEST, TORONTO,
"Feb. 28th, 1888.
"MY DEAR ELLA,

"We only returned home to day; but as we, with Pearl, leave for Jacksonville on to-morrow, I must do myself the pleasure of a one-sided written chat with you to-night. My pre-arranged plan is to be carried out; but with what a light heart do I carry it out as Elaine Blair—is it not a pretty name. But lest you think me insane at my age, I shall not go into raptures over my name, or my loving life companion, who has given it me.

"I have so much to say, that I am in a quandary what to begin with.

"The day after you left we went down quietly to the early morning Lenten service, and at its close were married by my good pastor, leaving the same day for Niagara. You remember I used to say in jest, that to make a marriage legal, we Torontonians must go thither! so Alec and I are fast bound; thank God for His goodness. How little I dreamed of this two weeks ago. Your good husband has worked a miracle in obtaining my release from Philip; I cannot but think I have been bought out of that regiment; what different colors I am under now; poor Philip. His letter to me, in freeing me, is so truly characteristic of the man, that I shall amuse you with a line or two:

"' . . . . . . in releasing you from your oath to be my wife, I repeat that you will long for me once and forever! I am sorry for you, Elaine, for I am the only man to make you happy. If you marry that cowardly fellow who has run me out, take my advice, and have the knot tied loosely in the States, for I prophesy you will want a divorce before a year has elapsed; and then, as I bear you no malice, you have only got into bad hands; send for me, even then, and I shall give up every other woman admirer for you. . . . . . .' Is it not typical of Philip? Poor fellow; he little dreams of my restful content at the steadfast, manly heart I have won. He came in the afternoon of the day you left; though, you are aware, your husband had handed me his letter releasing me the evening previous; but he came to try and persuade me to destroy it, waxing eloquent over *my folly*, and his regret for me and himself. Pretty Mrs. St. Clair calling while he was here, they left together. I again thought how well matched they would have been; she amused me—but I must tell you.

"You remember, we read in a city newspaper that a man suggested as a rabbit exterminator, fashion should decree that the ears of the aforesaid animal should be used in some manner of feminine adornment; but Mrs. St. Clair solved the problem of extermination; and if she and other leaders of fashion push it, the rabbit is a doomed creature.

" While the attention of Philip was momentarily given to Mrs. Tremaine and Miss Hall, she purred.

" ' Oh, Mrs. Gower, I do want a rabbit's paw more than anything else in the world.'

" ' A rabbit's paw ! what for ? '

" ' To put my rouge on with, it's just the cutest thing out, for that. Do you paint, Mrs. Gower ? '

" I fancy I see your lip curl, and Alec asks me what I am smiling at. I tell him above, on the rabbit ; and that my smile is the reflection of the laugh in your Irish eyes. He says I don't punctuate often enough to let him kiss me. Give me credit for a little sanity yet, Ella, for I know how foolish this sounds ; but our great happiness is so dazzling after our dark days of despair, that I dare say we are a little daft.

" And now, for a startling bit of news that I have been trying to keep for the last—but it won't wait— a telegram arrived here yesterday for Charlie Cole, from Grand Central Hotel, New York City, from Mr. Stone, running thus :

" ' C. BABBINGTON-COLE, ESQ.,

" ' Your wife, Mrs. Cole, died suddenly of malignant sore throat, on the twenty-fifth, and was buried same evening.

" ' TIMOTHY STONE.'

" The first thing on our arrival this a.m., Alec wired the information to the Tremont Hotel, Jacksonville, to Charlie. And so death has stepped in, freeing him from an unhappy union. Pearl is not as yet aware of this ; but we shall tell her on her coming over from the O'Sullivan's to-morrow. When we reach Jacksonville, she can procure the usual black robes.

" It appears that Mr. Stone has actually rented an office here, in which he will carry on the real estate business. We are informed that he and his late niece lived here some time ago, for a few years. A gentleman from the Grand Central, tells Mr. Smyth that Mr. Stone boasts of his large and influential connection here. And so, though some of our smart Central Bank men have skipped the line, we gain one that caps them all, in Timothy Stone.

"And now to a brighter theme, *our* firm of Dale, Buckingham & Blair, with my ain dearie as manager of our Toronto branch. Graham & Graham tell Alec the agreement is drawn. Will do business on the square in mineral lands, and should get a bonus from the city, for no one heretofore has known where to place or purchase properties of this kind. And so we had better set our chant to music, and sing to ' dream-faces '—

Oxides of Iron	66·23
Silica	21·20
Alumina	3·70
Lime	5·04
Magnesia	2·19

"Were you not glad to hear that Silas Jones is to be in charge of the office while we are away, and head clerk afterwards? I tell you, Ella, dear, when I think of winging our flight south together, thence to the Old World, in which fair Dunkeld stands out the brightest spot, I am half wild with joy. Barlow Cumberland, I am sure, thought me more than a little off when we were in buying our tickets.

"I verily believe I am growing egotistical; in all this letter, who has been foremost—self?

"Madame de Sevigne was right: ' One loves to talk of one's self so much, that one never tires of *téte-à-téte* with a lover for years. This is the reason a devotee likes to be with her confessor; it is for the pleasure of talking of one's self—even though talking evil.'

"But should we meet at New York on our way

south, I shall talk of nothing but your own dear selves, and Pearl will bring you news of Garfield; whom, I feel sure, she has seen every day during your absence.

"Thomas and Begonia (in days of yore, Bridget) will have everything snug for you any day you come. All our world seems so in couples linked, that though he is but sixteen, and she forty, I shall not be surprised to find them buckled, too.

"Times are changed, dear. I never even think of chains, bolts, or shutters. No more nervous evenings; no more starts at the bell; no more heart-aches; but arms leal and true to shield me, a heart fond and loving, all my own. Ella, Ella, with my faulty nature, I ask myself, am I deserving of this great happiness?

"My dear husband is bending over me; but lest you deem him a flatterer, I must not tell you his words he bids me tell you; but no, he must say it himself. But he has taken away the inkbottle, lest I burn the midnight oil. One says of Aspasia, writing in ancient days of her Pericles, that 'happy is the man who comes last, and alone, into the warm and secret foldings of a letter.' And so the name of my dear husband, Alec Blair, comes here, Ella, dear, and I say good-night to you as he holds me in his arms, his eyes, with love's steadfast gaze, resting on my face.

"From your happy friend,

"ELAINE,

"Who is affectionately and
"abundantly yours.

"To Mrs. Dale, c/o Henry Dale, Esq.,
"Hoffman House, New York City."